Shadow Sight

Also by E.J. Stevens

Ivy Granger World

Ivy Granger
Urban Fantasy Series
Shadow Sight
Blood and Mistletoe
Ghost Light
Club Nexus
Burning Bright
Birthright
Hound's Bite
Blood Rite (coming soon)

Hunters' Guild
Urban Fantasy Series
Hunting in Bruges

Beyond the World of Ivy Granger

Spirit Guide
Young Adult Series
She Smells the Dead
Spirit Storm
Legend of Witchtrot Road
Brush with Death
The Pirate Curse

Poetry Collections
From the Shadows
Shadows of Myth and Legend

Super Simple Guides
Super Simple Quick Start Guide to Self-Publishing
Super Simple Quick Start Guide to Book Marketing

IVY GRANGER PSYCHIC DETECTIVE

Shadow Sight

E.J. STEVENS

Published by Sacred Oaks Press
Sacred Oaks, 221 Sacred Oaks Lane, Wells, Maine 04090

First Printing (trade paperback edition), July 2012

Stevens, E.J.
Shadow Sight / E.J. Stevens

ISBN 978-0-9842475-8-5 (trade pbk.)

Printed in the United States of America

PUBLISHER'S NOTE
This is a work of fiction. Names, characters, places, and incidents either are the product of the author's imagination or are used fictitiously, and any resemblance to actual persons, living or dead, business establishments, events, or locales is entirely coincidental.

As always, to my mom and dad, for encouraging me to leap from Dr. Seuss to the wondrous pages of Edgar Allen Poe, Agatha Christie, J.R.R. Tolkien, and Sir Arthur Conan Doyle. You presented me with books for every special occasion in my life, instilling in me a love of reading—the most wonderful gift of all.

Deep into that darkness peering, long I stood there wondering, fearing,
Doubting, dreaming dreams no mortal ever dared to dream before;
                              —Edgar Allen Poe, *The Raven*

INTRODUCTION

Welcome to Harborsmouth, where monsters walk the streets unseen by humans...except those with second sight.

Whether visiting our modern business district or exploring the cobblestone lanes of the Old Port quarter, please enjoy your stay. When you return home, do tell your friends about our wonderful city—just leave out any supernatural details.

Don't worry—most of our guests never experience anything unusual. Otherworlders, such as faeries, vampires, and ghouls, are quite adept at hiding within the shadows. Many are also skilled at erasing memories. You may wake in the night screaming, but you won't recall why. Be glad that you don't remember—you are one of the fortunate ones.

If you do encounter something unnatural, we recommend the services of Ivy Granger, Psychic Detective. Co-founder of Private Eye detective agency, Ivy Granger is a relatively new member of our small business community. Her offices can be found on Water Street, in the heart of the Old Port.

Miss Granger has a remarkable ability to receive visions by the act of touching an object. This skill is useful in her detective work, especially when locating lost items. Whether you are looking for a lost brooch or missing persons, no job is too small for Ivy Granger—and she could certainly use the business.

We can also provide, upon request, a list of highly skilled undertakers. If you are in need of their services, then we also kindly direct you to Harborsmouth Cemetery Realty. It's never too early to contact them, since we have a booming "housing" market. Demand is quite high for a local plot—there are always people dying for a place to stay.

CHAPTER 1

Spectral light shone along my skin as I walked past the sideboard mirror. I hesitated, uncertain where the light was coming from. Raising a small, pudgy hand to my cheek, I stared back at the ghoulish reflection mimicking the motion. There was no ghost, only my own face staring back at me. Looking up and down the hallway, I spied the source of the unearthly glow.

It was only waning moonlight coming in from the skylight overhead. I released the gasping breath I'd been holding and tried to shrug. I had walked this hallway so many times that I'd worn a path down the carpet runner. I was safe in my home. There was no reason to be frightened.

It was a normal school day. My mom and stepfather were still asleep in their bed and I had to rush through my breakfast if I wanted a chance at the bathroom. I tiptoed past the narrow table with bowed legs that held a stack of mail and a porcelain dish overflowing with keys and loose change. I'd grab money for my lunch on the way back to my room.

I poured myself a bowl of cereal and filled my cat's dish with fresh food. Fluffy had been missing for six days, nearly an entire week. We let her roam around the neighborhood during the day, but she had always turned up at the kitchen door in time for her dinner. When she didn't come home before dark, I knew something was wrong. Fluffy was a huge cat who loved her food, she'd never willingly miss a meal.

I opened the back door and rattled the food in her dish, but Fluffy didn't appear. Setting the dish back on the tile floor, I decided to get my chores out of the way while my cereal got nice and soggy, the way I liked it. I lifted a full bag of garbage from the kitchen bin, tied it, and trudged out through the kitchen door.

It had rained during the night and the back steps were damp, but I didn't have far to go. The metal trash bins were kept lined up like suits of armor behind my stepfather's tool shed. I skipped across a patch of wet grass, dragging the bag of garbage. Fireflies lit my way, the sun still hovering along the horizon.

Halting at one of the empty bins, I reached out to lift the lid. My hand touched cool, damp metal and I let out a mew of terror as a series of images burst behind my eyes. It was like being trapped inside a disturbing movie—forced to watch, but helpless to do anything to stop the things you see happening. No matter how badly you want to change events, they continue to roll on before your eyes.

I didn't know then, what I know now. Maybe that's a good thing. Back then I still had hope. Hope that I was dreaming and the nightmare would soon be over. Hope that I had a fever and mom would make everything better. Hope that I just had an overactive imagination. I swore to never watch a scary movie again. It didn't help. Nothing did.

Nothing ever does.

In the vision, my parents' car backed down our driveway just as something loped behind them. The old Buick stopped quickly, but it was too late. My stepfather climbed out to discover he had run over something small and black. In horror, I watched him retrieve a towel from the car and wrap my dead cat into a small bundle that he carried across the lawn to his shed, where he placed her inside the trash bin.

Squeezing my eyelids shut, I screamed.

There are some truths better left unknown. The white lie that Fluffy was missing, maybe just on some grand cat adventure, had been a kindness. The vision of her death was not something a child should ever have to see.

I was having the dream again.

Not just any dream, but The Nightmare

The screaming in my head was useless. The events of the dream were driven by memory, and you can't change the past, no matter how hard you try.

Psychometry is a nasty gift. Unfortunately, it's not the kind of gift you can return for store credit. Lucky me.

*****

"Ivy, wake up," Jinx said. "You're going to be late for work."

"Five more minutes," I muttered.

"No way," she said.

I cracked my eyelids open to see my roommate with both hands on her hips. Crap. She looked serious.

"Tired," I whined, pulling a pillow over my head.

The Nightmare always left me feeling exhausted. I don't think adult bodies are equipped to deal with childhood terrors.

"Nope, nada, not going to happen," she said, deftly slipping the pillow from my sleep-weak grip.

"Come on, Jinx," I said. "Five more minutes."

Jinx was the most unlucky person that I had ever met. She never won anything, and if she bought a lottery ticket, they usually, accidentally, charged her extra. Jess, or Jinx as everyone called her, was known for falling ass over tea kettle for no reason whatsoever. When we first moved into our loft apartment, she tried hammering a lucky horseshoe above the kitchen alcove. It fell on her head, leaving a nasty bruise and a gash requiring six stitches. Since then, we set ground rules. No hammers or other dangerous carpentry tools for Jinx, ever.

Using her nickname only made Jinx more determined. She yanked back the covers, letting a gust of chill morning air do its work. I was out of bed, in the time it takes to bolt upright and gasp, and running for a hot shower. No matter that Jinx had been there first. After a year of living together, I knew that Jinx would always have the bad luck of a cold shower whether I hopped in first or last. She really was the unluckiest chick on the planet.

Fortunately for me, she could still make a mean cup of coffee.

After my hot shower, I slunk slow as molasses to slump onto a bar stool across from Jinx. She slid a steaming mug across the counter that separated the kitchen from the living room. Mmmmm, good and strong.

"You're welcome," Jinx said.

"Thanks," I said. "So why the rush?"

"You have a client in an hour," Jinx said. "I told you yesterday, but you were working a case. I knew you'd forget."

A lot had happened since the day I had my first vision. I wasn't the same innocent kid who believed everything her parents told her and wore little blue stars and pink hearts glued to her sneakers.

Yes, I remember what shoes I was wearing that day— just before I threw up all over them. Some memories stick with you. After gulping air, and crying for my dead cat, I pulled off those cute little kid shoes and tossed them away, along with my innocence and the person that I had been. I dropped my soiled sneakers into the same trash can that had delivered the cruel gift that Fate had bestowed on me. The kid who walked the garbage out that morning had been full of smiles and dreams. The haunted girl who scurried back to the house moved with careful steps, arms hugging herself, a tiny object in motion dreading the simple sense of touch—and the horrors that could now come with it.

I went from being a carefree kid to an introverted loner. I didn't like to be touched and the prospect of handling anything new to me filled me with dread. Have you ever watched a kid pass out in terror when they see a dodge ball coming their way? Okay, maybe you have. But I would shy away from a shared pencil, passed papers, and would totally wig out if I had to sit at a new desk. So I became the school freak. Junior High sucked. High School wasn't much better.

Being a loner left me time to do some research and experiment with my gift. It was during one of those experiments that I met Jinx. Like I said, she's really unlucky. No one should have walked in on me that day. I know I locked the door. Nobody should have seen me holding an old brass compass and writhing on the floor. Not a soul.

I knew from searching the internet that my gift was called psychometry, the supernatural ability to see events, usually traumatic, in an object's history. Jinx taught me how to use my gift to help others. With her help, I started working small cases. Jinx has the people skills and I have the raw talent. Together, after a lot of trial and error, we opened Private Eye, our own psychic detective agency.

Private Eye may sound goofy, but the sign kicks butt. Our friend Olly did the artwork, a graphic of a detective wearing an old-style hat with a third eye emblazoned across his forehead. It probably helps business that we get a lot of repeat customers too. I mean, there are some people who think I'm a crackpot or charlatan, but people who come to us for help, and don't run away, usually feel that our fee is money well spent. Like the guy I had been helping yesterday.

I tried not to shudder. I didn't want to spill my coffee. That case was creepy. Trust me. If I think a case is spooky, then it is beyond weird.

I wasn't surprised that I forgot Jinx telling me about a new client. Handling certain objects was especially difficult and left my mind in a fog. After telling yesterday's client what he needed to know, and collecting my fee, I had climbed the stairs to our loft and crawled into bed. I didn't even wake up to eat dinner with Jinx.

My stomach growled as the realization hit that I hadn't eaten anything since breakfast yesterday. Jinx laughed and passed me a slice of toast slathered with strawberry jam. She totally rocked.

Not only was I eating a delicious breakfast and washing it down with strong coffee, I didn't even have to touch the jam jar or bread bag. Bonus. You never know who has handled the wrapping and under what circumstances. All it takes is for a fat man to brush past the jam jar as he's having a heart attack and I end up gasping over my toast like a fish out of water. It's not fun and not good for the appetite either. Jinx is always trying to get me to eat more and removing food wrappers is one of her new tricks.

"So who is our client today?" I asked. "Anyone I know?"

"Don't think so," she said, drumming ring-covered fingers along her coffee mug. "He's not an old client. I checked."

"Any idea what he wants?" I asked.

"Just the unique services of Ivy Granger, psychic detective," she said, waggling her eyebrows. "But he was cute."

"Well, now I know why you forgot to ask," I said.

"My brain did turn to mush for a second," she said, winking. "He's total eye candy. Tall, nice smile, and when he turned around..."

"Okay, I get it, he's super cute," I said, rolling my eyes. "Did Mr. Hottie have a name?"

"That's the weird thing," Jinx said, frowning. "You know how organized I am, right?"

More like totally, obsessively, anal retentive. Her appointment book was her bible. No joke.

"Yes," I said.

"Well, somehow I forgot to put his name in the book," she said, blushing. "I just noted that you had an appointment. Plus, I know he gave me his name because I punched his name into the system to see if he was a former client. The database came up blank."

"Kind of like your brain," I said.

"Exactly like my brain," she said. "Weird, huh?"

"Freaky," I said.

What was really bizarre was the way Jinx bit her lip instead of rebutting my last few comments. I had totally baited her with the "like your brain" remark. She must be really worried about her lapse in memory.

"Maybe you need to take some ginkgo," I said.

The Chinese herb was used for improving memory, though I was sure my friend's memory was just fine. She just had trouble concentrating when hot guys were in the room.

"Damn, you know I always forget to take it," Jinx said, hitting her forehead with the heel of her hand.

It was an old joke and we laughed as I rinsed my dish in the sink and gulped the last dregs of my coffee. Too bad I didn't have time for another cup. I had a feeling this was going to be a very long day.

*****

I pulled on leather bike gloves, grabbed my keys from the dish by the door and left the loft, waving goodbye to Jinx on the way out. Heat blasted me as I stepped into the stairwell that led down to the street. The stairwell always smelled old, a stratosphere of building history. August heat brought out the scent of curry, vegetable soup, unwashed bodies, tobacco, fabric softener, mildew, and old wood—a pungent olfactory picture, like a patchwork quilt that each tenant contributed to over the years.

I loved our loft and office space. Fortunately for me, nothing really bad had ever happened here. Ever go apartment hunting and wonder, if walls could talk, then what would the walls of this place say about its past? Well, in my case, they can. All I have to do is pull off my gloves and place my hand against the plaster and wood. If something bad happened here, I would know about it. A stinky stairwell was something a girl could get used to. Nightmare visions? Not so much.

I took the steps two at a time, boots clomping against the hollow wood. Another reason to like this place—it was difficult to sneak up on Jinx and me. Not that I was especially worried, but it didn't pay to take any chances. I knew the monsters that walked these streets. Not all of them were human—another little treat that my psychic gift had given me.

As if the horror of seeing death and injury wasn't enough, my special sight also cuts through the veil of glamour that many fae wear...to show the true monstrous visage beneath. Why? Again, I say, Fate is a fickle bitch.

So, yes, I'm aware of the monsters that walk the streets of our city and have taken measures to stay safe. The old, iron lock on the front door was just one of those measures, but an important one all the same.

Turning the key to the right with a solid click, I slid it out of the lock and into my back pocket. From the front of my jeans, I dug out a small packet of salt blended with herbs which I sprinkled along the door sill.

Yes, Jinx would be coming down in about five minutes to make a run to the bank so our rent check wouldn't bounce. And yes, she would relock the door and sprinkle the same combination of herbs and salt along the bottom of the door. Were we over cautious? Perhaps, but this was our home and damn if we'd let some creature-feature nasty just waltz in. I'd *seen* what these things looked like. Trust me. They wouldn't make pleasant house guests.

No, some of the things that lurked in the shadows preferred human flesh, and they were so not getting a taste at this address. I was not coming home to a big baddy picking its teeth with my furniture after having my roommate for dinner. Not going to happen.

Finishing up my ritual, I turned to our office window. I didn't have to go far. The door to our loft was about fourteen inches away from our office. The location was another bonus to living here. I loved this place.

When Jinx found us the cool digs and the incredible office space downstairs, I jumped at the chance. It was a million times better than living at home with my parents. Living with Jinx meant being able to unburden myself of the guilt I always carried back home.

Why the parental guilt? Good question. After four years of intense therapy, I had a perfect macaroni Jesus (I liked to use our art therapy sessions to make religious icons out of pasta. It totally freaked out my therapist), but only an inkling of why I felt so bad about my relationship with my folks. I guess I figured it must be tough to have a daughter who started screaming and drooling when you handed her a birthday present, Christmas gift...or the mail.

Being around my parents and their wary, anxious looks, made me feel guilty. Jinx made me feel important—wanted, needed. Over the years, she had taught me how to be a human being again. Jinx saved me. Not only did she help to give my life purpose by coaxing me to use my gift to solve mysteries, and help people, she also saved me from myself. Jinx did the one thing that my parents, and kids at school, couldn't do, the thing even I hadn't been able to do since I was nine years old. Jinx accepted me for who I was—creepy supernatural gift and all. I totally loved her for that.

Jinx was also an amazing office assistant. Just don't call her my secretary. It pisses her off. Jinx usually runs interference at the front desk, greeting clients and preparing them for my brusque demeanor and touch phobia. She would have been there now, but we were behind on rent. She had to make that bank deposit this morning or we'd be in big trouble with our landlord. I'd have to face the hot mystery client alone. If I didn't know better, I'd think Jinx set the whole thing up. She liked to play cupid. You'd think she'd learn.

With a sigh, I looked at my reflection in the office window. I've been getting stray white hairs since I was in my teens. No big surprise considering the things that I've seen. It was amazing all my hair wasn't pure white. The white bits were adding up though, and looked weird on a twenty-four-year-old, so last week Jinx dyed my auburn hair an inky shade of black.

The face that stared back at me still looked like a stranger. I don't think I'll ever get used to the jet black hair. It made my pale skin and unusual, almond-shaped, amber eyes all the more pronounced. I slid on a pair of dark sunglasses, pulled a baseball cap out of my back pocket, and tossed it on my head. I felt less conspicuous, which helped me breathe easier. In my jeans and tank top, I just hoped the client didn't mistake me for a boy. I didn't have Jinx's curves or feminine rockabilly style. I envied her ability to pull off halter dresses, 50's era hair, and bitchin' tats. Even her heavy framed, retro glasses were super cute.

I didn't do cute, especially not first thing in the morning.

"Okay, enough stalling," I muttered to my reflection.

I unlocked the office door and switched on the overhead lights. My eyes scanned the room as the lights came on with

little pings and clicks. The phrenology head on the filing
cabinet, wearing an old-school fedora, always gave me a start.
Damn it, Jinx, that thing is creepy. I walked in and shoved the
hat down over its eyes. I leapt backward into a low crouch
when a pen I'd accidentally knocked rolled off the cabinet and
onto the floor.

I wasn't sure why I was so jumpy today, but it wasn't a
good omen. I hoped it was just the lingering effects of The
Nightmare. We needed today's case to go smoothly.

I walked the entire room, poking into corners and
shadows, until satisfied that I was truly alone. We really
should clean up some of this stuff. Private Eye was filled with
a weird collection of occult items and gumshoe detective
memorabilia from old books and film noir.

My partner in crime fighting, or at least in finding
Gran's lost cat, had a thing for anything retro. The big black
phone on her desk looked authentic, but I knew it was a
replica. I had to answer it once and didn't get any nasty
visions from last century. I scanned the wall behind her desk
and grinned. Jinx could totally be one of the actresses featured
on the movie posters that papered the wall by her desk—if only
those actresses had tattoos and septum piercings.

My desk had its own charm, though *charms* may be
more accurate. Over the years, I had researched protection
magic. I didn't have any real magic ability myself, other than
my second sight, but there were many items that the lay
person can use effectively. Herbs, crystals, talismans,
protection symbols, I had them all…and most of these were
heaped on or around my desk.

It's no wonder we barely had enough money to pay the
bills. I spent a fortune each week at Madame Kaye's Magic
Emporium, a Harborsmouth landmark run by Kaye O'Shay.
Kaye is a sweet old lady, and an incredibly powerful witch.
Don't let the tacky shop name fool you. She just plays up her
talents for the rich tourists who come in on the ferry each day.
Kaye wears more make-up than Jinx, and hovers over a battery
operated crystal ball when the day trippers are in her shop, but
she's the real deal. I've seen her magic work, which is why I
can barely find a place to sit at my desk.

You never know when you'll need a good protection
charm. With Jinx's bad luck and my gift for seeing things I

probably shouldn't, I was betting we'd need the junk on my desk sooner than later.

I lifted a basket from my chair and set it on top of the metal cabinet beside the phrenology head. A few rowan berries and a piece of stale bread tumbled out onto the floor. That basket of Kaye's goodies could keep a faerie of the Unseelie court at bay. Too bad the Sidhe weren't the only bloodthirsty creatures walking the streets of our city.

I sat back in my chair and waited for my mystery client to arrive.

CHAPTER 2

At precisely 9 AM, my mystery client walked through the door letting in a burst of August heat. I had a really bad feeling about this guy and it wasn't just the, "Jinx is trying to hook me up with a hot date" vibe. I looked closely at the handsome client, standing patiently at the door, and felt my skin crawl. The harder I tried to get a closer look, the more my eyes skittered to the walls, floor, ceiling...anywhere but at my client. Not good.

I wasn't born yesterday. I may be a lowly mortal with a marginally helpful psychic talent, but I knew about monsters. I'd bet a month's food money that this guy was one of the creatures who walked amongst us. One of the very, very old ones.

"It's rude to ask someone their age," he said, crossing his legs and steepling his fingers.

When the heck did he sit down? Or come inside?

"Look, drop the magic shield or glamour or whatever it is," I said, starting to feel dizzy. "If you want my services that is. I like to look potential clients in the eye, not get whammied with the, 'he's so hot' vibe."

"Very well," he said, a smile quirking the edge of his lip.

My eyes suddenly obeyed my brain and snapped to my mystery client's face. I wish they hadn't. He was handsome if you didn't count the fact that the flesh stretched over his Ken-doll face was rippling as if snakes, or something worse, was writhing and pulsating just beneath the skin. *Ew.* I swallowed hard and clenched my teeth. It was that or puke all over his expensive shoes.

"What are you?" I asked.

My second sight wasn't giving me any helpful clues. I'm sure there are plenty of baddies with writhing skin and enough magic to cover their gag worthy visage with a glamour, but I was at a loss. I needed more information.

I sniffed the air and smelled a whiff of sulfur. Oh,
Mab's bloody bones! My hand snagged a crucifix off the desk
and I started muttering the Lord's Prayer. I may not follow
any particular faith, but Kaye had taught me a trick or two.
Ten to one odds my client wasn't bothered by today's intense
heat.

Color me pixed—the guy sitting on the other side of my
desk was a demon. My hand, the one holding the crucifix in a
white-knuckled grip, started to shake.

"You seem to have some inkling as to my lineage,
however, I am not here for myself," he said. "Hell has no
interest in you...yet. I represent a client, someone very
powerful who requires your special services."

"You're telling me that you're some other dude's
lackey?" I asked. My hand steadied as I held the crucifix out
before me.

"Attorney," he said, shooting me a narrow-eyed glare.

"Lower than a lackey then," I said.

I was playing with fire, or brimstone. I should order the
demon to leave, but there was something intriguing about his
story. I couldn't help becoming curious. Someone had made a
deal with a devil, literally, to gain my services. I wasn't sure if
I should be flattered or die of fright.

At least I knew my instincts were good—this was
definitely going to be a long day and this really was a client
from Hell. I stifled a giggle.

"Really, Miss Granger, time is of the essence," he said.

"Wait," I said, holding up my empty hand. The other
still firmly held the crucifix. I may be curious, but I wasn't
stupid. "You can at least tell me your name."

There was power in a name.

"Forneus," he said with a sulfuric sigh.

This guy needed mouthwash big time.

Forneus...a Great Marquis of Hell. Not that that meant
much since nearly every demon was considered some form of
royalty or nobility. Demons were all about ego, which meant
that most demons had some kind of title. I think it made them
feel better about their tiny...pitchforks.

So, a minor ranked demon who the demonic history
books claimed was skilled at rhetoric and languages. If
memory serves, and I'm betting it does, then he also liked
taking the form of a huge sea monster. How messed up was

that? It was no wonder that his skin was shifting like the tides. There was a Kraken-like beasty inside that meat-suit just dying to bust out.

I was pretty sure I didn't want this job—no matter how much I needed the money. I draw the line at demonic sea monsters for clients.

Hopefully, he could contain himself while in the office. Demonic fish gunk was something I didn't want to have to explain to Jinx. Would making Forneus angry cause him to lose control? I was about to find out.

"I can give you my answer now, Forneus," I said, looking him in the eye. It was difficult to do. He may have dropped his spell, but my eyes still wanted to slide away from Forneus's grotesque, writhing face. "Whatever the job is, no matter how much it pays, the answer is no."

"But..." he said.

"No," I said. "I'm not going to be tricked into making a deal with the devil."

"I can assure you that I do not represent His Eminence..." he said.

"I don't care," I said.

"You should care," he said, eyes beginning to glow. "If you care one jot about your fair city and its inhabitants, your family, friends, and self included, then I suggest you hear what I have to say."

Threats? Wrong answer, halitosis dude. I shifted my weight to the balls of my feet.

"Can I get you a drink while I think it over?" I asked.

I didn't need to think over his offer, or his threats, but my crucifix suddenly seemed an inadequate weapon. I needed something more suited for throwing. I moved casually over to the office water cooler.

I had Father Thomas bless our Poland Spring water jugs each week. All I needed was a cup of water and I'd have the Holy Freakin' Hand Grenade. I tried to loosen my shoulders and look relaxed, but I must have telegraphed my intent. I only looked away for a second, but when I spun around with my water cup, Forneus was gone.

On the empty chair lay a smoking business card. I so wasn't touching that thing without super thick, industrial gloves. A ten foot pole would come in handy as well. I did not need tortuous visions from Hell to add to my nightmare repertoire.

My second sight is strange that way. I can see through a simple glamour, the type the average fae cast while walking our city streets, without any special tricks. Seeing the past history of an item though requires more effort. Psychometry only kicks in when I physically touch an item.

I'm guessing it's a built in safety mechanism for people like me. Otherwise, we'd all be gouging our eyes out, begging the visions to stop. Honestly, I didn't think eyeballs were required tools for seeing visions, but I can understand the impulse. That's why I own multiple pairs of thick gloves.

If they carried human size hermetically sealed bubbles at the corner store, I'd never leave home without one. I'd roll around the streets like a rodent in an exercise ball. Unfortunately, hamster balls for humans is a fad that hasn't caught on yet. It's not fair, rodents have all the fun. With no protective bubble, I had to settle for the next best thing.

I moved carefully to my desk and pulled the top drawer open with the tip of the cross I still held in a vice-like grip. A pair of large, black, rubber gloves sat on top of paperclips and candy wrappers. I needed to slip the heavy duty gloves on over my leather bike gloves, but I was still holding the cross and holy water. Juggling the plastic water cup onto the edge of the desk, I raced to pull on the gloves over shaking hands. My hands weren't the only thing shaking. I was trembling all over. The adrenaline was wearing off, allowing fear to catch up with me. It's not like I get demons for clients every day. *Thank God.*

I retrieved the water cup with clumsy, gloved fingers and walked around to the front of my desk. The chair where Forneus sat moments before reeked of sulfur and something like burning dirt that was most likely brimstone. I'd probably have to douse the chair with holy water and haul it to the city dump. Jinx was going to kill me.

Leaning forward I tried to read the cursive script on the card. No dice. Even squinting and bringing my face closer didn't help. The archaic writing was difficult enough to make out without being wreathed in a perpetual smoke cloud.

"Oberon's eyes," I muttered. "Here goes nothing."

I reached out and grabbed the card, cross still in hand. The script rippled and shifted into letters and numbers. It wasn't a vision, but it still made my skin crawl like spiders were racing up my arms and neck to nest in my hair. With grim determination, I forced thoughts of spiders away and focused on the writing that was now legible and beginning to glow.

Tomorrow 7 AM. Don't be late.

"Arrogant jerk," I said.

As I said the last, the card burst into flames. I wrote down Forneus' message and rethought my plan for the day. I better visit Madame Kaye before tomorrow morning and stock up on demonic protection charms. Looks like I had one hell of an appointment to keep.

*****

It was late afternoon before I could make a trip to Madame Kaye's. By the time I rolled the, now worthless and potentially dangerous, office chair behind the building and doused it with holy water, I had clients waiting.

I lit a stick of Nag Champa incense to cover the burning, rotten-egg stink of Forneus and cranked the table fan on Jinx's desk to high. It set the silver and iron spoon wind chime to a metallic tinkling. Hopefully, it would distract clients from the smell of demon butt. Seriously, did he have to ruin my chair? I left a voicemail asking Jinx to bring one of our dining chairs down from the loft and, with a heavy sigh, faced my clients.

After a demon with hellish halitosis starts your morning by destroying office furniture and leaving you with cryptic threats of looming danger, you'd think the day could only get better. Unfortunately, we were trapped in a heat wave that turned the city into an oven and boiled people's brains. Tempers flared and clients made ridiculous demands. If I were less scrupulous, I could have made decent money as a one woman hit squad. I swear every client wanted someone dead.

I made a few promises to look into potential cases of adultery and sent the rest home. When I suggested to one woman that she take her kids to the beach for a swim in the ocean to cool off (it seemed like a better alternative to bludgeoning her husband for forgetting to bring home ice cream), she acted like I was the psycho. She said something about me being a "child hater" and stormed out. Totally effing bizarre.

Jinx caught some venom from the woman's glare as she came in carrying a cheap ladder-back chair from our apartment. She raised an eyebrow and set the chair in front of my desk.

"What was that all about?" Jinx asked.

"I have no freakin' idea," I said, shaking my head. "All I did was suggest that the lady take her kids for a swim at the beach. I thought it might keep her out of trouble and give them all a chance to cool off."

"You didn't," Jinx groaned. She sank down onto the chair and put her perfectly coifed head in her hands. I suppose she didn't have to worry about messing up her hair. There was enough hairspray in those bangs to stop a bullet.

"What?" I asked. "Is swimming taboo now or something?"

"Swimming with man-eating sharks is," Jinx mumbled through her fingers. "Haven't you read the paper? Watched the news? It probably has its own Twitter hashtag by now."

"Mab's bones," I said, rubbing the back of my neck. "That bad?"

"People torn to bloody shreds," Jinx said, lifting her head. She shuddered dramatically, but I could tell it wasn't all theatrics. I'm glad I hadn't watched the news. "At first they thought it was some serial killer because of the livers that are left behind, but the coroner said the bodies were ripped apart in a way that a human couldn't have managed."

"Livers?" I asked. I really didn't want to ask, but that detail felt important. Sometimes when working a case there will be one thing that seems out of place. After a few years on the job, I've learned to pay attention to those anomalous pieces of information. The fact that someone, or something, was leaving behind human livers seemed significant.

"Yes, the bodies were completely shredded," Jinx said, wrinkling her nose. "All except for the livers which they always find floating on the water, or washed up on the beach, totally intact."

"Okay, that is completely disgusting," I said, swallowing hard.

"At least we know why your client was pissed at you," Jinx said. "You told her and her kids to go swim with sharks."

"I can't believe she thought I meant it like that," I said. I could be grouchy and stubborn, but I didn't go out of my way to be rude and yet people had been acting irritated and offended all day. "Well, actually I can. Have you noticed people acting really angry today?"

"Some guy at the bank had a short fuse," Jinx said. "It's the heat. It makes people crazy."

"Oh, um, speaking of crazy," I said. "You won't believe what happened this morning."

I told Jinx all about my encounter with Forneus and his pseudo threats about a needy client and a danger that faced our city.

"Shut up!" Jinx said. "That's, that's..."

"Inconceivable?" I said.

"Yes, but I believe you," Jinx said, tapping a red lacquered nail against her teeth. "You always have bad luck with men..."

She started to giggle. It was completely contagious.

When we finally settled down, I wiped watery eyes with the edge of my shirt and grabbed my shopping list.

"I better head to Kaye's now if I'm going to get back before dark," I said. "Can you lock up?"

"Sure," Jinx said.

We bumped knuckles and I walked to the front door. I felt the weight of the crucifix in my back pocket and fingered a small cross necklace that now lay beneath my tank top. I hoped leaving the safety of our building wards was a good idea. I guess I'd find out soon enough.

In fact, I was going to have to ask Kaye why the wards hadn't kept the demon out. I didn't like having a Forneus sized hole in our security. With one last wave, I stepped out into the sweltering heat and onto the city streets.

CHAPTER 3

From the west, Harborsmouth is a gleaming city of tall, glass and steel office buildings and swanky convention centers that sit along a ridge overlooking the harbor. Heading toward the waterfront, the modern city is quickly replaced by brick and stone. I often expect to hear the clop of horse hooves and see the flickering light of gas lanterns here in the Old Port quarter, and it's not just because of my visions.

I mean, I've seen what the Old Port looked like a century ago and it really hasn't changed much on the surface. The cobbles are still uneven, the brick sidewalks slanting toward the waterfront remain treacherous during our icy winters, and the alleys still reek of urine after dark. Even the shop fronts retain an old charm, but the wooden signs swinging from wrought iron brackets now advertise sex toys and internet cafes. So much for the butcher, baker, and candlestick maker.

I walked past a bar, dance club, two pubs, and a tavern before leaving Water Street behind. That is one thing you'll notice when walking the Old Port—we have no shortage of drinking establishments. One more reason for Jinx to close up early tonight. Monsters and demons weren't the only dangers after dark.

I turned up Wharf Street and kept to the middle of the pavement. There is little traffic here, most cars won't attempt to weave through the pedestrian hordes, and I didn't want to bump into anyone or anything that could induce a vision. I had enough on my mind without adding someone else's emotional baggage. For the first time today, I was in luck. Most locals were indoors, minding shops or pints, and the tourists that braved the cobbles were keeping to the shade of the buildings. I strode up the sun-scorched street unmolested.

At the top of Wharf Street sat Madame Kaye's Magic Emporium. It was impressive. The entrance was located on the corner and Kaye's shop encompassed the store fronts leading in both directions. The wood and brick façade had been painted royal purple and midnight blue with astrological symbols carved around the door. Huge gold-trimmed windows displayed witchy (and kitschy) wares.

I walked though the doorway and into a riot of sights, sounds, and smells. Every surface, from floor to ceiling, was covered in displays of magic and non-magic merchandise. Baskets of glow-in-the-dark rubber skeletons sat beside tarot cards. Glass jars filled with herbs cluttered rows of shelves that covered an entire wall. Need ingredients for a basic spell, potion, or tisane? You'd come to the right place. Require the really potent stuff? You had to speak with Madame Kaye directly.

At this time of day, Kaye would probably be working in the back of the shop. I looked for one of her staff who I could ask. I didn't have time to waste wandering the aisles of The Emporium.

A blond girl stood so still beside the door, I nearly mistook her for a mannequin. I suppose that was one way to keep customers from asking questions. I wonder if she's given anyone a heart attack yet today. I stifled a smile and walked up to Arachne, Kaye's newest employee.

"Hi, Arachne," I said. "Kaye here today?"

"Hey, Ivy," Arachne said. "How'd you know it was me? I was, like, totally invisible, right?"

"Um, not totally..." I said.

"But Kaye told me to drink an invisibility potion and stand by the front door..." Arachne said.

"Ever wonder why people don't work here for long?" I said. "Kaye likes to mess with her employees. Don't take it personal."

"Oh, okay," Arachne said, brow wrinkling. "So, I'm not invisible at all? Not even a little transparent?"

Arachne was completely visible. Everything from her purple headband holding perfectly straight, blond, shoulder length hair, to the black bowling shirt with purple piping, black skinny jeans, and purple converse. I guess she was in her purple phase.

I just shook my head and tried to look apologetic. Kaye was a total trickster. I don't know what she told the kid, but Arachne seemed pretty disappointed. Maybe Kaye promised ninja powers. If so, I'd be disappointed too.

"Is she in the back?" I asked.

"Yes, she's in the kitchen working on potion mixing," Arachne said. "Go on back."

"Thanks," I said.

I left Arachne puzzling over her lack of concealment and strode to the back of the store. I had to dodge past an urn filled with plastic and foam reaper scythes. Ducking low, I almost missed the dark shape that flitted through the shadows to my right. I jinked left and twisted in a spinning crouch only to face a black cat with huge emerald eyes.

"Meorow," Kaye's cat Midnight said, rushing forward to brush against my leg.

I tensed, but no visions flooded my mind. I wasn't used to anyone touching me, even a cat. Thankfully, Midnight hadn't witnessed anything heinous…or if he had, it hadn't bothered him enough to leave an emotional imprint. It probably took a lot to faze a cat.

Now that I was claimed by the ritual leg bump, a rightful mode of cat ownership, I no longer mattered. Midnight sat at my feet grooming his shoulder with a bright pink tongue. He looked at me disdainfully as I scratched behind his ear and returned to his grooming.

I pushed myself up and resumed my trip to the back room. Kaye didn't make it easy. Obstacles slowed my progress and I had to stop and climb under the counter arm at the end of the Oddments and Accoutrements display case, since it was bolted shut from the inside.

Once behind the counter, I pushed a button marked with an Eye of Ra symbol on the cash register and the door behind me clicked open. I slipped through the door and passed through a beaded curtain laced with tiny silver bells. I was all for security, but there was no way that anyone could sneak up on Kaye. The current store layout seemed excessive.

Then again, there was a demon in town. With the failure of my own security, I should probably consider making my clients run such a gauntlet. Somehow, I didn't think Jinx would agree to remodeling our office.

I stopped at the opening to the kitchen where Kaye was busy frowning over an old tome on the stone counter. The leather-bound book rested against a large mortar and pestle that seemed to be created for giants. A trail of large muddy footprints led from the kitchen to a huge wooden door at the rear of the room. Ah, not giants…trolls.

Madame Kaye employed a number of fae creatures, including trolls. Trolls were strong and well-skilled in the art of lift and fetch, but they lacked the finesse of the domestic fae. They were also devoid of basic personal hygiene. If I had my choice, I'd stick with Brownies and Hobgoblins.

A steaming cast iron pot bubbled on the nearby industrial stovetop. I tried not to look too closely at its contents. With Kaye, and her troll helpers, there was no saying what could be in that pot. Best to ignore the strange burbling and tapping and look away from the stove. *Fewer nightmares that way.*

My wandering gaze took in the beautiful, cavernous room. Kaye's spell kitchen always made my chest constrict with envy. I wasn't one for drooling over material objects, you could fit my personal belongings in a steam trunk and my entire wardrobe in a cake box, but I would give anything for a kitchen like this.

A large protective circle was carved deeply into the floor. It was lined with silver and completely encircled the cooking area. If you made a mistake while brewing a potion in this kitchen, which was always a likely possibility due to the delicate and sensitive nature of most spell ingredients, the city outside these doors would remain intact. The same couldn't be said for the person standing inside the protective silver ring— another reminder to take every possible precaution.

There's a good reason why Kaye's potions are so expensive. The danger to the person brewing a spell potion increases exponentially with the potency of the final spell and Kaye's brews are very, very effective. Her potions always pack a wallop. Most new customers are often surprised to discover that Madame Kaye herself is so small and frail in appearance, since her spells kick such major butt. They assume that a person must be a physically large goliath to wield the power necessary to wrestle the very elements of nature into submission, a specialty of Kaye's, but the truth is that true power resides within. Kaye uses her sharp mind to combine years of wisdom and an iron will to brew her spells. One minute under Kaye's intense, owl-like gaze will teach you that.

Those eyes were currently turned inward...rolled completely back inside her head. Kaye's arms were lifted, palms turned upward to face the constellation and rune-marked ceiling, and her spine was ramrod straight. Low guttural sounds escaped her lips.

Probably not the best time to bother her with questions.

I skirted the spell circle and walked to the old stone hearth across, but worlds away, from the modern stove. This section of kitchen closely resembled an old roadside inn with long, wood benches and a comfortable chair where someone could sit by the fire. The gaping mouth of the hearth was large enough for three grown men, or one troll, to stand upright with arms outstretched. Trolls, however, avoided this section of kitchen. The hearth was the demesne of the kitchen's resident brownie, Hob-o-Waggle.

Hob was a crusty old coot. The shriveled little brownie was moody enough to make a PMS-ing Jinx look like a purring kitten. Hob could be a sweetheart, but if he thought you'd slighted him, even the teensiest bit, he'd torment you for a week.

Ever been pinched by a wizened old man in rags whose hat didn't reach your knee? It may not sound dire, but trust me—after the first hour you won't have an inch of skin that isn't black and blue. Souring milk, tying your shoelaces together, putting spiders in your bed, and tangling your hair into faerie-locks are a few of the more innocent pranks in Hob's bag of tricks.

I went to a small fridge and retrieved a glass milk bottle. Opening cupboards, I found a small porcelain tea cup and filled it with sweet cream. I put the bottle back in the fridge and carried the cup to the hearth where I set it carefully on the mantel. I'd learned the hard way that it was worth the extra effort. Hob was a tiny, angry, time-bomb—filled with the potential to destroy my day, but easily diffused with a cup of cream.

Plus, bringing Hob's cup to the hearth before knocking on his door was a sign of respect that brought a smile to his gnarled face. I liked making Hob happy. Over the years, he had become a friend.

If anyone but Kaye had been in the room, they would have thought I was completely crazy. Only humans with strong magic or second-sight can see fae folk like Hob. Hob's front door was also in an unusual location, though common for a domestic brownie, hobgoblin, bwbach, or bwca. I knelt down in front of the large fireplace, careful not to kneel directly on the old stones, and rapped three times on the hearthstone. It probably looked like I was talking to the floor.

"Go 'way!" shouted Hob. "Eem not a comin' out 'till de foul troll go e'way!"

"Hob?" I asked sweetly. "It's me, Ivy. The troll appears to be gone, for now, and I have a cup of cream here. It would be a waste to see it spoil."

Spoiled milk was something Hob wouldn't tolerate, not unless he used his magic to spoil it himself. Brownies take great pride in the tidiness of the home and hearth they attach themselves to. If he let the cup of cream curdle on the mantel, he'd never be able to live with himself. And I hadn't lied. There were no trolls in the kitchen at present though there were plenty of signs that at least one troll had been here recently.

The edge of the hearthstone lifted an inch to reveal a gleaming eye beneath a furry caterpillar-like eyebrow.

"'Tis it be sweet cream?" Hob asked.

"Yes, your favorite," I said. "But maybe I should go now. If this isn't a good time..."

"Gawww!" Hob shouted. He sprung out of his faerie home and shot straight up into the air to land on the pot hook. He was now able to look down his nose at me from his perch. "Human-folk! Always rush, rush, rush. Sa quick ta leave."

"I don't have to leave, Hob," I said, slowly.

Talking to a grumpy brownie is a bit like calming a Tasmanian devil after stealing its dinner. There tends to be lots of screeching and posturing—you just hope to come away without a case of rabies and with all your fingers intact.

"Dinna bring a gift for Hob?" Hob asked.

He was sitting in the crook of the pot hook, straddling it like a saddle. His stumpy legs swung in the air, but I was sure to keep the rising smile off my face. We were entering into a ritual that was older than time itself. It was best to remain serious. Fae rituals were never something to scoff at.

"I brought your cup of cream," I said, nodding toward the mantel.

"Wha 'bout my payment," Hob asked. He placed his fists on his hips. He was trying to look stern, but the effect was diminished as he began to lose his balance. Hob was listing dangerously to the right.

"Um, yes, I do have something here," I said.

I reached into my back pocket and made a show of rummaging through my wallet. I always kept something on me for Hob. Brownies are curious creatures by nature and Hob was leaning even more precariously in his effort to see inside my wallet.

"Hob don't want yer pocket lint," he said. Hob crossed his arms across his barrel chest, but continued to lean forward eagerly.

"It's a good thing then that I brought something less dull and dusty," I said.

I pulled out a shiny silver pin. It was the shape of a feather with a stick pin on the back. Brownies like shiny things, especially silver, but anything resembling clothing can cause them to become angry or leave a hearth for good. I just hoped that Hob liked the gift and didn't think of jewelry as clothing.

I held out my hand, with the tiny silver feather resting on my palm, and crossed my toes. Crossing my fingers would have been rude. If Hob took offense to my gift and Kaye lost her hearth brownie, I'd have worse things to worry about than Hob's departure. There was only one thing scarier than an angry brownie…and that was an angry witch.

"Ah, a respec'able gift," Hob said, furry brow rising in admiration. The grey caterpillar-like eyebrow looked ready to spring into the air and complete its metamorphosis into a butterfly.

"Can I set it beside your cup?" I asked.

It was never prudent to step within a brownie's hearth without his permission, no matter how wide his smile.

"Aye, lass, set it dere," Hob said, rubbing his knobby hands together.

As soon as I set the down the pin, it was gone. Hob shot up to the mantel, lickety split, and held the shiny bobble up to the light. Brownies could move so fast that you'd swear they could fly or had access to teleportation.

I tried not to picture Hob in a spandex Trekkie uniform demanding, "Beam me up, Scotty!" I failed. The image was so ridiculous that I had to cover my laughter with a cough. Fortunately, Hob was distracted by the gleam of his new gift.

If this heat wave didn't abate soon, I'd end up getting myself into trouble. It was never a good idea to let your mind and imagination wander when dealing with the fae, and now there was a demon in town. Time to buck up and stay alert, or die.

There were, of course, worse things than death.

I shook my head to clear the mental cobwebs and nodded at Hob.

"Mind if I grab a cup of tea while I'm here?" I asked. The tea was really Kaye's, but Hob ruled the kitchen…and Kaye was still busy cooking her spell.

"Pour ye'self a cuppa and tell ol' Hob about this purty bit o' silver," Hob said. "Jus' be sure to mind which pot ye pour from. Wouldn't do ta have ye turn into a spotty toad or slimy slug, now would eet?"

Hob let out a wheezing laugh and slapped his knee.

"Um, thanks," I said.

I swallowed and tried not to look green. Hob was right. Checking, and double-checking, the labels on Kaye's ingredients was always a good idea. Belladonna tea would kill me just as quick as Forneus—and then I'd never know what the demon was up to.

A quick search through the cupboards turned up a teapot and a tin of Earl Gray. I was lifting the teapot down gingerly, the handle wrapped in a linen napkin, when the back door crashed noisily against the wall. I nearly dropped the pot.

A huge form came lumbering through the opening, his head (I'm guessing it was a male since there aren't many female trolls) so wide it nearly didn't fit through. The troll was bent at the waist, his long, greasy hair dragging across the floor. A loud fart exploded from his direction and the troll scooted forward, quickly kicking the door closed behind him.

Great. Trolls always smell bad. I can't imagine what a troll fart smells like. If it was bad enough to make a troll try to put a door between him and the foul odor, then I was sure I didn't want to find out. I pulled the front of my tank top up over my mouth and nose.

"Nasty, smelly, filthy!" Hob screamed. "Take yer stink hide 'way from me kitchen!"

Hob was red with rage, his hand fisted over his treasure.

"Me fetch," the troll said.

He smiled and pointed at the lumpy sack he carried over his shoulder. The troll's smile was a nightmare…and I've seen some very scary things. Large, broken stumps of rotten teeth stood crookedly like old headstones in a neglected graveyard. His tongue lolled to the side and drool slid to the floor.

Oh, and the smell! Gangrenous teeth are much nastier than troll farts—or maybe I was catching the odor of both through my shirt. I grabbed the tin of Earl Gray, lifted off the lid, and stuck my nose inside. I'd buy Kaye a new tin of tea later. For now, I inhaled the sweet smell of bergamot.

Hob bounced up and down on the pot hook screaming about filth in his kitchen. This troll obviously didn't know the rules of dealing with brownies. By the looks of him, I wasn't all that surprised that he wasn't acquainted with many domestic fae. The troll was filthy, even by troll standards, and looked like he had climbed out from under his bridge only to wallow in a mud pit and jump around in a mound of trash.

Rule #1 when dealing with brownies—never make a mess in their demesne. Brownies take tidiness very seriously. Like, you know, deadly serious.

Rule #2 when dealing with brownies—don't appear to be lazy. Brownies know how to motivate, and it's not a pleasant experience.

Rule #3 when dealing with brownies—bring them a gift. Nearly any item will suffice.

The troll dropped the sack from his shoulder and onto the floor. A dark, noxious substance seeped through the cloth and trickled out the open sack. Something within the bag flopped twice, like a disheartened fish out of water, then the cloth went still.

Addendum to rule #3—brownie gifts should be something nice, preferably shiny. Brownies have a strong dislike for clothing, cold iron, and stinky, vile bags of muck.

Hob rushed toward the troll, silver pin thrust out before him like a saber.

Mab's bloody bones. I brandished my tin of Earl Gray and leapt forward. I didn't stand a chance against a troll, or a brownie, in a fight, but I wasn't about to let Hob kill himself over a dirty floor. Some things friends just don't sit idly by and let happen.

"Stop!" Kaye shouted. Her voice was like a thunder clap and held a note of authority. Heck, it contained a whole damn symphony. "Halt, Hob-o-Waggle son of Wag-at-the-Wa and kin to Gwarwyn-a-Throt! Poke that dear troll and I shall poke you thrice."

There was power in a name, especially to the fae folk, and Kaye had used Hob's full name and the names of his family. She wasn't one to mess around.

"But, madam, dis vermin be filthying de floor and foulin' the air besides," Hob said.

He lowered his arm, though I noticed he hesitated as his eyes flicked to the disgusting heap at the troll's feet. At a brisk nod from Kaye, Hob reluctantly slid the pin inside his shabby pocket.

The troll shuffled over to Kaye and lay at her feet like a big, smelly dog—or a grizzly bear with mange. He sighed contentedly and I thrust my tin of Earl Gray back over my nose. I suddenly regretted eating breakfast this morning. Throwing up now would be very bad. I didn't want to offend Hob. He wouldn't like any more disgusting mess on his polished floors.

"This *vermin* as you call him has a name, and you shall show him some respect," Kaye said. "Marvin lost his papa last year and is having a bad time of it on his own. He's taken to living under a very unsanitary bridge and now has sores on his skin and is losing his teeth. Life is rough for orphans living on the street, even those with fae blood. You'd do well to remember that."

"Aye, sorry madam," Hob said. He hung his head and blushed.

I felt guilty too. A moment before, I was ready to blind Marvin with my tea tin. Poor kid. I wasn't volunteering for the job or anything, but Marvin needed help. The guy could use a break—and a bath.

I shuffled my feet, straightened my shirt, and tucked the tea tin behind my back. The stench in the room was so bad that I could taste it, but I'd been rude enough. I had plenty of experience with being the odd kid that everyone drew away from. Marvin may be the size of a VW Beetle, and smell like a backed up sewer, but he was just a messed up kid and I was determined to make the guy feel welcome.

"Hey, Marvin," I said, waving. "Nice to meet you. My name's Ivy."

I pointed to my chest and smiled. Hob shot me a scowl that screamed traitor, but I kept smiling. It wasn't easy. The troll funk was making me queasy.

"Poison Ivy?" Marvin asked.

"Um, no, just Ivy," I said.

Hob snickered.

"I think he's making fun of you, dear," Kaye said, smiling.

Wonderful, I was being outwitted by a troll.

"Ah, a funny man," I said. "So, um, Kaye...is this a bad time?"

"No, I'm done with my spell and Marvin has brought me the items I need to make a poultice for his sores," Kaye said. "If he doesn't mind taking a nap here in the kitchen, we can retire to my office. Marvin?"

"Me tired," Marvin said. "Sleep here. Me wait."

"He's sleepin' ere...in de kitchen?" Hob sputtered. "Wha' 'bout de mess?"

"If you must clean, dear, just be quiet about it," Kaye said. "Marvin really does need his rest. He's agreed to do some labor for me in exchange for the poultice and the mending of his teeth. Poor thing has been out fetching items all day."

"Aye, madam," Hob said.

Kaye bustled to the shop door, lifting her layers of skirts as she went.

"See you later, Hob," I said, turning to follow Kaye out the door. "Fresh breezes and safe travels."

"Safe travels, lass," Hob said absently.

He was already walking toward his mop bucket. I heard Hob whistling a tune and Marvin's snores as I closed the kitchen door and stepped into the cramped hallway. Kaye's office door was open and I took a steadying breath before stepping inside. Kaye was a friend, but she was also owner of Madame Kaye's Magic Emporium and the most powerful witch in the city. I needed advice on how to deal with Forneus and his supposed client.

But first, I had to inform a force of nature that there was a demon in her back yard. I was pretty sure that would piss her off. I was right.

CHAPTER 4

We were in Kaye's office, where she kept everything from shop inventory records and accounting ledgers to astrological charts on her friends and business associates. The room was small, but functional...if you were a pixie. Filing cabinets were pushed against the walls and cardboard boxes were piled everywhere, their contents spilling out to litter the floor. No brownies were allowed in here. Poor Hob would have an apoplectic fit and die of shock if he ever witnessed this mess.

Kaye rolled her wrist, gesturing at the paper sky scrapers, and a path cleared in the record-keeping chaos. One thing was certain; Kaye didn't trust technology to maintain her important records. A lot of magic users are old-school like that.

Kaye looked to be in her late sixties, though she was much, much older. I don't know exactly how old she is. With magic users, it's hard to tell and Forneus was right about one thing—it's impolite to ask someone their age.

She sat balanced atop a pile of boxes behind her desk, the path to her side of the small room already disappearing beneath the detritus. In her shop attire of head kerchief over a tumble of silver-threaded dark curls, long, layered skirts, and excessive jewelry, Kaye looked like a keen-eyed raven perched on its nest of treasures.

"A demon?" Kaye asked, leaping upright and raising her hands in the air with a jangle of bracelets.

We'd already been over this, like, a million times already. Kaye could really go in for theatrics and she was milking the demon drama to the freaking max.

"Look, I was hoping you could tell me," I said.

"Okay, dear, start again at the beginning," Kaye said with a sigh. "And don't leave out a single detail. I want to know how the bastard got through my detection wards. A demon shouldn't be able to pop in and out of this city without so much as an as you please, not on my watch."

Kaye had a fiery gleam in her eye that belied her age and hinted at a past that involved wielding something more dangerous than a long-handled spoon to cook spells (though the one she was waving around could probably cause a broken bone or two). I didn't know all of the details, but I had come to share the secret of Kaye's past. The old woman who stood before me had run with hunters in her wilder days.

The story of her taking down a rogue barghest, a monstrous black dog the size of an overgrown mastiff with glowing eyes, razor claws, and the ability to strike fear into the hearts of men twice her size, is a legend among those who hold the magic secrets of the city. Not that there are many of us left. According to the old-timers there used to be nearly as many city dwellers with magic ability as those without, but times have changed. So when a blood-thirsty barghest started hunting the city streets, there were few who could do anything about it.

A barghest isn't always malevolent. In fact, the beasts are usually set with the task of portending doom at the request of a higher ranking fae master. Barghests wander the crossroads and back alleys searching for the man or woman marked to die. When the barghest looks into their eyes, they see their own death and die of fright. Not a particularly pleasant faerie beast, but not one of the purely evil monsters who enjoy the suffering of others for their own delight. I mean, heck, the barghest is just a messenger...and we don't shoot the messenger no matter how bad the news, right?

Unfortunately, this particular barghest's heart had turned black as midnight. He left the shackles of his master and went on a killing spree—for fun. The beast enjoyed tormenting and killing those souls he could stalk at night. Men and women leaving the pubs, bars, and dance clubs to stumble home to their beds were a particularly fun and tasty treat. Someone had to do something to stop the beast.

Once a barghest goes rogue, there are few options left. This one was a few centuries too old for obedience training. You just can't teach an immortal black dog new tricks.

The barghest was a creature of habit and stuck to his usual hunting grounds—crossroads and dark alleys. This made hunting him easy. It was the killing that was damn near impossible. Kaye was in charge of taking it down, and keeping it down, while the others tried to destroy it or banish it back to the Otherworld.

Ten magic users went out that night to catch and kill a rogue barghest. By morning only one mage was left standing against the beast. The one magic user who lived through that battle was the same woman who now stood before me shuffling papers and fuming over the audacity of a demon in her city. Kaye was one tough witch.

Kaye worked binding magic throughout the night while the other mages tried every offensive spell at their disposal, but man after man fell before the barghest. The beast reacted as if the mages were flies to swat away. He was just too strong.

As Kaye's body weakened and power faded, she did the unthinkable. She cast a spell that was sure to immolate her own body. But she didn't die a fiery death—she became a Hero.

In a final act of desperation, as the morning sky lightened to the east, Kaye called upon the one power source that no magic user in their right mind would dare touch. She wrestled with the sun. Kaye drew tendrils of blazing energy from the rising sun to cast one final spell. What she cast was something akin to the Holy Fire of legend.

It should have burned out her mind and left nothing but cinder, smoke, and ash. Instead, Kaye forced solar fire to obey her will and wrapped the bound barghest in a cocoon of flame hot enough to rival the fires of Hell. Kaye may have been crazy to tap into the energies of the sun, but one thing was certain— she gave a whole new meaning to solar powered.

Writhing in ropes of blue-green witch flame and encased in a pillar of white-hot celestial fueled fire, the barghest's eyes still burned red, flickering with hellfire. The ancestry of most fae is too old to be remembered, but there are those who say the barghest are the unfortunate offspring of a female mauthe doog and a male hell hound. According to Kaye, that rumor is well founded.

The barghest started offering a boon of unlimited wealth and power in exchange for his release, but Kaye continued to channel the sun's power to fan the flames. She was one woman who was not going to be bought. His promises turned to curses as the fires rose up to swallow him whole. The angry red dots of the beast's eyes winked out, and he was gone. Whether sent back to the Otherlands home of his fae mother or the pits of

Hell where his father is rumored to reside, the barghest was gone from Harborsmouth and Kaye became an instant legend within the magic community.

That living legend was now sitting across from me, giving me the stink eye. Soulless barghests with the powerful mixed blood of fae and demons may be able to wheedle and bargain under her gaze, but I was just a lowly human. I coughed up the goods, making sure not to leave out the teensiest detail.

"So, I'm supposed to meet Forneus back at my office at 7 AM tomorrow morning," I said, sighing and holding my head in my hands. "What should I do?"

"Pray?" Kaye said.

"Very funny," I said.

"You could bring a priest," Kaye said. She raised her hand to stop my snarky reply in its tracks. "Actually, I'm being serious on this one. A man of Faith can be a powerful ally against a demon."

She sounded like she spoke from experience. Knowing Kaye, she probably was.

"You really think I can find a priest who can help?" I asked, dubiously.

There was the guy who blessed our office water cooler, but that was just a business arrangement—one that Kaye helped negotiate. I didn't know any priests personally. It's not like they'd been knocking down my door for psychic detective services. For all I knew, there was a commandment against it. I didn't belong to a church and I wasn't one for making friends. No, I couldn't think of a priest willing to rush to my aid. If I lived through this, maybe I'd be nicer to men of the cloth in the future.

Heck, I didn't think I'd even be able to roust my own roommate to come to my aid on such short notice. We were heading into the weekend. The appointment with Forneus was scheduled for 7 AM on a Saturday. No sane person would be up at that hour. How was I supposed to enlist the last minute services of a priest?

"I know a priest who works possessions and banishings," Kaye said. "He'll come if you ask."

"Really?" I asked. "That would be awesome. I hope you're right."

"Oh, I think he'll help defend a fair maiden against an evil demon, if you ask nicely enough," Kaye said, winking. "Plus, Father Michael is very handsome."

Oberon's eyes, she was nearly as bad as Jinx.

"You think I can seduce a priest?" I asked. "Me. The girl who never dates? You give me way too much credit."

I didn't have any intentions to begin dating, but I'd wasted enough breath trying to explain that particular quirk. For some reason, Jinx and Kaye couldn't understand why I wouldn't be delighted to get intimate with someone when the slightest touch could send me into a paroxysm of pain, with some serious potential for insanity. Right, I'm the crazy one.

"Just don't corrupt the poor man before facing your demon visitor," Kaye said. "A deflowered priest wouldn't have the same level of power as a man securely entrenched in his Faith."

Did she just say deflowered? Yuck, yuck, yuck.

"Right, I'll try not to do that," I said, dryly.

"Good," Kaye said. "And, Ivy?"

"Yes?" I asked.

"Don't forget that Forneus walked right through your wards and into an office filled with protection charms," Kaye said. "I think this calls for a little more than a few Hail Mary's."

"Never bring a knife to a gun fight?" I asked.

"Something like that," Kaye said, retrieving a packet of charms. "Here, take these. They may be useful if things go badly."

"Thanks," I said, slipping the packet of charms into my bag. "So, what now?"

I was starting to feel antsy. Fatigue was warring with nerves. Today had been long and crappy and it was far from over. Tomorrow's appointment would come way too soon. I didn't feel prepared. If the room wasn't so cramped, I'd have paced a groove into the floor already. I settled for bouncing my knee up and down at the rate of a hummingbird's heartbeat.

"I'll call ahead to let Father Michael know you are coming," Kaye said. "You'd best be on your way if you hope to get there before dark."

"Which church am I walking to?" I asked.

Maybe it would be St. Mary's on Congress Street. Congress Street was uphill from here, but the walk would only take me about ten minutes, if I hurried.

"Sacred Heart, on the hill," Kaye said. "Now, run along dear. Don't keep Father Michael waiting."

Mab's bones! She was talking about Joysen Hill. If Congress Street was an uphill walk from here, then Joysen Hill was a veritable mountain and Sacred Heart was the creepy, gothic, stone peak. I wasn't going to make it to Sacred Heart before dark. Not without taking a cab or hitching a ride. I wasn't a fan of getting into taxi cabs, too many strangers leaving their psychic imprint on the upholstery, but hitching a ride was out of the question. I knew the monsters that preyed on lone, female hitchhikers. No, I'd rather face the dark.

*****

I left Kaye to her phone call and stepped back out into the stark service corridor. I considered making a detour to ask Hob for advice, but I just didn't have time. A foul stench tickled my nose as I approached the kitchen door, making me almost glad I didn't have a minute to spare. For Hob's sake, I hoped he was hiding deep in his home beneath the hearth. Marvin was one smelly troll.

Hand covering my nose and mouth, I rushed past the kitchen door and through the beaded curtain into the store itself. I dodged skeletal hands and pointy witch hats, nearly poking my eye out twice. The clutter of occult items and labyrinthine shop layout was frustrating. I wished that my second sight came with built in GPS. Now that would be a useful talent.

Arachne's face as I rounded the corner of the front counter was priceless. Her eyes widened like saucers and her mouth rounded into an O of fear. She squealed and jumped, knocking over a display of wind-up vampire teeth.

"Sorry, it's just me," I said, waving.

"Oh my Goddess, Ivy," Arachne said. "I forgot you were here."

I walked over and scooped a chattering pair of vampire fangs from the floor, setting them back on the counter. They were a good reminder that demons and faeries weren't the only scary things that walked our streets.

"Thought you were alone?" I asked.

"Yes, I just locked up," Arachne said. She chewed on a lock of hair, which made her look awfully young.

"Don't know how anyone can tell in this place," I muttered. "Hey, it's almost dark. Someone walking you home?"

"My brother should be here any minute," Arachne said, nodding.

Arachne came from a large Wiccan family who lived a few blocks away. They wouldn't have far to walk.

"Cool, see you later," I said, rushing for the door.

Color was returning to the kid's face and her hands were barely shaking. With her brother on his way to walk her home, and Kaye, Hob, and Marvin in the back, she was safe as houses. Now that I knew Arachne was free from danger, I could leave.

"Safe travels, Ivy," Arachne said.

"Safe travels," I said.

Exiting through the front door, I left the cool air conditioning of Madame Kaye's Magic Emporium behind. It took an act of will not to rush back inside. Well, that and the door being locked.

A wall of heat hit me like a ton of bricks straight from the kiln. The sun was low in the sky leaving lengthening shadows in its wake, but temps remained in the triple digits. Great, if the night had to bring out the clawed and creepy, couldn't it at least provide some relief from the heat? Life was so not fair.

I pulled a baseball cap out of my back pocket and tugged it down low, hiding my eyes. Monsters were a danger, but eye contact with the wrong street punk could get me just as dead.

I started walking up toward the East End and felt sweat trickle down my spine after three steps. A few more loping steps and my shirt, now soaking wet, stuck to my back. This heat was absolute misery. The air was completely still, a rarity for a harbor city. Not for the first time, I wondered if this heat wave was truly natural or if it had a paranormal cause. Strong magic could mess with weather patterns; Kaye says it snowed for three days after she called on the Barghest killing spell. I'd have to ask Kaye about it after my meeting with Forneus.

If I lived that long.

CHAPTER 5

Joysen Hill has a bad reputation. According to Kaye, murders, rapes, and muggings on The Hill were daily news headlines back in the 1980's. The new millennium brought beautification and gentrification to sections of the East End, but The Hill still drives fear into the hearts of most long-term Harborsmouth residents—as it should. Shiny new building façades are just the candy coating, created to hide a rotten, oozing center. These days there's a shortage of journalists brave enough to bite into that story and get to the festering heart of the matter.

Faeries and other supernatural nasties, that's the real problem with The Hill. Most of the fae who live in our city find homes on Joysen Hill and its environs. The hill warrens make an ideal paranormal habitat—plenty of dark places to slink away or hide in plain sight, glamour optional. The poor folk who live on The Hill don't have time to care if their neighbors have too many limbs or drip ectoplasm. The few human property owners are too greedy or apathetic to be bothered by fangs and fur. So long as you mind your business and pay your rent, you don't exist; a situation which suits the fae and other beasties just fine.

Crime may not make the daily headlines anymore, but that doesn't mean Joysen Hill is safe. Monsters, both human and supernatural, continue to thrive on the desperate and impoverished people who end up on The Hill. The baddies have just become better at hiding their messes.

Residential streets are packed with dilapidated tenements and moldering low-income housing that landlords should be ashamed to collect rent from—that is, if they had souls. In Harborsmouth, calling your landlord a soulless leach may be more accurate than you think. The worst slumlords of this city? Vampires. I guess it's hard to understand why your tenants want trivial things like heat and running water when you've been dead so long you don't remember warmth...and running water is something to be avoided.

Unfortunately, the fanged creeps are known for their stake (har, har, har) in local real estate. A coven of vampires entered Harborsmouth in the 1800's and bought up large tracts of land for pennies. They now own most rental properties in the East End.

These landlord scum will bleed you dry in more ways than one. Most vamps make their money from the genteel properties on the edge of the East End that overlook the scenic waters of Back Bay. So why bother renting to the poor on Joysen Hill? You know that saying, "You can't squeeze blood from a stone?" Humans will do a lot to keep a roof over their head and, unlike stones, they contain a nearly sufficient supply of blood. Wealth and dinner; I guess sometimes it pays to be immortal.

Think the dank, over-populated apartments are bad? You haven't seen the true evils of The Hill until you've explored the less traveled places that exist shrouded in perpetual shadow. A warren of side streets and alleys lay like a tangled spider web over the hill. It is in these dark back streets that the drunk, unwary, and downright stupid find themselves mugged, knifed, or worse. It's not unusual to wake up anemic and penniless after a night partying on Joysen Hill—if you wake up at all.

Market Street, the main thoroughfare, runs up Joysen, from top to bottom, like it was cut into the hill with a straight razor. Walking up Market Street after dark gave me the willies. Fluorescent lights in grimy windows flickered on, as the hill got ready for business. Joysen Hill may no longer house the farmer's markets of a hundred years ago, but one thing hasn't changed in the last century—on Market Street, everything is for sale.

There were plenty of people poking their curious heads into shop stalls searching for bargains and treasures. I shuddered and looked away. The hungry leers they attracted were a constant reminder that not all of these happy shoppers would make it through the night unscathed. Of course, most humans can't see the true forms of the creatures hawking their wares on Market Street. They're the lucky ones.

I edged into the road, dodging cars rather than jostle the reaching legs of a huge arachnid. I jinked left, as a driver in a rusty old Thunderbird honked his horn angrily, and caught a glimpse of human-sized cocoons writhing and wriggling, hanging from the fire escape of the building to my right. Gorge rising, I gulped down car exhaust laced air, and skipped farther away from the "weaver" selling tie-dyed tapestries.

My second sight is a peculiar thing. If I look directly at a magic veil or faerie glamour, I can see the true monster that lies beneath. When I cast my gaze to the corner of my vision, the images swim together and I can make out the illusion that most people see. The glamour usually takes advantage of existing details and elaborates on the given theme.

For example, the arachnid with black, furry legs looked like a Rastafarian with long, black dreadlocks. The average passerby would see a man with round mirror glasses weaving tie-dyed tapestries, but I saw the spider, eight shiny eyes gleaming, as he wove a web soaked through with blood as it encased another victim. And that wasn't a spliff hanging out of his mouth. Spiders don't smoke. No, he was nibbling on a tiny cocoon wrapped snack—probably a small dog, but it could be the body of a small child.

I'd have to let Kaye know about the increased monster activity on The Hill. She needed to notify any hunters in the vicinity about the blatant feeding on humans. We didn't have the manpower to keep all of the predators at bay, but you have to draw the line somewhere. Taking a flamethrower to creeps who perform bloodletting in the streets, and hang their human meals to ripen like prosciutto, seemed like a good place to start.

I sped up, calves burning, determined to make it to the top of Joysen Hill in one piece. If I kept moving, and didn't touch anything on the way, I'd probably make it to the church safely. There were easier pickings in the crowd and the night was young.

Sacred Heart sat at the pinnacle of Joysen Hill, the highest point of the city. From the bottom of the hill, with its steeple silhouetted against the rising moon, Sacred Heart appeared to be high enough to whisper in God's ear.

Hopefully, Radio G-O-D would send up a prayer for a certain psychic detective. Heck, I may not subscribe to any religion, but if I knew the number, I'd dial up a request. The night denizens of Joysen Hill were slithering and lurching their way onto Market Street...and they all looked hungry.

I walked as fast as I could without technically running. Running in the presence of predators is always a bad idea. If you run, they have to give chase. And there is no shiny trophy or colored ribbon at the end of that race. No, all you'll find at that finish line are pain and terror...and the answer to what appetites that particular monster is looking to satisfy. Getting eaten? Not always the worst case scenario.

"Oberon's eyes," I muttered.

Gripping the charms in my pocket, I stifled a shiver and trudged further up the hill.

*****

I don't know if it was due to Kaye's charms, Radio G-O-D, or my Don't You Dare Come Closer glare, but I made it to the steps of Sacred Heart unscathed. The towering stone façade would have been imposing, if I hadn't just walked the front lines of Joysen Hill.

With a sigh, and more than an ounce of trepidation, I started the ascent to Sacred Heart's front door. I hoped it was unlocked. Skulking around at night searching for a back entrance would likely get me killed.

I raised my gloved hand, but hesitated. If I couldn't pray on the steps of God's house, where could I ever? I bowed my head and sent up a prayer to the man in charge. I figured it was like leaving milk and cookies for Santa long after you'd left your belief in the jolly old elf on the school playground. You may not be a believer, but it couldn't hurt, right?

Reaching forward, I pressed the latch and pushed inward. To my relief, the door was unlocked. Scanning the street one last time, I stepped inside the church lobby.

I wasn't struck by lightning. Fancy that.

Stepping into the church narthex was like plunging into a cold pool of water after an hour in the gym sauna. After being outside in the heat, it felt damn cold. Encircling stone walls radiated cool air that chilled the sweat on my skin and sent a shiver up my spine.

The large wooden door swooshed shut behind me, leaving the sounds of Market Street behind. A hushed silence descended like a heavy velvet theatre curtain, signaling a beginning and an end, and choking off my surprised gasp. Doors closing themselves? Creepy. Dead silence? Even creepier. I froze in place and waited to see what else the church had waiting for me.

When nothing happened, I rolled my shoulders and tried to loosen muscles threatening to strangle my neck. The point between my shoulder blades burned like someone had dropped a cinder under my bra strap. I stretched each arm across my chest, trying to work out the kink in my back, letting my arms drop with a shrug.

"Okay, Ivy, get a grip," I muttered.

Now that my breathing and heart rate were easing back to normal, I felt foolish. The idea of the door closing itself was silly, right? That thought should have calmed my jangling nerves, but instead it raised an alarming question; if the door didn't shut itself, then who closed it?

I turned a slow pirouette on the ball of my left foot—the right was poised for action. Kick, foot sweep, or run—I was ready for anything. I stared into the ink-black shadows, trying to determine my next move.

I may work out most days, but I wasn't overly strong. Rather than weight training, I focused on muscle toning and cardiovascular endurance. Valuing lean muscle over muscle bulk meant I didn't look threatening, but I could run like a gazelle. My theory? Always be aware of your surroundings, and if you have no other options...run like the hounds of Hell are hot on your tail. Odds are good that they probably are.

Of course, running wasn't always the best option. Most beasties like to play with their food, especially when their chosen meal plays chase. Sometimes you had to get your hands dirty. I could hold my own in a fight, so long as it was quick and dirty. Again my strategy was, get away from the big baddy. I knew numerous moves to disarm and immobilize, but I preferred not to get into a fight on holy ground. I may not be religious, but some things just seem wrong. I spun around one more time, hoping I wouldn't have to get into fisticuffs with whoever closed the door.

No one was there.

The lobby was dark, lit only by two shaded lamps that did little to keep the night at bay. One of the lamps had a faulty bulb, or bad wiring, and the flickering light created shadows that danced eerily along the walls. Eager to leave the creepy vestibule, I plastered a fake smile on my face and entered the church proper.

Stepping into the nave was like staring directly at the sun...without sunglasses. White light shone brightly from the front of the church and I blinked tears from my eyes. Shapes moved within the light, but I couldn't make out who, or what, they were. Turning my head to the side, I snuck a sideways glimpse at the area surrounding the altar.

As I suspected, the light subsided to the golden glow of reflected candlelight. The bright light was of supernatural origin. Good to know. A priest, Father Michael I presumed, stood at the edge of the chancel. He was leaning forward and talking quietly with a huddled form dressed in rags who I guessed was one of the unfortunate East End homeless.

I left the priest to his private discussion and headed to the nearest pew to wait my turn. My knees protested as I genuflected stiffly, before taking a seat. Next time I visit this place? I'll take my chances with nightmare visions and catch a cab.

I bowed my head, trying to look properly respectful, and fell asleep. So much for getting off to the right start. In my defense, it had been a very long day.

I woke to someone shaking me and did a double-take when I realized that person wasn't Jinx. Pulling away, and putting some distance between us—I did not want to see any freaky priest visions—I mumbled an apology.

"No need to apologize," Father Michael said. "Can I help you?"

"Um, yes, my name is Ivy Granger," I said, handing him a business card. "Madame Kaye was going to call ahead..."

"Yes, we've been expecting you," Father Michael said. "Kaye mentioned you had an encounter with a demon."

A gleam entered Father Michael's eye and a smile quirked his lips. He rubbed his hands together and looked positively delighted. Crazy priest.

"Yes, earlier today," I said. "But he's coming back tomorrow morning and I need to be prepared."

"Tomorrow?" Father Michael asked. He fidgeted with his hair, leaving his glasses slightly askew. His birdlike features, pointy nose and chin, bony wrists and ankles, and eyes too small for his face, were accentuated by constant, nervous nodding. He looked like he was excitedly pecking seed from the ground, or hesitantly head banging. Kaye thought this guy was cute? I had no idea her taste in men ran so...avian. "Oh wonderful, wonderful. Follow me. We have so much to prepare. Come, tell me all about this demon. I cannot wait to make his acquaintance."

I bit my lip and groaned inwardly. Leave it to Kaye to find the one priest in the city who actually enjoys showdowns with demons. I was glad that he was willing to help, but his eagerness worried me. What if he couldn't handle Forneus? It wasn't like this was some routine exorcism. Crap. I didn't even know if he had ever performed an exorcism. For all I knew, Father Michael's entire experience with demons could be rolling twenty-sided dice behind a dungeon master's screen. It was no wonder he seemed excited.

Mab's bones! Was I about to lead a priest to his death?

I followed Father Michael down the central aisle, past rows of pews, toward the white light. It wasn't as blinding now, but I wished the supernatural thing causing the light had a dimmer switch.

Father Michael was rambling on about holy water, vestments, and other demon-fighting gear—I think—waving his hands enthusiastically. I stumbled along behind him, shielding my eyes with one hand, until we reached the raised section at the front. The toes of my sneakers bumped the wooden steps leading up onto the bema, a portion of the church that was surely reserved for priests only.

I hesitated, wondering if I should follow Father Michael any further. The priest, oblivious, continued on. He was enthusiastically reciting demon hunting theory and wasn't even paying attention to his surroundings. I sucked in a breath as he waved his arm through a candle flame and nearly lit his vestments on fire. Chances were good that this guy would get himself killed.

I followed Father Michael up the wooden steps and completely forgot about my worry for the man's safety. Something else held my attention. The white light retreated, narrowing into the form of a white horse sporting a gleaming, spiral-shaped horn from the center of its regal head.

I stared, slack-jawed, trying to remember how to speak. "Is that a freaking UNICORN?" I asked.

"What?" Father Michael asked, startled from his rambling. "Oh, you can see Galliel. Curious. It is a rare thing for anyone to see a unicorn."

Father Michael was starting to look at me greedily, like a lab rat or a specimen in a Petri dish. Oh no, this amoeba had a mind of her own and I had no intention of being this guy's new plaything.

"Look, I don't know what Kaye said about me, but I'm just a human with a barely useful psychic gift," I said. I folded my arms across my chest and tried not to tap my foot. I didn't have any patience for people who saw my gift, rather than me. It was an old beef that still stung. "If you can't stick to the demon problem, then I'll find someone else."

Who was I kidding? I was lucky, thanks to Kaye, to find this guy on such short notice. There was no way I'd find another priest who could help me deal with Forneus before the demon showed up for his 7 AM appointment at my office. I held my breath and hoped he'd back off. I needed his help, but I'd be out that door if he kept treating me like his own personal science experiment.

"No, wait..." Father Michael said. He lifted his hand, as though to grab me, but dropped it with a sigh. "I'm sorry." He ran his fingers through his hair and flashed me a sheepish smile. "I am not very good at this. You may have noticed I'm not all that good with people."

The admission was odd, for a priest, but he seemed sincere. Now that I had a chance to look him over, he did seem like more of a book person than a people person.

"Please, let me help you," Father Michael said. "Demons are not something you should face alone."

I pinched the bridge of my nose and squeezed my eyelids shut tight. He was right. I was overtired and letting my temper get the better of me, but going to that meeting without a priest would be a mistake. Trusting people didn't come naturally to me, I wasn't a people person either, and I was being pretty hard on Father Michael. I took a deep breath and tried to clear my head of pesky demons, smelly trolls, man-eating sharks, nightmare visions, the bogey monsters of Joysen Hill...and unicorns.

Okay, the unicorn was a bit more difficult to ignore. Especially since he was staring right at me.

Galliel was a beautiful creature. His body appeared to be carved from white marble, yet he moved with a sinuous grace. I know, marble doesn't move like that, but I suppose when you're a mythological creature you don't have to follow the rules of nature. I, on the other hand, do have to obey the laws of physics. Galliel clomped forward to nuzzle my hand and the warm, moist breath on my palm was too much for my brain to process. My legs gave out and my butt hit the pew behind me.

Galliel took the opportunity to kneel down at my feet and put his head in my lap. He looked so content, I expected him to purr. Do unicorns purr? I stroked his head and looked up at Father Michael for answers.

"That..." Father Michael said, nodding his head at Galliel and clearing his throat. "That is even more unusual."

"So, you're telling me he doesn't take to all new visitors like this?" I asked.

Awestruck, I realized that I was touching a strange creature and hadn't even worried about being invaded by visions. I looked down into Galliel's eyes and saw complete adoration. I smiled back, feeling totally relaxed for the first time in days. Huh, I wasn't one for pets, for obvious reasons, but he was pretty cool.

"Unicorns are nearly extinct," Father Michael said. He was speaking in hushed, reverent tones as though afraid to disturb Galliel. "So it is rare to encounter one, even in a house of God, but it is rarer still to have the ability to see one."

"Wait, back up," I said. "Why are they so endangered?"

"Alicorn, the substance that makes up the horn of a unicorn, has many magical properties," he said.

"So they were hunted," I said, anger edging my voice. Galliel nudged the hand that fisted on my lap and I went back to stroking his silky mane. How could anyone kill something so magnificent for a stupid piece of bone?

"Yes, they were hunted nearly to extinction by humans and fae alike," he said. "Alicorn is an essential ingredient in some high ritual magic. It is also rumored to make any food or drink it touches safe to consume."

"You mean safe from poison," I said, eyes narrowing.

"Yes," he said.

"That would be a valuable item for the faerie courts," I said.

"Mab and Titania both drink from goblets made of alicorn," he said. "At least, they did before they disappeared."

The Seelie and Unseelie courts still gathered, but their queens had not been seen in over a century. The word of either queen was law in her realm, but I wondered how long they could rule from afar. For their sakes, they better stay away for another decade or two. I was pretty steamed about their flagrant slaughter of unicorns.

I bent down and murmured to Galliel, "I won't let them get you."

I don't know what possessed me to baby talk in a unicorn's ear. Something so majestic was probably used to more reverent treatment, but I couldn't help myself. Galliel lifted his head long enough to give my face a "thank you" lick. Okay, I'll admit it, this bundle of marble and fur was growing on me.

"So, humans and faeries all wanted alicorn, but how did they manage to kill so many unicorns?" I asked. "I know Galliel is being super cute right now, but aren't unicorns supposed to be fierce in battle?"

"Extremely," Father Michael said. "They have no equal on the battlefield."

"Then how?" I asked.

"Unicorns have a weakness and those hunting them exploited that," he said.

"A weakness?" I asked. "Like an Achilles heel?"

"Yes, ahem, unicorns are attracted to warriors who are true of heart and…virgins," he said.

"Oh," I said, blood rushing to my face.

Father Michael was blushing to the tips of his ears and my face was burning with embarrassment. My virginity? Not something I wanted to discuss with a priest. So. Awkward.

"I hate to pry, but…" he asked.

His question hung in the air between us.

"Yes," I answered.

Fear of being touched had a downside. I didn't get close to many people and had never dated. I was a virgin. Admitting that was embarrassing, but heck, I got to snuggle with a unicorn. That was something, right?

"I believe Galliel has two reasons to adore you then," he said. "He does seem quite taken with you."

Maybe it was because all the blood had rushed out of my brain and into my burning cheeks, but I wasn't quite following.

"Huh?" I asked.

"You are a lady of supreme virtue and a warrior with a pure heart," he said.

Me, a warrior? Not likely.

"I'm no warrior," I said.

Father Michael raised an eyebrow and a smile quirked the edge of his lips. "Really?" he asked. "I would tend to disagree." He raised a hand to stop my rebuttal. "You demonstrate great courage and are willing to face a demon to get answers about the fate of our city."

"Oh, well, when you put it that way..." I said.

"So, as to that demon," Father Michael said, grinning happily. "Tell me all about him."

*****

It was past midnight when I dragged myself from Father Michael's car. He waited for me to get inside the door to my stairwell before driving away. Nice guy, but he definitely had a thing for demons. If I hadn't insisted that I needed a few hours sleep before facing Forneus, I'd still be at the church.

After much complaining, Father Michael agreed to let me get some sleep so long as we met back at my office by 6:45 AM. He would be bringing his bag of demon fighting tricks and I promised not to be late. I'd feel safer if Galliel were joining us, but after talking to Father Michael about the value of alicorn on the black market, I agreed that it was too dangerous for the unicorn to leave the safety of consecrated ground. He would have to remain in the church, for now. Saying goodbye to Galliel was the hardest thing I'd done all day—and this day ranked high on the crap-o'-meter. Who knew unicorns could be so darn cute?

I was having visions of bringing a unicorn home as a pet when Jinx whipped the loft door open. She glared down at me and crossed her arms over her chest. I was still a few steps from the top landing and she made an imposing figure as she towered above me. The mermaid tattoo on my roommate's bicep twitched her tail impatiently as Jinx hugged herself. With a sinking feeling in my gut, I realized that this day's crap-o'-meter rating just went up. Lucky me.

"Dude, where the hell have you been?" Jinx asked.

"Um, Kaye sent me to see a priest," I said.

"Yeah, well, you may need a priest when I'm done with you," Jinx said.

She tried to increase the scorch-factor of her glare, but the corner of her eyes wrinkled and a smile spread across her cherry red lips. I knew they were that exact shade because Jinx was wearing a sleeveless white robe covered with red cherries over a night slip that sported a cherry appliqué. It clashed with the flamingo pink, fuzzy slipper tapping the floor impatiently, but I wasn't going to say a thing. I was just glad that she wasn't staying mad at me—I didn't have the energy to deal with a crazed roommate tonight.

I needed to crawl into bed before someone reported a zombie sighting. At least now I know why zombies are always shuffling around trying to gorge on brains. They need to replace all the brain matter that sleep-deprivation steals away. Don't believe me? Then ask yourself this; have you ever seen a zombie sleep? Yeah, me neither.

"I'm so glad you're okay!" Jinx said.

She looked like she wanted to throw her arms around me in a bear hug, but we don't hug. I don't do the touching thing. Well, except when it's a unicorn.

"Yeah, me too," I said, trudging up the last step and dragging my feet across the landing. I was doing the zombie shuffle. "Sorry I didn't call."

"It's okay," Jinx said, looking sheepish. "Actually, Kaye called me after you left The Emporium. So, I sort of knew where you were."

"I still should have called," I said.

"Kaye had you covered," Jinx said, shrugging one cherry covered shoulder. "Come on in. I promise not to bite. You look like you're about to drop dead."

"If only I could be so lucky," I groaned.

I trudged into the loft and dropped onto the sofa. One foot made it onto the cushion, but the other dangled above the wood floor. I was too tired to lift it the rest of the way onto the couch. I tossed one arm over my eyes, knocking my hat off onto the floor behind me, and sighed.

"That bad?" Jinx asked.

I winced. Jinx was my roommate, business partner, and best friend. She had stayed up worrying and waiting for me to come home when every sane person in this city was resting in front of a very big fan. I owed her an explanation, but I had no idea where to start. My head was swimming with demon lore, alicorn hunters, and an almost primal need for coffee.

"Yes," I said, letting my arm flop down to my lap and meeting her eyes. "It's bad. I have a 7 AM appointment with a demon and no idea what to expect. Kaye wasn't much help; not really her magical bailiwick. Father Michael, Kaye's priest contact at Sacred Heart, is book smart, sure, but I don't have a lot of confidence that he can hold his own in a face-to-face rockem' sockem' show down with Forneus."

My mouth filled with something warm and salty. Gross. I tasted blood and realized I must have bit my lip, hard.

"You're worried," Jinx said.

"Yes," I said. "I am."

Jinx ran her tongue over her lips, leaving it there while her eyes stared off into space. I recognized the look.

"I'm in," Jinx said. She'd returned from Deep Thinking Land with a satisfied grin. "I'll make sure you're up in time to make our meeting with Forneus. Go ahead and catch some Z's."

"Wait," I said. "*Our* meeting with Forneus?"

"Of course," Jinx said, smiling. "Everyone knows you're lost without me. If I'm not there, how will you find anything? Organizational skills are not your strong suit."

It was kind of scary, but she was right. I had the raw talent and a nose for trouble, but Jinx did all of the real work that kept our little business afloat. Early morning appointment with a demon attorney? Not the best time to rock the boat and leave my first mate on shore.

"Okay, you win," I said. "See you bright and early."

"Goodnight, Ivy," Jinx said, settling a blanket over me.

It was already too late for this night to be good. I just hoped it wasn't our last.

CHAPTER 6

Sunrise was spectacular, the sky all vibrant shades of red, orange, and pink. Who knows, maybe it's that amazing every morning. If so, I've been missing something by waking long after dawn. Not that I was planning on changing my sleep schedule. Getting up early is for roosters...and demons. When all this is finally over, I'm sleeping for an entire week.

Even an hour after sunrise the sky reflected brilliant blush hues in the east facing shop windows across the street from Private Eye. Jinx had kept to her promise. She woke me early—too damned early—and made sure I stayed upright. No going back to bed for this detective. Oh no, not if I wanted to stay sane. Jinx had dangled a signed copy of an Elvis record over my bed, told me it was from his drug-using, lounge singing days, and watched me squirm. I was up, dressed, and out the door with toast and coffee in hand in less than twenty minutes. My BFF may look like a cute extra from the set of Happy Days, but she was pure evil.

I started to slouch and nearly impaled myself on the stakes and crosses lining my belt. Forneus may not be a vamp, but the army style nylon equipment belt slung low across my hips made me feel better. In addition to the stakes and crosses, it held iron nails, vials of holy water, and a pocket knife. The side pouch contained a few white candles and quick-strike matches.

I rearranged a few of the pointier objects—still within easy reach, but in a less uncomfortable location. Turning myself into human shish kebab would give Forneus an unfair advantage. I didn't want that. Plus, I was wearing my favorite bad-ass, black vinyl tee and black cargo pants. The shirt was a gift from Jinx and she'd kill me if I put a hole in it.

Of course, she might have to get in line.

"Red sky at night, sailor's delight," Jinx sing-songed. "Red sky in morning, sailor's warning."

A chill went down my spine, all the way to my toes. She had no way of knowing that I'd been abstractly thinking of our morning meeting as a sailing adventure. It was silly, but the old maritime shanty felt like an ill omen.

Red sky in morning, sailor's warning.

I jumped as Father Michael pulled up in front of our office, nearly spilling my coffee. Now that would have been a disaster of epic proportions. I downed the last of the caffeine goodness, and went to unlock the office. Our priest was here and a demon was on his way. Time to get to work.

*****

Jinx bustled around the office, trying not to hover, but failing entirely.

"It's cool," I said, waving her over. "You should hear this too."

She nodded and came to stand beside my desk with both hands gripping her pink feather duster like it had remembered the bird it used to be and was struggling to fly away. Any other day I might have smirked, but my own white-knuckled grip on the object in front of me described our situation aptly. We were up a creek and heading for the rapids. Our lizard brains were screaming at us to hold on tight, so that's exactly what we did.

"So what the he..." I started to ask.

"H-E double hockey sticks," Jinx interjected.

Okay Mom, I wanted to snark, but maybe she had a point. We were about to make nice with a demon. Mentioning its home turf may not be the brightest idea. Words have power.

"Right," I said. "So what does this clockwork monstrosity do?"

Turning the brass and copper object over in my gloved hands did nothing to shed any light on the subject. The object was about the size of a pocket watch and resembled a mutant compass. I didn't think the device got its looks from any of Father Michael's tinkering. It had the patina, and aura, of something very old. If it wasn't for the urgency of our situation, and the thick leather gloves covering my skin, I wouldn't have dreamt of handling it.

"You hold in your hands, The Deffakus," Father Michael said reverently.

That fanatic gleam was back in his eye and I was glad the good father was on our side. There was something scary about people with that much brains being so obsessed with the supernatural. It didn't take much imagination to picture him in the vestments of the Spanish Inquisition.

Jinx started giggling, leaned forward, and tripped over her own wedge-sandaled feet. We don't call her Jinx for nothing. She collapsed against the file cabinet, creepy phrenology head teetering precariously above her prone form.

"Ouch," Jinx said, rubbing the knee she'd landed on. "So what does the Almighty Deffakus do, detect bullshit?"

"I can assure you that The Deffakus has nothing at all to do with vulgar cuss words," he said. "The artifact was named for Horatio Deffakus, the man who discovered it."

Great, we'd ruffled his feathers. In fact, he was flapping his arms agitatedly in a decidedly birdlike motion. If I didn't put an end to this train wreck, my friend would put her foot even further in her mouth and Father Michael would expound upon the linguistic differences between feces and the metal object still resting in my hand. I didn't think I'd survive that conversation, especially since our demon would be here in ten minutes.

"Please," I said. See, I can play nice. "What does the compass thingy do? Will it help me deal with Forneus?"

"Yes, yes, it will," he said, nodding his head. "See this knob here? Turn it thrice widdershins."

I knew from hanging out with Kaye that widdershins meant counterclockwise. It was a direction that, when used in magic, was likely to precede something negative or an undoing. That was fine if you were working to dispel an item or disperse excess energy after a rite, but moving something widdershins to twist a curse was old-school traditional black magic.

A demon attorney may be high on the freak out scale, but I wasn't letting my morning meeting turn me to the dark side. They may have cookies, but I had a freakin' unicorn. No way was I changing sides this early in the game.

"No," I said. "Not until you tell me exactly what it does."

"It can determine whether or not a demon is telling a lie," he said.

Huh, Jinx was right. It really was a bullshit detector.

"Is it black magic?" I asked. Might as well get straight to the point. We were running out of time and I needed to know if I could use the thing or not.

"Of course not!" he exclaimed.

"Don't get your panties in a bunch," Jinx said, waving a hand at Father Michael. Her red lacquered nails froze mid-wave as she realized that she'd just said the word "panties" to a priest. Oopsie.

"Okay, if it doesn't run on black magic and has the ability that you say, how come it's in your possession?" I asked. "Shouldn't it be locked up in the Vatican or something?"

Yes, I have trust issues. When someone tries to hand me something that sounds too good to be true, I hesitate. No bridges hiding in my closet. No buyer's remorse either. Of course, if The Deffakus was the real deal, I'd use it. I just wanted to be sure.

"It was in the safe keeping of the Vatican, until a young archivist signed it out for study," he said.

"You were a Vatican archivist?" I asked.

"Among other things," he said.

Interesting.

"Have you tested it?" I asked. I didn't intend to be this guy's numero uno guinea pig. That was a role for some other sucker.

"Yes," he said. "According to my calculations, The Deffakus is 99.975 percent accurate. It is also entirely safe to activate. I detected no magical side-effects as a result of using this artifact."

99.975 percent was good enough for me. I turned the knob widdershins and settled in to wait for my first appointment of the day.

*****

I didn't have to wait long. Forneus's sins could line the shelves of Hell's larder, but I could say one thing for the demon—the guy was punctual.

He was wearing his own face today—a slender humanoid face, not the horrific sea monster visage. That was interesting, since manifesting fully in our realm was difficult for most Hell spawn. Even if they could manage the trip, there were potential dangers. Appearing corporeally, without the aid of a human vessel, often left a demon vulnerable. It was the reason why most demons used possession for their trips topside.

Goat-slit eyes stared out of a handsome face that no longer rippled with the shared features of a human meat suit. His gaze was unsettling, but I didn't feel the urge to upchuck toast and coffee. We were making progress.

Forneus pulled gloves from his fingers and stepped gracefully up to the reception desk. No zapping himself into my office and giving me a heart attack. Well, well, I guess his manners had improved with his face. I wondered if it had to do with demon rules. His use of the door, rather than making a grand magical entrance seemed significant. How much was Forneus risking by coming here today?

Why would a demon even hazard coming into an office filled with wards and charms? I had the feeling that Forneus was about to reveal something big, and unpleasant. Whatever deal he was about to propose, it couldn't be good.

Jinx went to her desk to greet our client. Her smile was pure sugar, but the tiny wrinkle in her brow gave away her anxiety...and determination. That girl was tough as nails.

"Welcome to Private Eye Investigations," Jinx said. "Please follow me."

Jinx walked Forneus to my desk, acting, for all the world, like demon clients were an everyday occurrence. I hoped that never became the case. No, this was a one-time only meeting. I would hear Forneus' story, then send him on his way.

I was glad to have the benefit of Father Michael's unique knowledge. The priest was here to guide me through the demonic legal mumbo-jumbo, and save me from any ignorant missteps. His clockwork artifact was an added bonus.

I looked down to see a set of needles on the face of The Deffakus spinning leisurely. According to Father Michael, the needles were made of different metals that each resonated alchemically to the words of a demon. When a demon lie is told, the needles will spin until their rotation is synchronized, pointing to a symbol representing falsehood. Time to see if the thingamabob really worked.

"Hi, Forneus," I said. I gestured at the chair in front of my desk, but didn't rise to greet my guest. "Have a seat."

"Doing a bit of redecorating, are we?" Forneus asked. He raised one brow and cast a disapproving eye at the mismatched chairs. "I can't say it's an improvement."

"You sonofa...," I said.

That guy had some nerve. First he destroys my chair, then criticizes its cheap replacement. If he wanted an aesthetically balanced collection of furniture that was pleasing to the eye, he should have stopped at the Ethan Allen store on Congress Street. Jinx and I ran this place on a budget. We were low on funds and I was running even less on patience.

Father Michael placed a calming hand on my, thankfully clothed, shoulder and I sat back down. He didn't know how lucky he was that I didn't bop him in the nose. How many times does a girl have to say, no freakin' touching? Was everyone trying to piss me off?

"Ivy," Jinx said. I looked up to see her twitch her head in a quick, micro shake of negation. "He's working his demon mojo..."

Crap. I squeezed my eyes shut tight, drew in a deep breath, and tried to think about the past few minutes objectively. Sure, I have a temper, but I don't usually consider attacking both a demon and a priest within ten seconds of each other. That was extreme, even for me. I sucked in one more calming breath and opened my eyes.

Forneus looked even more smug than usual. The creep was used to manipulating people into making foolish deals, and I almost fell for it.

"You can't blame a man for trying," Forneus said.

"No more mind control spells," I said.

"As you wish," Forneus said.

He spread his long-fingered hands wide and batted dark eyelashes innocently. Yeah, right, like he'd stop using magic to mess with my head. I checked the gauge on The Deffakus. I even shook the device to be sure. Huh, he was telling the truth. Not that I trusted him. Who knows, maybe the holy lie detector wasn't working. That would be just my luck.

"Why the meeting, Forneus?" I asked.

"Yeah, what was so important that we had to get up at the butt-crack of dawn?" Jinx asked.

I tried to hide my grin. Butt crack of dawn? Jinx had a way with words.

"There are things afoot in your dear city and time was of the essence," Forneus said. "To tarry any longer would have been foolhardy...and dangerous. My clients are not the kind to be kept waiting."

"You still haven't answered my question," I said, fixing Forneus with a stare. Most people found looking into my amber eyes unnerving, but he seemed immune.

"And that would be...?" Forneus asked.

"Why are we here?" I asked.

"Ah, I didn't realize you were interested in philosophy, Miss Granger," Forneus said.

I sighed and waved my hand in a, "get on with it" gesture and Jinx rolled her eyes. Demons were so annoying. They were right up there with telemarketers and politicians.

"May I make a suggestion?" Father Michael asked. "Perhaps asking the creature who he is working for would be helpful. If you ask the question three times, he will be obliged to answer."

"Who is your client?" I asked.

"Come now, that isn't entirely relevant..." Forneus said.

"Who is your client?" I asked.

"Dude, who are you working for?" Jinx asked.

"Ladies, ladies, please," Forneus said. "If you would just let me explain..."

"Who is your client?" I asked.

A small popping sensation of pressure in my ears indicated the thrice asked question had worked.

"You are all terribly vexing," Forneus said, casting his glare around the office. "Very well, if you insist on knowing, I am currently in the employ of kelpies who dwell in the waters off Harborsmouth."

"Kelpies," I said, agog.

"Who or what's a kelpie?" Jinx asked.

It wasn't surprising that Jinx didn't know what a kelpie was. Kelpies could be found throughout faerie folklore, but the tales were often brief and bloody. Not the kind of stories to be told at bedtime to sleepy children.

Kelpies were a type of water horse, an Unseelie fae with a dark and dangerous reputation. They were rumored to lure human riders onto their backs, and then plunge deep into nearby river, lake, or ocean waters. Some folk tales claim that kelpies devour their victims after drowning them.

"You're working for kelpies?" I asked. "The same monsters who drown and eat humans?"

"Only when times are hard," Forneus said. "Even the fae folk can become down on their luck, and starvation is a powerful motivator."

"So you represent a client, who sometimes gets hungry and eats people, and you want me to do a job for them, why exactly?" I asked.

"Because your city is in danger from a much more terrifying foe," Forneus said. "And believe me when I say that, in this situation, kelpies are the lesser of two evils."

Mab's bones! What could be worse than kelpies? I was pretty sure that I didn't want to find out.

Then it clicked, pieces of the puzzle coming together. Jinx had relayed news of shark attacks at local beaches and around the bay. Something was attacking people, tearing them apart, and leaving their livers to float to shore. I had a very bad feeling about this.

"Is there something in the sea that's hunting humans?" I asked.

"Indubitably," Forneus said.

"It's not a shark, is it?" I asked.

"No, absolutely not," Forneus said. "I regret to inform you that the *each uisge* have come to your waters."

Father Michael gasped and muttered a prayer behind me. I hadn't read anything about *each uisge*, but apparently the priest had and he didn't sound too happy to hear the news that they were here in Harborsmouth.

"Who are the *each uisge* and what are they doing eating humans?" I asked.

"It's what they do," Father Michael said. "They are bloodthirsty creatures who live to rend flesh from bone. They devastate everything in their path, like a plague of locusts, leaving nothing but discarded livers in their wake."

"Yes, an apt description," Forneus said. "Usually, in the waters of a city this size, the local fauna would keep the *each uisge* in check. The worst butchery is always in remote locations. Except here we are with humans being eaten, the perpetrators continuing unchecked."

"Why?" I asked. "Who usually keeps them from overrunning cities?"

"Yeah, why aren't they doing their job?" Jinx asked.

"Excellent questions," Forneus said. "The kelpies, with the assistance of nearby selkies, mermaids, and other allies, would normally defend the city from attack. It does these fae no good to bring human attention to their home waters."

"But they're not keeping the *each uisge* away," I said.

"No, they have a problem, a quandary that they need your help to fix," Forneus said. "Ceffyl Dŵr, King of the Kelpies, has gone missing."

"So, the kelpies want my help to find their missing king?" I asked.

How was I supposed to find a lost kelpie king? This whole thing had to be a bad joke, right?

"Not the king, an artifact," he said. "A bridle. His bridle. My clients have hired me to formally ask for your assistance in this matter. If you can locate their king's bridle, then they will defend the city from the *each uisge*."

Locate a missing bridle? Maybe the job was more plausible than finding a faerie king, but it still sounded crazy. How could I find something like that? It was probably in the ocean, and that was one place that I couldn't go. With a bay filled with flesh eating *each uisge*, a dip in the ocean wasn't high on my to-do list.

"Look, I'd love to help you guys out, and save the city and all, but this job is way above my pay grade," I said. "Sorry."

"Perhaps this will help," Forneus said.

He withdrew a small, cloth covered item from his coat pocket. His slender hands carefully unwrapped the bundle to reveal a piece of leather intertwined with seaweed and woven threads of silver. The piece was ragged on one end, either cut or torn from a larger item.

"What is it?" I asked.

Power seemed to emanate from the item, slapping against me like waves crashing upon a rocky shore. Whatever it was, the thing in Forneus' hand was imbued with some seriously potent magic.

"This is from Ceffyl Dŵr's bridle, the only remaining connection we have to the kelpie king," Forneus said.

"Let me guess," I said, raising my hand. "You want me to touch that remnant of the kelpie king's bridle and tell you what I see."

"Precisely," Forneus said.

"Forget it," I said. "No deal."

Touch an item that had been worn by a flesh eating, human drowning, Unseelie water fae? No freaking way.

"Fine," Forneus said, wrapping the item and setting it on my desk. "You and everyone you care about will die a horrible death and you will leave this world knowing that you had not done everything in your power to stop it from happening."

"Ivy?" Jinx asked, tentatively. Her voice sounded small and scared.

I looked down at The Deffakus. Forneus wasn't lying.

"Crap," I said. I stood up and reluctantly nodded at Forneus. "Jinx? Father Michael? Meet our new client, the demon Forneus, Great Marquis of Hell, representing the interests of the kelpies of Harborsmouth."

God save us all.

Forneus grinned like the Cheshire cat who ate the canary. I just hoped that I wasn't the canary in this arrangement.

CHAPTER 7

father Michael stayed to help Jinx write up the formal job paperwork. Entering into a contract with a demon was potentially disastrous, so we needed the expertise of someone versed in demon legalese.

I was responsible for handling the fae side of things.

Eventually I would have to touch the piece of bridle, now wrapped safely away in my bag, but first I needed information. My knowledge of kelpies and *each uisge* was minimal, but there was one person I knew who could fill in the blanks. With a little luck, she'd be willing to help.

With a wave to Jinx, I left the office and headed to Madam Kaye's Magic Emporium. Father Michael had assured me that I didn't need to sign the deal in blood or anything, but Forneus was arguing that point. At least, I think he was arguing. I don't speak Latin. One thing I was sure of—I'd go crazy if I remained at the office any longer. If they needed me, or my blood, I was just a phone call away.

Our office had been unbearably hot and claustrophobic, but stepping out onto the sidewalk was like entering the outer ring of Dante's Hell. If it wasn't for the demon contract pow wow going on, I probably would have gone running back inside. With a sigh, I pulled on a baseball cap to shade my face and started the walk to Madame Kaye's.

Harborsmouth held its collective breath against the stifling heat that continued to plague the coast. I walked alone, the city seemingly devoid of life, except for the raucous sound of arguing crows and seagulls overhead. The buildings appeared to waver in the heat-shimmer that rose from the pavement and stone surfaces. It was easy, in that moment, to imagine the city besieged by carnivorous fae, the streets running red with blood.

I clutched the strap of my bag, wringing the fabric with sweaty gloved hands, and blinked back hot tears. My chest felt tight and each rapid breath burned like my lungs were scorched raw. I knew that feeling, all too well. Signs of a panic attack are something a kid with the gifts of psychometry and second sight come to quickly recognize.

I staggered over to an old style lamp post and leaned against it as I slid to the ground. The black metal radiated painful heat through my t-shirt, but I pressed hard against it. Pain was good; it meant I was still conscious. I tried to control my breathing, and failed. Little sparks of light flashed in the darkness and I realized that I had squeezed my eyes shut tight against the panic. In a city filled with monsters and desperation, closing off any of my senses was a bad idea. I forced my eyes open with a gasp.

Lashes thick with tears blurred my vision further and, for a moment, my skin appeared to glow. Glowing skin? That thought, more than anything, shocked me out of my spiraling panic. Who knows, maybe I had been bitten by a radioactive spider or blessed with saintly powers. I felt a giggle rising at the absurd image.

"You're really losing it," I muttered between clenched teeth.

I gulped in air and pulled myself up onto wobbly legs. There was no time to waste. I had to save the city and that meant getting information from Kaye, having nightmare visions, and deducing the location of the missing kelpie king, before a bloodthirsty band of *each uisge* got hungry or bored. Tick tock.

The remainder of the walk to The Emporium was uneventful. My breathing was a bit ragged, but that could have been attributed to an uphill slog in the oppressive heat. The dizziness that plagued my walk was, aside from a few sparklies in my peripheral vision, mostly gone.

Arachne was busy with customers, a group of ladies in sundresses probably just off the ferry, so I waved and headed toward the back. The shop was cluttered, as usual, but I managed to make it to the oddments counter without tripping or getting lost. A small victory, but I'll take what I can get.

Once through Kaye's security protocols, I headed to the spell kitchen and rapped on the open door frame. Kaye's colorful form was missing from the cooking area, so I wasn't surprised when I heard a voice call to me from her office.

I found Kaye, wrapped in her usual multi-hued layers and kerchiefs, atop the chair behind her desk. She was reading a large leather covered tome, with gold stars and moons along the spine that winked in the flickering candle-light.

"Hey," I said, standing just outside the office door. I felt embarrassed to be asking for her help again, so soon.

"Well, don't stand on ceremony, girl," Kaye said, waving a jangling, bangle covered arm. "Come in and sit yourself down. You look like you are about to drop dead on your feet."

"Sure, um, thanks," I said. "Did Jinx or Father Michael call ahead?"

"Yes," Kaye said.

I pulled off my baseball cap and moved a stack of books, so I could sit on a low stool beside the desk. I fidgeted with the cap, wringing it as I held it between my knees. Where in the world to start? Had my roommate or the priest explained the day's events and what I had come for? Perhaps it was best to let her speak first.

I waited patiently as Kaye scrutinized me over small, gold-rimmed glasses. Her sharp eyes widened as her gaze took in the space around my head, the book she was reading forgotten on her lap. Was she reading my aura? If so, I didn't like the reflection of what she saw there.

"Well, I'll be a faerie's uncle," Kaye muttered.

"What?" I asked.

"Nothing, nothing, just the ramblings of an old woman," Kaye said. The ramblings of an old woman? Now that was hard to believe. "Father Michael tells me you've had your meeting with the demon and survived. He also tells me you are in dire need of information."

"Yes," I said. "Somehow I've ended up in the middle of a local turf war between two types of water fae that I know almost nothing about." I took a deep, slow breath and clamped down on the already rising panic. I needed to face my fear and stay in control. Fear would only help our enemy. "I could really use some information about kelpies and *each uisge*— strengths, weaknesses, habits, allegiances, that sort of thing."

"So what is the job?" Kaye asked. She got right to the point. "The demon vermin wanted you for a specific task, correct?"

"Yes, he...the demon, is working for kelpies," I said. "They want my help to find their missing king. The kelpie king, Ceffyl Dŵr, left this behind. I'm told it's from his bridle."

I pulled my bag onto my lap and slowly lifted the wrapped bundle, containing the piece of kelpie bridle, onto Kaye's desk.

"Ah, they want you to use your Sight to see who has taken their king, or if he is even still alive," Kaye said.

"Yes," I said, swallowing hard. "Though my primary job is to locate the remainder of Ceffyl Dŵr's bridle."

"Did the demon bother to mention the significance of a kelpie's bridle?" Kaye asked. I shook my head. The piece emanated powerful magic, even I could tell that, but Forneus hadn't shed any light onto why. "No? I didn't think so. Demons are such frustrating creatures. They are so terribly verbose when they wish to be and unbearably laconic when details would be welcome."

"Is it significant?" I asked.

"Well, the kelpies probably don't want you to know, in case you were to use the information against them, but most of their power is in their bridle," Kaye said. "If you manage to steal a kelpie bridle, you have absolute control over their actions for as long as it remains in your possession. Of course, a kelpie bridle is not an easy thing to steal."

Mab's bones. I had a very bad feeling about this.

"There's more you should know," I said. I ran a gloved hand through my hair and sighed. "*Each uisge* are here, in the bay, and they've started hunting humans. I was told that kelpies and other local water fae usually defend their home waters against an *each uisge* threat..."

"But with the blasted kelpie king missing, they don't have the guts to stand against them," Kaye said.

"Right," I said. "The kelpies need their king to return, if there's any hope of fighting the *each uisge*. But if the *each uisge* abducted Ceffyl Dŵr and have possession of his bridle..."

"When he returns, it won't be to lead his people against the *each uisge*," Kaye said. "He'll be fighting for the enemy. Even if they are attacked directly, the kelpies will not put up much of a fight against their own king. Unless his bridle is retrieved from the *each uisge*, Ceffyl Dŵr's people will not survive this battle."

"Neither, will we," I said. "Forneus and Father Michael seem to be in agreement that, if left unchecked, the *each uisge* will slaughter every human in this city. With the kelpie king leading them against us, we don't stand a chance."

"Did Forneus say how much time we have?" Kaye asked.

"No, just that the *each uisge* are already testing the waters with these individual attacks," I said. "Once they're convinced that the local kelpies and their allies aren't willing to oppose them, they'll swarm the city in a killing spree."

"Then there is no time to lose," Kaye said. She stood up with a flurry of skirts and tinkling of jewelry and began shuffling about the tiny room, thrusting dusty books into my arms. "Take these books to the kitchen. We have spells to brew and a bridle to find if there's any hope for this city."

"Do you think we can find the king's bridle in time?" I asked.

I had been afraid to ask, but if she answered while I was standing with watery eyes behind a pile of dusty books, I wouldn't have to see the fear in her lined face.

"We best find it, and find it quick, or there will be war," Kaye said. "And this is one battle that the humans of Harborsmouth have little hope of winning. A few of us will fight, we always do, but there are not enough of us. Not anymore."

I expected fear, but Kaye sounded tired and perhaps a bit melancholy. I suppose that's what happens when you watch everyone around you die. If we went to war with the *each uisge*, it wouldn't be Kaye's first, but it could be our last.

I peered around the stack of books to see if Kaye was done giving me stuff to carry. She didn't just sound tired, the old woman looked exhausted. There were dark smudges circling her eyes and deep worry lines around her mouth and below her kerchief that weren't there before. This threat was taking its toll.

I vowed then to do everything that I could to find the lost kelpie king and end this thing, fast. I felt guilty for involving Kaye. The demon had hired me to do this job, so the problem was mine to deal with. I desperately needed information regarding the monsters, information that Kaye had, but hadn't she already done enough for this city?

"Stop daydreaming and carry those books to the kitchen," Kaye said, snapping her fingers in front of my face. "In case you haven't noticed, we have a lot of work to do."

"Yes, ma'am," I squeaked. Kaye was right. This was no time for getting lost in thought. No, it was time for action. I ran for the door.

*****

Kaye's battle experience and iron will made her an excellent general for our little ragtag army. Her spell kitchen was quickly transformed into our war room. Maps of the city and surrounding waters were spread across an enormous oak slab table.

Hob had been coaxed out from beneath his hearthstone to help mark locations of *each uisge* attacks on the maps before us. He was the only one nimble enough to flit around the table without disturbing the arrangement of markers, but I kept a close watch on his pockets. The rapt look he gave the colorful pieces of sea glass we were using to mark the map revealed his true nature. I was sure that Kaye had promised a gift of sea glass to enlist Hob's help. I just hoped he could wait until we were actually done using them. Brownies, though long-lived, are not known for their patience.

I split my attention between watching Hob and studying the pile of books I'd borrowed from Kaye's personal library. Thick tomes covered the carved plank bench I was straddling. A few lay open to the section on *each uisge*. I wished I could close them and run away screaming.

The reproduced paintings and anatomical renderings on those pages were almost too terrifying to believe. I rubbed already tired eyes with gloved fingers. Great, even with my eyes closed, I could see the horrifying, gore-filled, pictures. Disturbing images of *each uisge*, and their disgusting habits, had burned themselves into my brain. I was definitely going to have new nightmares to add to my repertoire. Oh, joy.

Turning back to the books, I skimmed the pages trying to glean something useful.

According to Kaye's books, an *each uisge* is a dark skinned water horse that appeared to suffer from a bad case of mange. Either the *each uisge* depicted in the pictures were a sickly representation, or these fae weren't overly healthy. Who knows, maybe a diet consisting wholly of human flesh, sans livers, isn't very nutritious. The beasts were slender to the point of emaciation, with patchy fur and slimy skin pulled tight over hips, ribs, and cheek bones.

Diseased or not, the *each uisge* were formidable. Though slender, the average height of an *each uisge* was documented at around seventeen hands, six feet, high at the

withers, where the base of the neck meets the back. Their hips
are hinged so that they can also stand upright on their hind
legs. The better to disembowel their victim, I suppose.

They were, in fact, designed with a disemboweling tool
similar to that of a velociraptor. A sickle claw on each hind leg
extended from the sesamoid, or fetlock, bones. The rear legs of
the *each uisge* ended in hooves similar to those of other equine
creatures, but the front legs were an abomination. The forelegs
of an *each uisge* appear horse-like until you reach the carpus,
or knee, where they sprout a fan of needle-like protrusions.
These black spines contain a toxic cocktail of poisons and
neurotoxins designed to paralyze their prey. Below the spines,
the legs are covered in chitinous layers of exoskeleton. Where
the layers of exoskeleton overlapped, hard, razor sharp
projections, similar to mussel shells, provided additional
protection. The forelegs were capped with barnacle and
seaweed covered hooves.

The head of an *each uisge* resembled a horse with the
exception of red gill slits along the elongated neck, fin-like ears,
milky white eyes, and the upper jaw of a dire wolf. The bottom
jaw could dislocate while eating, allowing it to distend, in order
to swallow large prey whole.

I don't know how they ate around, or regurgitated, the
livers that they leave behind. The book, some kind of
encyclopedia of monsters, wasn't clear on that point. Perhaps
they use their sickle claws to disembowel their prey first then
proceed to eat the remainder of the body whole. Honestly, if it
wouldn't help with keeping the beasts from killing everyone in
Harborsmouth, I really didn't want to know.

The most impressive, and horrifying, thing about an
each uisge was their teeth. Damn, those things would give the
most ancient vampire a whopping case of fang envy. Two
large, black fangs, easily the length of my forearm, protruded
from the upper jaw. But that wasn't all. The mouth, when
opened wide, revealed a lower jaw filled with two alternating
rows of long, pointed, needle-sharp teeth, similar to those of an
anglerfish.

These monsters were about to invade our city? I was
already nostalgic for this morning when my biggest worry was
tangling with a demon.

A flitting motion to my left made me raise my head from
the book of horrors. I was just in time to see Hob thrust a

knobby hand, clutching a piece of blue sea glass, into the
pocket of his little brown coat.

"Put it back," I whispered. I eyed his pocket knowingly.

"Don' know wa' ta lass speaks of," Hob said. He was
blushing from his neck to his furry brow, but his hand
remained in his pocket.

"As soon as this is over, I'll buy you a big bag of sea
glass," I said. "But for now, we need to track the movements of
the *each uisge*. It's important."

"Oh, dis bit of purty?" Hob asked. He held it out and
when I nodded he started rubbing it on his sleeve. "'twas dirty,
lass. Hob was jus givin' it a bit o' shine."

Right, and I'm the tooth faerie.

"Okay, just be sure to put it back exactly where it
belongs," I said.

Hob sighed, but put the piece of blue glass back on the
map. The pieces of blue glass indicated areas of missing
persons. There were a lot of them. I hoped that they didn't
represent more *each uisge* attacks. We had enough violent
deaths that matched *each uisge* hunting habits marked with
pink glass. So far they were sticking to the area around the
bay, but how long would that last?

My hand strayed to the pouch that held the piece of the
kelpie king's bridle. It was time for me to face the reality of
what Forneus had hired me to do. The colored sea glass
spreading out over the maps of Harborsmouth, were a clear
indication of just how little time we had left. The *each uisge*
were in position for a mass invasion, and they were hungry for
flesh and blood. My money was on a full-scale attack within
forty-eight hours—and that was a conservative bet.

I removed the pouch from my backpack, holding it
gingerly by the pull-string handles, and set it on the bench. My
hands were barely shaking. Go me.

"So, I guess I'm ready to touch the, um, piece of bridle," I
said, turning to Kaye. "Do you have your spells up?"

Kaye had offered to set a dampening spell to keep
customers from hearing my screams. I'm sure she could have
made some excuse about banshees or some other nonsense, but
she knew me well enough to know I'd be uncomfortable with
the attention. I appreciated, and accepted, the offer. The lack
of control over my visions was always frustrating, but when it

led to screaming and drooling, it could be downright embarrassing.

"Just a moment," Kaye said. She closed her eyes and spoke a few words under her breath. When she opened them again, the walls of the room seemed to shimmer. "The spells are set. Okay, Ivy. You may proceed whenever you are ready."

Ouch. I tried not to wince, but Kaye sounded overly formal. She only talks like that when she's nervous, which is, like, almost never. *You may proceed whenever you are ready.* At least she didn't call me ma'am. If that ever happened, I might as well go jump in the *each uisge* infested bay.

With a jerky nod, I faked a smile and reached for the small, draw-string bag. Setting it gingerly on my lap, I closed my eyes and counted to ten. Therapy may not have improved my relationship with my parents, but it had helped me cope with anxiety. With one last slow, deep breath, I opened my eyes to stare at my hands resting at either side of the small bag.

Mab's bones. Even with the breathing exercises, I was far from calm. I tried to ignore my heart trying to beat its way out of my chest. With a shrug, I yanked the wrist strap open on each glove. I continued to remove my gloves, tugging them off one finger at a time, and set them on top of the book I had been reading. Cool air tingled across the backs of my hands. I felt vulnerable, naked.

The small pouch on my lap was next. The purple Royal Crown bag was cinched at the top. It was difficult to untie the knot with trembling fingers, but, after a few tense minutes, I was able to ease the bag open. Tipping the velvet pouch upside down, I slid out the cloth-wrapped bundle, so small yet filled with the potential to crack this case...or leave me a dribbling mess.

I was rooting for the former, but if I couldn't solve this and help the kelpies find their king, then I might as well be a mindless, gibbering fool. I'd rather not be in control of all my senses when the *each uisge* come. The slaughter of Harborsmouth was not something I ever wanted to experience.

I unwrapped the final layers of the cloth bundle until a small piece of leather lay exposed. I took a shuddering breath.

"Now or never, Ivy," I goaded myself.

I licked trembling lips, but my mouth was dry. All the moisture seemed to have gone to my hands. I wiped sweaty palms on my thighs and reached for the piece of bridle. Time to discover what happened to Ceffyl Dŵr—why he went missing. I gripped the leather, fingers pressed against silver-threaded engravings, and Kaye's kitchen disappeared.

*****

Just when the pressure in my head and blinding fog seemed unbearable, my ears cleared with a pop and my vision came into focus.

It's a good thing kelpies aren't as horrifying as *each uisge*. I stood in a flooded cavern, water dripping ceaselessly from stalactites that projected from the limestone ceiling. I was completely surrounded. Hundreds of kelpies milled about the rocky outcroppings and swam in the dark waters. *My people...*

Kelpies were gorgeous creatures. In their natural form, the kelpies were slender, yet well-muscled, resembling impressive racehorses. They didn't share the more horrific mutations of the *each uisge*, but they did have fin shaped ears that flared from the sides of their head, seaweed woven into mane and tail, and gill slits along the neck. Their dappled grey coats were glossy and smooth like a harbor seal's.

I wondered if they shared origins with selkies who also sported seal-like skins. I had learned that anyone who stole the bridle of a kelpie, gained control over them completely. Selkies, similarly, fell under the power of the person who stole their skin. There were many tales of human men stealing and locking away the skin of a selkie woman, forcing her to become his bride. The similarities were intriguing, but the scene before me was more important.

I studied the kelpies as they moved to attend their king. A few in their human form moved with otherworldly grace, as though they retained the underlying strength and abilities of their equine bodies. Though similar to human men and women, I would never have mistaken them for anything other than water fae. Their lithe movements were not the only thing to give them away. Each kelpie appeared to have a piece of seaweed entwined in their beautifully sleek hair. I'd have to ask Kaye about the significance of that later. The kelpies also had unnaturally large eyes. Their eyes at first glance appeared to be colorless black, but closer inspection revealed a shade of green, midnight dark, but green nonetheless.

I was receiving a particularly close look at those eyes, as a large male kelpie knelt before me. He was in his natural equine form and the subservient pose looked awkward to hold. My chest constricted as he leveled his pleading gaze on mine. *My son...*

I nodded and the young kelpie's head was severed. I don't know exactly what the king's son had done, but the word that battered my senses was *traitor*. This was something that happened a long time ago, but a strong psychic impression had been left on the bridle. Ceffyl Dŵr's pain was intense. I gasped for breath and, with a vertiginous tilt, the scenery shifted.

This time when my sight cleared, I was the one on my knees. I knelt, in the form of a man, before a strikingly attractive woman. Rage made her blue eyes flash, but even the twist of her full lips into a snarling grimace couldn't mar her beauty. She had to be fae. No human was that seductive without even trying.

She paced back and forth behind a low wall of stones and dangled something that cried and wailed as it swung out over the low fire pit. Ceffyl Dŵr was pleading for the woman to stop.

"Please, Melusine!" he begged. "Let our child go. We have already lost one son. Do not kill our only remaining heir."

"Sons, sons, oh your precious sons!" she shrieked. "That is all you've ever cared about. Never me, no, never your beloved."

"This is crazy," he said. "You know I love you. I am your husband."

His words rang empty, even to my ears.

"There was a time that I thought being your wife would be enough," she said. "I was wrong."

Something splashed in the water behind Melusine and the resultant hiss of steam on the fire made the child's sobs increase.

"You're scaring me and frightening the child," he said. "Please, set the babe down away from the fire. We can talk about this."

"No, the time for talk is long gone, my love," Melusine said.

She pulled herself upright, moving closer to the fire, and for the first time I could see her tail. Melusine had a voluptuous female body from the waist up and a fish tail from

the waist down. She was definitely fae, probably a nix or
mermaid, though her behavior tickled a memory of my own.
Wasn't there a story of a lamia who had killed her sons?
Another bit of monster history to ask Kaye about, if I made it
out of this vision.

Distracted by the firelight reflecting off rainbow hued
scales, I nearly missed what happened next. Ceffyl Dŵr's pain
pulled my eyes to Melusine's hand, where his attention was
riveted. Their child writhed in his mother's grip, face red from
crying. *My son...*

Melusine cast the child into the flames. She savored the
anguish on her husband's face, then, with a splash, she was
gone. A sob burst from my chest and the vision changed again.

My eyes took in a different time and location, the cry of
gulls and the kelpie child still ringing in my ears. The cries
died away to blessed silence.

I had worked hard to slip away from my guards. They
were bound to my service, and served me well, but their looks
of adoration and respect became downright claustrophobic,
especially on this day of the year. I reveled in the silent night,
a rare stolen private moment for a king perpetually surrounded
by guards and courtiers.

I was walking alone along a gravel footpath. Moonlight
reflected off a stream that trickled over smooth rocks to my left,
bushes and tall trees blocked out the city lights to my right,
and a stone bridge loomed ahead. The space beneath the
bridge, like a gaping mouth, was inky black, but something
large stirred within.

I tensed, straining my senses to detect what lurked
within the shadows of the bridge, when a twig snapped on the
path behind me. I slid a long knife from its sheath on my belt,
and spun to face my potential attacker. A horse-like creature
stood on the path behind me, but it was not one of my people—
it was an *each uisge*. The *each uisge* were our enemy, but they
rarely left the ocean waters except to feed. Even then, they
traveled in packs, hunting the commercial wharf areas along
the water's edge. What was it doing here alone, so far into the
city?

Surveying my options, I took a step back and the bushes
to my left rustled as three more *each uisge* joined my assailant.
Hooves and chitin clattered on wet stones, indicating more

enemies closing in from the stream bed. This was no random encounter. No, it wasn't even a routine mugging.

It was an ambush.

I cursed my foolishness. Slipping my royal bodyguards was going to get me killed, or worse. I swung my knife in an arc, slashing a warning to keep my assailants at a distance. I was skilled with a blade, but my knife wouldn't keep them away for long. These creatures came armed with their own claws, poisoned spines, razor sharp chitin, and deadly fangs. I could call on the water of the stream, but its power was small. The recent drought had reduced it to a sluggish trickle. I tried anyway.

I was feeling desperate.

My skin became luminous as I called the water to me. I might as well have painted a target on my back. Singing a trilling, bubbling song, I coaxed the water into a slender rope and whipped it at the *each uisges'* ankles. One of the creatures let out a guttural whinny that tore at my eardrums, as he stumbled.

Hope swelled my chest, but it was trampled as something hit me from the side. I staggered and felt the slash of a sickle claw slice open my hip and cut through the bridle that hung from my belt. No, not that. Not my bridle. I couldn't, wouldn't be a slave to the *each uisge*. I tried to roll, looking for an escape route, but nothing happened.

I was frozen in place.

The *each uisge* snickered, a sound like a beast coughing up rocks and nails. Movement from the shadow of the bridge caused them to stop. Their violent, shrieking laughter died on blood encrusted lips. All heads turned, eerily as one, to glare at the creature foolish enough to interrupt my torment, and spoil their fun.

A large figure unfolded from a heap of clothing, a blanket still wrapped around his shoulders. From my angle, I could tell that the figure appeared to be a troll, probably a bridge troll judging from where it had been sleeping. Unless it had lots of friends, it didn't stand a chance against a pack of *each uisge*, but I had no way of warning him off. I had lost the ability to speak, unless ordered to by my captors.

"What going on?" the troll said, yawning and rubbing his face.

An *each uisge* hissed and launched itself at the troll. Trolls are huge, but this one didn't put up much of a fight. The *each uisge* had it on the ground in seconds. Once it was down, a second *each uisge* used its hooves to kick in the poor creature's teeth. I tried to block out the wet tearing sound and the whimpering that followed.

Fortunately, the two *each uisge* quickly lost interest in the unmoving troll and trotted over to a tall figure that I assumed was their leader. They paced in restless circles, like aquarium sharks at feeding time. One of the *each uisge*, shorter and heavier set than the rest, finally began to speak.

The language they spoke was like hissing steam and rusty metal grating against a chalkboard, but I understood the words.

"Hungry," the stout one said. Drool oozed from his fanged mouth to pool on the stones at his feet. "Trollsss tassste bad. Kill humansss now?"

"Patience, B'al," the tall one said. "Sssoon, we will take this cccity, ripe with tasssty humansss."

"Yesss, my lord," B'al said.

They turned to face me, or rather Ceffyl Dŵr who stood rooted to the spot where his bridle had been removed.

"Come kelpie," the tall one said. "We have plansss for you."

As Ceffyl Dŵr turned to follow his new masters, I caught a glimpse of the crumpled form beneath the bridge. Mab's bones. The large victim they had been abusing was Marvin. Sweet, innocent, child-like Marvin.

Something inside me shattered.

*****

It was a good thing that Kaye had set a dampening spell on the room. I woke to shrieking cries that I belatedly identified as my own. Clamping both hands over my mouth, I rocked back and forth trying to silence the eerie howls and wailing rising from my throat. Even with the help of Kaye, who draped a blanket across my shoulders and whispered promises of safety, it took me a long time to stop.

Only when my lungs were spent and I had no air left to scream, did the silence come. My ears were ringing and my throat was raw and sore, but I was back in my own body. I was Ivy Granger again, and I was slave to no one.

During the final moments of the vision, I felt like I was losing my sense of self. That, even more than the kelpie king's abduction, was terrifying. What would have happened to me if I had remained lost in the vision, believing I was Ceffyl Dŵr? Would I have relived that moment of his enslavement and Marvin's attack, forever?

Oh, Oberon's eyes, poor Marvin. I needed to tell Kaye about how the kid had received his injuries. He wasn't mugged by wannabe gangsters or assaulted by teens out drinking and looking for trouble. No, Marvin was brutally attacked by *each uisge*. That kind of thing could leave lasting emotional scars. The kid was going to need therapy.

I sucked in a shuddering breath and wiped tears on the knees of my pants. My legs were drawn up to my chest so tight that the muscles felt cramped and my joints protested as I eased my feet back down to the floor. How long had I sat here, in fetal position, rocking and screaming like a madwoman?

I opened my eyes and realized I must have been acting crazy long enough to freak out my friends. Worry was etched into Kaye's face and Hob's cheeks were sparkling with shed tears.

"Lass?" Hob asked. "Ye' be a'right, now. Ye' safe."

Leaning forward, he hesitantly patted my blanket covered shoulder, brow raised as his eyes searched my face. He must have been reassured by what he saw there, because he pulled away, drew himself up to his full height, and smiled.

"How long..." I asked. I started to speak, but was wracked with an uncontrollable coughing fit. My mouth was dry and my throat felt like it had been sandblasted. I licked cracked, bleeding lips, tasted blood, and tried again. "How long was I out?"

"From the time you touched the bridle, about nine hours," Kaye said. "You could probably do with a cup of tea. Hob?"

"Yes, ma'am," Hob said. He shot me a nervous grin then flitted off to bustle with the kettle and teapot.

Tea sounded wonderful and I started to relax into a hazy post-shock lassitude, but something was bugging me. Nine hours? Mab's Bones!

"I have to call Jinx!" I said, starting to panic.

I bolted upright and nearly fell over. My legs were tingling with pins and needles and my feet felt like cement blocks. Thrusting gloved hands (huh, someone must have put my gloves back on while I was incoherent) into my pockets, I searched for my cell phone. I needed a phone, like, yesterday.

If I had been unconscious for nine hours, then it was already getting dark. I had left Jinx at the office with a priest and demon. After last night, there was no way I'd risk staying out past sunset without calling her...not unless I was kidnapped or dead. I was in so much trouble.

"Calm yourself, child," Kaye said. "I've called your friend Jinx, and Father Michael. They know you aren't out wandering the streets, dead, or injured."

"Oh, um, thank you," I said. That was a relief, but I still needed to talk to Jinx. I didn't want her to worry. "Did someone, like, borrow my phone?"

"We set it over here, dear, out of the way," Kaye said. She bustled, skirts swishing back and forth, to a ceramic jar on the counter. My phone was in Kaye's cookie jar? "You were thrashing about quite a bit there and I worried you might damage yourself or the phone. I have your belt as well."

My belt? That was quick thinking. There were enough pointy objects on my tool belt to impale me ten times over.

"Thanks," I said, cheeks warming.

I took my phone from Kaye and dialed Jinx's number. She answered on the first ring.

"Hey," I said. "Everything okay at the office?"

"Oh my God, Ivy," Jinx said. "Shit." She sniffed, and I could tell that she'd been crying. "I was so worried about you."

"Kaye said she called," I said. Damn, I knew Jinx would worry. When your luck is as bad as hers, you don't always look on the bright side. I mean, Jinx was one of the most positive minded people I know, but she knows enough to worry when things start going wrong. "Didn't she tell you that I was okay?"

"Oh, yeah, right," Jinx said. "She said you were 'safe as houses,' but I could hear you *screaming*. It didn't take a psychic to know you weren't okay. You barely sounded human."

She said the last in a muffled whisper, probably trying to keep my mental breakdown a secret from Forneus and Father Michael. I shivered and pulled the blanket tighter around my shoulders.

"I'm okay, now," I said. "How are things at the office? Any luck with the job contract?"

"Are you freaking kidding?" Jinx asked. "Dude, we're, like, only on page one."

"Seriously?" I asked. Demons, they made everything complicated.

"Seriously," Jinx said.

"Well, I have to get back to things here with Kaye, but hang in there," I said.

"You too," Jinx said. "And, Ivy? I love you, but if you ruin that top, I'm going to kill you."

"Right, I'll try not to get any blood stains on it," I said, rolling my eyes.

"Good, girl," Jinx said. "Later."

She hung up and I put my phone on vibrate. It was time to answer Kaye's questions, and drink copious amounts of tea. There was a lot to tell, and not all of it was good.

So, Ceffyl Dŵr, King of the Kelpies, had been betrayed by his eldest son whom he had put to death, married a bitch who murdered their other son in a jealous rage, and was recently attacked and abducted by a bloodthirsty group of *each uisge* bent on turning our city into their own gory buffet in their first move to control the eastern seaboard.

The attack on the kelpie king had happened near a stone bridge on a footpath by one of the streams that feeds into the marsh. We knew where the attack took place, but more importantly, we had a witness.

I also had a new reason to stay in this fight. No monster was going to beat up and torture an orphan kid in this city and get away with it. Not on my watch.

I was going to help the kelpies find their missing king and his bridle. Then I planned on kicking some *each uisge* ass.

CHAPTER 8

Kaye made me repeat every detail of my vision, like, a gazillion times. Even with Hob attentively filling my teacup, there was no way I could keep this up. My eyelids were on strike and my voice had gone past that sexy, gravelly, raspy sound that comes from a lifetime of whiskey and cigarettes, hours ago. It was now bordering on nonexistent.

"No more," I rasped. "Too tired. Need sleep."

"Too tired?" Kaye asked raising her eyebrow until it disappeared under her head kerchief. "We do not have time for sleep, we are at war."

"Beg pardon ma'am, but ta lass be only human," Hob said, gesturing at me with a knobby hand.

A strange look crossed Kaye's face, but she nodded, finally acquiescing.

"Perhaps a good nights' sleep will do us all a bit of good," Kaye said.

Giving in to peer pressure was not normal for Kaye, probably something to do with having no real equal in this city, but I wasn't going to argue. I desperately required sleep. I just hoped she wasn't sick or something. We had a lot of work to do in the morning.

"Um, Hob, want my help cleaning this up?" I asked, gesturing at the table.

I was bone tired, but I didn't want to anger the little guy by leaving a mess in his kitchen. I sent up a silent prayer that the maps and books could stay out on the table a bit longer.

"No, lass," Hob said, with a heavy sigh. "Looks like we'll be needin' dis a while yet."

"Yes, the battle has only just begun," Kaye said.

I didn't like the sound of that.

Tired as I was, I still picked up my teacup and saucer and placed them in the sink. They looked so small and fragile, easily chipped and altered forever. I lay my palms on either side of the sink and let my head hang down, breath bouncing off my chest to return in warm puffs of air. I didn't like what I had to do next, but I couldn't see an alternative.

"I'll be back in the morning," I said. "But, um, can you have Marvin meet me here? I have some questions for him."

I hated bringing up the night of his attack, especially when the kid had been through so much and it would be a fresh hurt, but we needed information. If I had any hope of picking up the kelpie king's trail, then I needed to know where that bridge was located. In the vision, it looked like Marvin had been living there, beneath one of the stone arches. It's what trolls do. With a bit of luck, he'd still remember where it was, even if he had blocked out the memory of the *each uisge* assault that forced him from his home.

"Of course," Kaye said. "Now take yourself home, before you drown in my sink."

I had slouched further forward and the tips of my hair were floating in dirty dishwater. When had my hair come undone? I'd wrestled it into a ponytail at an unholy hour this morning, hoping to keep the heat at bay. The fine hair must have slipped out of its elastic during my vision induced fit.

"Very funny," I said.

I pushed the hair from my face, twisting and pulling it up into a loose ghetto puff style bun. The ends were still wet with tea and dirty water. I also felt sweaty and sore from my nine-hour panic attack. I'd take a bath once I reached the loft, if I could stay awake long enough.

I turned around and dragged myself to the bench where I'd left my stuff. Grabbing my bag by the shoulder strap with one hand, I said my goodbyes, waving to Kaye and Hob. Hob looked worried, but let me go. He could nag me about wandering the streets alone after dark, when I returned in the morning.

I staggered home in a zombie-like fugue. Fortunately, the sweltering heat continued to keep most people indoors, enjoying the benefits of air conditioning, and off the streets. No one ran screaming, worried that I'd try to eat their brains. In fact, I barely remembered leaving The Emporium and walking across the city.

Blinking, I realized I was already on my street, just a few doors from home. My keys were in my gloved hand, ready to let myself into the apartment stairwell. All I had to do was walk past Private Eye.

I hesitated, unsure if I should stop by the office first. I needed to check in with Jinx, but I couldn't bear facing the priest or the demon. If they were still working on the job contract, I'd have to sneak up to the loft.

Sticking to the shadows cast by shop awnings and lamp posts, I stepped down from the brick sidewalk onto the cobblestone street. Water Street was narrow here, so I was across the smooth stones in seconds. I ducked into the doorway of a shop that sold handmade tapestry bags. The glass door panel and storefront were dark, the shop closed for the evening.

Pressed into the darkest corner, I remained unseen, but I couldn't quite see inside Private Eye. A semi-circle of golden light shone from the office window, putting our business emblem in stark relief, but the angle was too sharp to see what was going on inside. Holding my breath, I inched forward peeking my head out around the corner and into the street.

Craning my neck, I could just see Jinx sitting at her desk. She was chewing on a pen and looking down at something in front of her. Maybe she was alone? If they had taken a break for the night, then she might just be wrapping things up. I could head inside and help her close up the office, then catch up on the day's events over a cup of tea. I would even skip my bath.

Movement to her right, made Jinx look up and an angry look crossed her face. Crap, she wasn't alone and she obviously didn't like whoever she was now talking to. Even at this distance, I could see her nostrils flare. She was definitely angry at the person, and I was betting it was Forneus.

I tiptoed forward, heart hammering in my chest. A handsome man in an expensive suit stood glaring down his nose at Jinx. His posture was pure confidence and if I were standing closer, I knew that I'd be able to see the goat-slitted pupils of his eyes. I was right, it was Forneus.

I clenched my hands into fists to still the shaking from fear or exhaustion, take your pick. Inching past the bag shop with tapestry totes hanging forlornly in the darkened window, I froze as I heard a strange humming come from my left. Demon magic? I jumped forward as a lamp flickered to life at the corner. A squeak did not slip past my lips—it was totally a mouse, I swear.

From my new vantage point, I could see Father Michael joining the argument, his birdlike movements quick with obvious agitation. I did not want to get trapped in that office right now. Oberon's eyes, I was tired. I was jumping at street lamps and ready to hit the dirt over the tiniest movement. I needed to get to bed before I gave myself a heart attack.

With a momentary pang of guilt, and a silent apology to Jinx, I crab-walked speedily to the apartment door. The key slid home, and with a quick turn of the knob, I ran inside. I clicked the door shut, flipped the lock, and sprinkled a line of salt and protection herbs across the threshold. I finally let out the breath I'd been holding and breathed in the stale odors of past tenants.

Climbing the flight of stairs was like the ascent up Mt. Everest, without the blessed cold, but eventually, I dragged myself to our apartment. I swung the door wide and smiled at the aroma of old coffee and wet dog. The wet dog smell was coming from a colorful woven tapestry that Jinx made when she took a crafting class, the heat and humidity bringing out the pungent oils of the wool. The loft was hot and stuffy, but at that moment I wouldn't have changed a thing. It was home.

I started toward my room, but hesitated. Sleep isn't an escape for me, and it hasn't been for a long, long time. I considered waiting up for Jinx and working through the events of the day, trying to make sense of my vision, but changed my mind. I knew, from experience, that if I stayed awake for too long, I'd become completely useless. I was already having difficulty stringing more than two words together and my eyes were blurry and unfocused. Soon, even my second sight would become unreliable.

No, I didn't want to reach that point. The resulting double vision was disorienting and this day had been baffling enough. I needed to get some rest while I could. I continued walking to my bedroom.

It didn't take me long to shrug out of my soiled clothes, tossing them on the floor, and crawl into bed. The sheets were cool and clean against my skin, but sleep didn't come right away.

Something had been weird about Kaye's behavior today, but I was too exhausted to figure out what exactly. I tried to forget about it, I mean, come on, we had some serious faerie crap hitting the fan, but the feeling that something was out of whack with our relationship nagged at me like a toothache. I felt like I had come close to figuring it out once, but every time my mind started to form a theory, it fragmented and slid away. It was like grasping at reflections on the surface of a pond.

Had I done something to anger her while I was having my vision, or suffering the screaming aftermath? Somehow that didn't seem right. Kaye had started acting strangely when I first arrived. Oberon's eyes, I was getting nowhere. Something was discordant about my friend's behavior and as soon as we both had a free moment, there were some tough questions I needed to ask.

I rolled over, pulling my blanket up under my chin and fell into the shadowy world of sleep. My nightmares were waiting for me in the dark. They're always lurking nearby, biding their time knowing that they'll get their chance to torment me again. Sleep always comes, no matter how hard I try to fight it.

CHAPTER 9

I woke to the heavenly smell of coffee. Too bad it was being held by a demon. Okay, not really a demon. Forneus hadn't found a way past our wards and into the loft, but Jinx was doing a damned fine imitation. Her red lacquered nails were tapping a staccato against the porcelain mug while her other hand rested on a curvaceous hip. She looked pissed.

"Sorry," I said.

It came out like, "shmorffrree" from beneath the tangle of blankets. I must have been battling my bedding in my sleep. If my sheets were the *each uisge* army, the war would be over by now. I had wrung all of the life from them. Go me.

"Get the hell up," Jinx said.

"Just a minute," I said.

I tried to disentangle myself from the sheets and blankets, but gave up, pushing them all onto the floor. There, I was free. Now if I could just find some clean clothes. I know there was a basket with clean laundry around here somewhere...

"No, Ivy," Jinx said. "You don't have a minute. Get your ass in the kitchen, now."

Mab's bones. She was well and truly ticked at me. Well, this day was starting off just peachy.

"Okay," I said, pulling on a hooded sweatshirt and yoga pants. It was too hot for the sweatshirt, but I wasn't going to take the time to look for something more weather appropriate and risk making Jinx any madder than she already was.

Jinx stormed to the kitchen, her mary jane pumps clacking against the floor with each angry step. I followed, hands in my pockets, feeling like a little kid awaiting punishment. This was so unfair. My head was pounding with each strike of Jinx's heels on the hard tile. It was enough to make me wish we had wall to wall shag carpeting.

With a wince, I shuffled to the opposite side of the bar that divides the kitchen from the living room, and pulled

myself onto one of the retro soda fountain stools. I felt safer
knowing there was a counter between us. Jinx looked ready to
pounce.

"You left me with those jerks all freaking day," Jinx
said. "What do you have to say for yourself?"

"Sorry?" I asked.

Oops, wrong answer. Jinx slapped a hand down on the
counter, making me jump. I hoped her tantrum would wind
down soon. My head was ready to split open.

"All day, Ivy," Jinx said. "You left me with bird man
and horn dog, all day and most of the night."

"What can I do to make it up to you?" I asked.

I sighed, knowing that my bank account was going to
take a sucker punch. A little maneuvering might keep my
checks from bouncing, but it had been a tough month.

"These," Jinx said. "I want these."

Jinx slammed her hand down on an open magazine. She
tapped her finger against a page displaying a pair of pricey
platform sandals, circled in black marker. The cherry pattern on
the fabric and red bows were cute, but the price nearly made
me throw up. Unfortunately, Jinx had a point. I owed her, big
time.

"Sure," I said. "If you can wait until the money from
this job comes in, they're yours."

"Really?" Jinx asked.

"Yes, they'll look amazing on you," I said.

I meant it too. She was the only person I knew who
could pull off wearing those shoes without looking cheesy. And
Jinx loves shoes. She has an entire wall of shelves in her room
devoted to them. Me? I have one pair of black Doc Martens
boots and an old pair of cross trainers. It was amazing that
Jinx and I were friends. We were total opposites.

Thankfully her bad temper doesn't last long, especially
when she gets her way. A smile broke out on her face, shifting
her features from dangerous to cute, in a flash.

"I know, right?" Jinx said. "I have the perfect dress to
wear them with. They'd be perfect for the Old Port Festival."

"So long as the *each uisge* don't eat us first," I said. Jinx
blanched and I immediately felt guilty about opening my big
mouth. "Sorry, I'm feeling grumpy. I'm still recovering from
yesterday, and haven't had any coffee yet."

"Oh, right," Jinx said, looking chagrined. She poured a mug of coffee and slid it over to my side of the counter. "I keep blocking out the whole being eaten by monster water horses thing. So, how did it go at Kaye's? Get any leads?"

I decided not to go into any more detail about my vision induced breakdown. It was nothing Jinx hadn't seen before and I didn't want to make her worry. I added cream to my coffee and focused, instead, on the positive.

"Yes, I learned a lot about kelpies and *each uisge* from the books in Kaye's library," I said, nodding. "And we got a lead from my vision. There was a witness to Ceffyl Dŵr's abduction, a friend of Kaye's."

"Wow!" Jinx exclaimed. "That's awesome news."

"I'm actually supposed to meet our witness at Kaye's this morning," I said, squinting at the hands on our Felix the Cat clock. "I should probably go change and get going. I don't want to end up on Kaye's bad side. I think she's already a little peeved with me."

"For what?" Jinx asked.

"I have no idea," I said.

With a shrug, I went to prepare for my meeting with Kaye and Marvin. I wasn't sure who I wanted to see less. Kaye's weird behavior was making me feel awkward, like I didn't know where we stood anymore, and I was dreading talking to Marvin about his attack.

I walked past my bed and let out a heavy sigh. Even with the blankets strewn on the floor, my mattress looked awfully tempting. I suddenly wished this day was already over with. The feeling grew stronger when I found my one basket of clean laundry.

In this heat, there was no getting away with wearing something more than once, not unless you wanted to be arrested by the stink police, and my clothing selection had dwindled to a short black skirt, spaghetti strap cami, and gray long-sleeved top. I wasn't even sure if the skirt was mine, so I steeled myself for a vision when I pulled it from the basket. When nothing happened, I blinked at the black fabric in my hands and felt my shoulders ease.

The mystery garment was either mine or something Jinx wore without incident. Time to see if it fit. I shimmied into the skirt, zipping it up with a satisfied grin. I wouldn't have to run around town in yoga pants and a sweatshirt after all. I passed over the cami and grabbed the gray shirt. I was already showing more leg than I was used to. I didn't need to show off everything else as well. Plus, bare skin meant a higher probability of accidental visions. *Gray top it is.*

"Heading to the skate park for a few," Jinx hollered from the living room. "I'll be at the office by nine. I want to warn some of the guys to stay away from the docks. They like to do rail slides on the north end stairs and sometimes they party down at the pier."

Oberon's eyes, I hadn't even thought about the pier. A lot of kids hang out down there, especially now that the heat of the city was so oppressive.

"Good idea," I said. "What reason are you going to give?"

It's not like she could tell the truth. "Dude, don't hang out on the docks, the water's infested with flesh eating faerie horses," doesn't sound plausible, no matter what you're smoking, and there were rules about talking to civilians. I didn't always follow the rules established for hunters and magic users that Kaye had told me about, but they were created for a reason. You don't cause panic among the ignorant masses, even if some of them were cute guys that Jinx likes to flirt with.

The sound of Jinx's shoes on tile preceded her leaning in to peek around my doorway.

"I'll tell them that we're working on a case investigating a rise in hepatitis around the docks and pier," Jinx said. "They knew that guy who was hospitalized when he stepped on a needle last year. I'll tell them that someone's dumping medical waste again and dirty needles are washing up on the beach. Storm tides sometimes push the surf up over the pier and sections of the wharf, so if they think the water's contaminated, they won't skate down there."

She was right. Those guys are always covered in cuts and bruises from skating and if what she was saying was true, it would only take a scratch to get infected.

"Wow, that might actually work," I said. "Ollie will probably think the reports of shark attacks are all part of a conspiracy to cover up the waste dumping."

Our friend Oliver, or Ollie, was majorly into conspiracy theories. If he could wear a tin foil hat while skating, he totally would.

"He'll probably be disappointed it doesn't match his original theory," Jinx said, giggling.

"Which was?" I asked.

"Sharks with fricken laser beams..." Jinx said, laughing. "...on their heads! He said it was part of a military experiment."

"Of course, he said that," I said, rolling my eyes. "He thinks *sea monkeys* are part of a military experiment."

"Too bad I can't tell him about the mutant shark-like faerie horses," Jinx said. "He'd totally freak."

"Yes, that's the problem," I said, sighing. "Everyone will freak and then there'll be rioting in the streets."

"I know," Jinx said. "Don't worry, my lips are sealed." She mimed locking her lips and throwing away the key.

I flashed Jinx the universal thumbs up sign and a smile. She waved, sashaying to the door, her ponytail and the pleats of her halter dress swinging in time to the song she was humming.

*****

Shutting the door on my messy bedroom, I surveyed the loft. I was way behind on my share of roommate duties, but saving the city would have to come first. Maybe I could get Hob to stop by and tidy up the place. He could keep anything shiny he found in my room and all of the couch change that he could carry. I tossed a bottle of water in my bag and grabbed a piece of cold toast from where Jinx had left it for me—right next to the shoe catalog.

I sighed around the toast in my mouth, Jinx wasn't subtle and she was never going to give up on those shoes. I brushed crumbs off my shirt and headed for the door. I needed to get across town before rush hour traffic had angry drivers trying to use Wharf Street as a short cut. It wasn't, but there were always a few drivers desperate enough to brave the narrow cobbled streets. If I wanted to avoid my fellow pedestrians by walking down the middle of the street, then I needed to hustle.

I made good time and managed to avoid the throngs of people that gathered at the coffee cart on the corner of Water Street and Baker's Row, but bumped into a kid as I rounded onto Wharf Street. It wasn't my fault. The "kid" had run headlong into me, probably due to the red hat pulled down low over his eyes.

He hit my hip, knocking him to the ground and spinning me to the side. I braced myself for a vision that didn't come. Realizing that he had only hit the fabric of my skirt and top, not any exposed skin, I breathed a sigh of relief and turned to tell him to watch where he was going. He was, after all, lucky that I wasn't a cyclist. A bike courier would have sent him to the hospital.

He was glaring at me from beneath his hat and one thing was certain—he was no kid. No, the thing flashing pointy, razor sharp teeth at me was a redcap. Redcaps are fae who get their name from the unsavory habit of dying their hat red with the blood of their victims. Kaye once told me that every redcap is on a continuous murder spree, because if they let the blood on their hat dry out, they weaken and eventually die. Judging by the eager gleam in this one's eyes, I'd say that she was right.

The redcap slid a tiny black blade from its belt and crouched low, hissing at me. Dwarflike, he stood with a wide stance, his short legs shod in heavy boots the tops of which nearly reached the bottom of his dark wool coat. A warm breeze shifted toward me and I nearly gagged at the carrion and slaughterhouse smells the redcap wore around him like a cloak. I tried breathing through my mouth, wishing that I could lather vapor rub cream on my upper lip to block the smell. Not that I had a free hand, vapor cream, or time.

I watched the small fae warily, knowing that his diminutive size didn't mean he wasn't deadly. But what the heck was he doing here?

Redcaps are nocturnal, residing in ruins and stone towers during the day. Abandoned forts and lighthouses that dot the coastline provide ample living quarters for the vermin. Usually, they don't travel far from their nest in their quest for blood, preferring the easy kill of vagrants and hikers. Sometimes, when fresh meat doesn't come to them with enough frequency, they turn on each other.

But here was a lone redcap walking the city streets in broad daylight. Something was very wrong with this picture.

The redcap sneered and lunged forward, snapping me out of my thoughts. I skipped to my left and stole a look around the street. People walked by, looking wilted in their business casual attire. A few even stubbornly wore suits, though moisture already ringed their armpits and collars.

I wouldn't get any help from passerby. They would only see a kid in a red hat playing around. His knife probably looked like a Gameboy, or a lollipop. Damn faerie glamour.

A heavy boot stomped on my foot, sending a flash of agony to my brain that stole the air from my lungs. I tried to limp out of knife range, and catch my breath, but my injured foot slowed me down. The evil little black blade lashed out, grazing my arm.

I stumbled to one knee, clutching my arm where red liquid, warm and wet, spread across my shirt like a flower seen blooming with time lapse photography. The blade bit through skin, triggering a tirade of visions that vied for my attention. Each vision was more gruesome than the last—and the common element in these little vignettes of terror? Blood, an endless sea of blood.

I gasped for breath, blinking against the visions to see the redcap grin and run his tongue along his blade, tasting my blood. Fighting the urge to vomit, I fumbled with the small pouch stuffed inside my boot. The pouch, containing salt and iron shavings, had slid out of range of my fingers, but I felt the loop of the string that held it together. *One more second...*

The cruel twist of the redcap's lips faltered and his mouth fell open. Eyes wide, he swept the blood caked hat from his head and bowed low until his large nose brushed the cobbles.

"Beg pardon, Mis...mis...tress," he stuttered. "Take this blade in recompense."

He reverently set his knife on the stones at my feet, and bent double, began moving away. Bowing vigorously, he stepped into a shadow cast by a nearby building and was gone. *Well, that wasn't weird or anything.*

Unfortunately, his nasty little blade remained on the ground before me. Why couldn't his knife have disappeared? I did not want to touch that thing again, but couldn't leave it for passerby to find. If the redcap's glamour was still active, it probably continued to look like a child's toy. I definitely couldn't just walk away.

I unlaced my boot and retrieved the pouch from where it lay nestled in the crook of my ankle. I needed to get my utility belt back from Kaye. I had it yesterday, so must have left it in her kitchen. Hopefully, Hob hadn't gone exploring for trinkets. If so, he'd get a nasty surprise. There were some items in that belt that were like kryptonite to the fae.

Unwinding thread, I upended the pouch above the knife sprinkling salt and iron shavings over the blade and handle. I tried to pretend the red liquid that remained in the grooves, where the cross-guard met the blade, was ketchup. Bile rose in my throat. My attempts to see the blood—my blood—as ketchup wasn't working. I didn't see a burger and fries in my near future.

I needed something to wrap around the knife before picking it up. I didn't trust my bike gloves to keep me from a string of gory visions. With a sigh, I pulled off my sock. The inside of my boot felt rough and uncomfortable against my skin, but it was better than facing those visions again.

Biting my lip, I repressed a shudder, and gingerly lifted the knife in my sock covered hand. I wrapped the rest of the sock around it, and holding it away from my body, started up Wharf Street to The Emporium. The run in with the redcap made me nervous. What was he doing in the city and why did he run away after tasting my blood?

I needed to talk to Kaye. Her knowledge of the fae far exceeded my own. Squinting against a headache, I stomped up the hill. She'd have information, but I had a feeling that I wouldn't like the answers to my questions.

CHAPTER 10

Kaye was staring at the blade like it was a venomous snake. It could easily be just as dangerous, but at this moment I didn't really care. It was safely in Kaye's hands and no longer my responsibility. Finding the kelpie king and saving the city took priority.

I crossed my arms and winced. The cut on my right bicep was taped with gauze and wrapped with a bandage, but it still hurt. The throbbing in my arm matched my injured foot, forming a thumping baseline to the background music of my life. At the moment the soundtrack consisted of the rhythm of my tapping foot, the one not stomped on by a crazed redcap, and heavy sighs.

I was irritated with Kaye's reticence. I couldn't persuade her to talk about the redcap and his peculiar reaction to my blood. So far, she had stubbornly ignored all of my questions. My patience was becoming thin as wet tissue.

"Oberon's eyes, I'm tired," I said. Okay, I was whining, just a bit, but I was weary with fatigue. The adrenaline from the surprise confrontation with a redcap was fully flushed from my veins and I was left feeling exhausted. "Where's Marvin? I thought he was meeting us here this morning."

"You swear like a pixie," Kaye said, pulling her gaze from the redcap blade. She was giving me that scrutinizing look again. It made my skin crawl. "Mab's bones, and Oberon's eyes? These are faerie words, girl. Where did you learn them?"

Hob, who had cleverly been staying away from Kaye's glare and my tapping foot, edged forward in curiosity.

"From my mom," I said, but I knew that wasn't the full truth.

As soon as the words left my mouth, I realized that the sayings reminded me of my dad. Those faerie phrases were remnants from my past, part of another lifetime, when I was happy and my family was whole.

Apparently, Kaye could read the realization on my face. She fixed me with a knowing look, cocking an eyebrow, and put her hands on her hips. Her message was clear; spill it, Ivy.

"...and dad, my real dad, before he left," I said.

I tried to unclench my jaw, the muscles in my face starting to ache. A twinge of pain at my temples warned of a looming migraine.

Kaye's intense stare made me uncomfortable. I didn't like talking about my real dad. He left us when I was just a toddler, but it still hurt. Why did he abandon us?

It's totally irrational, I know, but I wondered if my psychic curse would have awakened if my real dad hadn't left us. Everything was so perfect before. Bad things didn't happen to us when he was still around. He always made me feel safe.

I could use that protection right now. Kaye's hand was fisted in her lap, dangerously close to the wand at her waist, and she looked pissed.

"And you never thought it peculiar that your ma and da spoke faerie words?" Kaye asked.

"What?" I asked. "Of course not! My mom was taking a seminar in Shakespearean plays when she met my dad. They studied A Midsummer Night's Dream. I'm sure those phrases are just from the play. They both loved Shakespeare. It's what brought them together."

"That may explain it," Kaye said. "The fae folk can't resist The Bard."

What the heck was she talking about?

"Are you trying to say that my parents hung out with faeries at the Shakespeare seminar?" I asked. I couldn't believe I was having this conversation, it was crazy.

"Something like that, yes," Kaye said. "What do you remember about your father?"

"Not very much," I said. My palms started to itch and sweat trickled down my back, making my shirt stick to skin. "I remember playing in the garden after dark, my mom and dad laughing as I spun and clapped and chased the fireflies that danced around my father's legs."

My head ached and my vision blurred as the room spun. Kaye moved forward and helped lower me to the floor. She knelt at my side and muttered strange words in a sibilant tongue. Pulling a slender wand from the waist of her skirt, she waved it over my head then tapped me on the temple and chest.

"Forget," Kaye said.

I felt a pressure growing, as if my skull was shrinking, and the memories of my father and the summer garden started slipping away.

"Wha' di' you do ta the lass?" Hob asked.

"Patched up an old spell that's been on the girl for most of her life," Kaye said. "I imagine a geis not to ever speak of her former lover was placed on Ivy's mother, while a spell to block all memories of her father was placed on Ivy. A child would not have understood the dangers of a geis. It had the taste of fae magic, but the memory spell was simple. I would guess that Ivy's father used the geis and the spell to protect Ivy and her mother, but Ivy's memories were leaking and she was starting to remember. Her nervous outbursts of faerie slang were what made me suspicious. That, and her aura."

"Her aura?" Hob asked. "Ta lass not be sick, or cursed?

"No," Kaye said. "Don't worry. I saw no darkness to indicate a curse or threads of green for illness. But her aura isn't normal for a human. It burns too brightly, much too brightly, as if she were on fire."

"Will ta lass be a'right, then?" Hob asked.

I held onto consciousness, willing myself to hear Kaye's answer. What was wrong with my aura? Did it have something to do with the redcap's reaction to my blood? Would I be okay?

"I hope so," Kaye said. "I dearly hope so."

Her words echoed as I slipped into oblivion.

*****

I cracked my eyes open, confused. Had I dozed off? Kaye was still at her workbench, glaring at the redcap knife, and Hob bustled about the kitchen with his dust cloth. I rubbed my face and stretched. I seriously needed a caffeine fix.

"May I make a cup of tea?" I asked.

I asked the question to the room, but directed my gaze to Hob. The kitchen may belong to Kaye, but this was the hearth brownie's domain.

"Aye, lass," Hob said.

He didn't look up from his dusting. The hearth was so clean it nearly sparkled, but domestic fae were fastidious to the point of obsession.

I felt slightly hurt that Kaye and Hob were both ignoring me. They could examine knives and dust kitchens later, right? I tried not to let Hob's back bother me, but failed. I was tired and needed the smiling face of a friend right now.

I pulled a canister down from the cupboard, checking the label twice, careful not to spill any leaves onto the clean counter as I scooped tea into the pot. I nearly dropped the teapot, leaves and all, when the silence of the kitchen was broken by someone rapping on the back door.

The door opened with a thump and a large, shaggy head poked under the lintel. A young troll smiled, showing a mouth filled with broken teeth. The *each uisge* who viciously attacked Marvin had kicked him in the face, damaging his teeth and gums.

Though still sporting injuries, he looked better today. Kaye had tended to the troll's wounds with magic and herbal treatments. The swelling and bruising on his face was less widespread and the infection, that had caused puss and bleeding during out last visit, seemed under control. He even smelled better. But I knew that the worst damage from such an attack was the kind that couldn't be seen, so I was relieved to see him smiling. He seemed like a good kid. I didn't want to see him suffer.

"Hey, Marvin," I said, waving. "Glad to see you're feeling better."

"Hi, Ivy," Marvin said shyly.

He was carrying a huge pot of honey under his arm and scooping the sugary liquid with large, blunt-tipped fingers, shoveling it into his mouth at an alarming rate. I guess growing bridge trolls like their sweets. I knew a local shop that sold real maple syrup. Maybe I'd buy a jug for Marvin. The stuff was expensive, but Jinx's shoes were already going to set me back a week's pay. What would it matter? Broke was broke, right?

"Eat up, I've got a job for you," I said. "You too, Hob, if you're interested."

Marvin sat on the floor, honey pot between his tree trunk legs, and Hob came to hover by my shoulder, standing on the hook that stuck out from the hearth. Kaye continued to stare at the knife, but her ears pricked and I was sure she was listening. I ignored her.

As gently as I could, I brought up the kelpies, the *each uisge*, and the recent attack on Marvin. He stared into his honey pot and his shoulders started to shake. I think I made the kid cry—either that or I gave him the hiccups. I felt like a heel. Hob handed him a hanky, which I thought was awfully nice, but it may have just been to prevent tears and honey from marring his clean floor.

I continued talking, wanting to just get this over with and vowed to buy Marvin as much syrup as he could eat. Hopefully, Jinx and Father Michael were able to negotiate a hefty payment for this job. I was going to need a sizable payout, judging by the size of that honey pot.

When I explained that the man Marvin saw abducted was the kelpie king, he understood our need to find more information and put a stop to the *each uisge* invasion. The kid caught on quick. He didn't want to encounter another *each uisge* again, ever. That meant making sure they didn't have a chance to wage war on our city. I had to admit, he may stumble over the English language, but Marvin was a smart kid.

I sketched out a plan to have Marvin show me the bridge where Ceffyl Dŵr was last seen. The bridge had been his home until the *each uisge* attack and Marvin seemed almost eager to return. He had left in a hurry and hoped that a few of the possessions he had been forced to leave behind remained. We agreed to walk there together and, if we had enough daylight, stop to question a few of the fae who lived near the river.

There was a variety of levels of intelligence amongst the fae. Some like elves, hags, brownies, and banshees were highly intelligent while hinds, wisht hounds, and nuckelavees behave more like animals. Pixies are the worst, being the fae equivalent of insects.

If I wanted to gain information more illuminating than how thick the dew was the night of the *each uisge* attack, then we needed to go looking for some of the more intelligent fae. Unfortunately, smart faeries are usually more dangerous. I was hoping that the water hags who live in the vicinity of the bridge would be more accepting of my presence if I came in the company of a bridge troll.

So Marvin and I would search the area of the kelpie king's abduction and, with a bit of luck, glean something helpful from the hags. That is, if something didn't eat us.

Hob's job was less risky, but just as important. The brownie was tasked with sneaking into local pubs, the ones with chimneys and no resident fae, and spy on conversations. I suspected that there must be some gossip about the recent "shark" attacks, especially amongst dock workers. With a bit of liquid courage to loosen tongues, I hoped that Hob might catch wind of where the *each uisge* were focusing their attentions.

Perhaps, between us, we could discover the location where the *each uisge* were holding Ceffyl Dŵr.

"Ready to go?" I asked, turning to Marvin.

"Smell funny," Marvin said, sucking the last of the honey off his fingers.

"Sure, kid, you do, but I don't hold it against you," I said. "Come on."

Hob and Marvin exchanged a look and burst out into chortling laughter.

"Okay, you two, what gives?" I asked.

Marvin just pointed a sticky finger at me and laughed a sound that resembled rocks in a cement mixer. Hob held his belly and let out a last wheezing gasp.

"Lad tinks you smell strange, lass," Hob said. "Not 'ta other way 'round."

"Very funny," I muttered.

"Smell glowy," Marvin said.

Smell glowy? What was this kid smoking?

I narrowed my eyes at Hob. He better not be teaching Marvin bad habits. The kid had enough troubles.

"Have you two been sharing a pipe with a pooka?" I asked.

My question made Hob laugh harder. Oh well, I'd have a serious chat with him later.

"Safe travels," Hob wheezed.

"Safe travels, Hob," I said, shaking my head. "Come on, kid. We have a job to do."

I waved to Kaye and exited out the back door.

CHAPTER 11

Marvin was a good walking companion. He didn't talk a lot, but when he did it was usually to point out something that I would have missed. My adult brain filters out things like rainbow shimmers caused by water sprinklers, the way truck brakes on the nearby highway overpass sound like a machine gun, and butterflies hovering above a honeysuckle covered trellis. He was also the first to notice the pixies roosting under the bridge.

Great, it just had to be pixies. I hate pixies. They were like a flamboyant marriage of mosquitoes, wasps, and peacocks. They buzzed about their nest, darting in and out of the hive in irritation. The flutter of their iridescent wings was beautiful as they flit in and out of sunbeams, but I knew better. They may be pretty, but I'd been pixed before and, let me tell you, it sucks. Pixies are armed with a stinger the size of an elephant hypodermic needle. One sting will knock a grown man out for at least ten minutes, plenty of time for the evil bugs to have their fun.

Pixies live on salt—it's why they usually nest near brackish streams and ocean waters. They can survive on the residues that build up on dock pilings and bridge abutments, but their favorite salt lick is a human victim.

Once incapacitated by the neurotoxin injected by their stinger, the pixie prey is then swarmed by members of the hive who...lick the salt from their skin. I stifled a shudder. Not only is the attack repulsive, but a compound in their saliva is an allergen to humans. The victim is left with a burning rash, from head to toe, and an eternal dislike for pixies.

I'm pretty sure that Jinx was attacked by pixies last summer. Her description of "evil stinging hummingbirds from Hell" fit with my experience, and pretty flocks of tiny birds was probably what the creatures looked like to regular humans. She had jumped, when a black cat ran out in front of her, and slammed into a nest. Her rash was so bad that she missed an entire week of work.

I wasn't going anywhere near that bridge, not without a Kevlar beekeeper's suit. Instead, I searched the ground where Marvin indicated the kelpie king had last stood. Though daytime, the landmarks were recognizable from my vision. This was definitely the place.

While I inspected the gravel footpath and surrounding bushes for clues, Marvin went off to gather his belongings. He laughed at my concern over the pixies. Apparently, troll skin was too tough for the stingers to pierce. Lucky kid.

My search yielded a bubblegum wrapper filled with a wad of chewed gum, a condom wrapper which thankfully did not contain any used latex, and an empty water bottle. Sighing, I kicked a nearby bush in frustration and was surprised when an arcade token struck the ground, rolling to rest at my feet.

Had it belonged to Ceffyl Dŵr, or one of the *each uisge* attackers? There was an arcade down by the pier that used tokens. I was suddenly very happy that Jinx had warned her friends away from the area. An image of *each uisge* eviscerating children crept to the surface. If the *each uisge* were spending time down at the arcade, then no one was safe.

I pulled out my cell phone, snapped a picture of the token, and sent it to Jinx. Maybe she could find out which arcade it came from.

I dreaded what I had to do next. I waved Marvin over and sank to the ground. We didn't have time to go back to The Emporium or my apartment. Here would have to do.

My stomach twisted in protest, but I started pulling off my gloves, preparing to touch the golden coin. It was stamped with a harlequin wearing a jester hat, similar to those seen on Mardi Gras party favors. The smiling, masked face was supposed to look festive, but it filled me with dread. It was as if the harlequin was laughing at me, a fool about to risk her sanity for information.

"What you find?" Marvin asked, squinting at the coin.

"I'm not sure, but it might be a clue," I said. "It looks like an arcade token."

He looked at my bare hands, now shaking in my lap. I tried to brace them against my thighs, but it made my teeth chatter, so I gave up. I was scared, and the kid should probably know that.

"You touch?" Marvin asked. "Get vision."

"Yes, at least, I'm going to try," I said. "Um, Marvin? If I start screaming, stick a sock in my mouth. If I pass out, go get Kaye."

I took off my boot and handed Marvin my remaining sock. At least I was symmetrical now. The kid clutched my sock and nodded sagely. He was taking his role seriously, good.

I reached forward and picked up the gold token, now warm from sitting in the sun. The heat of the day vanished as chill water covered my skin. I was looking out through the eyes of an *each uisge* and I didn't like what I saw.

A man was tethered to a barnacle-encrusted pylon, wrapped in heavy iron chains. His skin sizzled from the iron and the smell of burning meat met my sensitive nose...and venomous drool poured from between my lips. No, not my nose and lips, these belonged to the *each uisge*, but it was already difficult to tell the difference. The *each uisge* moved toward the injured man, licking his fangs, hungering for the flesh that he could not have, and quivering at the anticipation of the torture he was allowed to inflict.

I screamed wishing there was a way to end the vision, an off switch for my talent, when I was suddenly blinking up into Marvin's worried face. He was holding the arcade token in one of his large hands. Told you he was a smart kid.

Panting, I rolled over and heaved up the coffee and toast I'd had for breakfast. Marvin was watching me and started wringing his hands. He looked concerned, and scared.

"Sorry, Ivy," Marvin said.

"You did good, kid," I said. "That was a seriously bad vision and there was no way for me to make it stop. You probably just saved my life." *Definitely my sanity.*

He shuffled his feet, but looked pleased. Gee, he was probably worried that I'd be mad at him for abruptly ending my vision.

I started to get up, but didn't make it far before sitting back down with a thud. Everything was spinning, forming a kaleidoscopic combination of sky, bushes, and pixies. And Marvin had a twin who was miming his every move. It might have been entertaining if my stomach wasn't trying to match the spinning movements of the sky.

Marvin may have removed the token from my hand, ending the vision, but I had seen enough to fill a lifetime of nightmares. The sensation of drooling in hungry anticipation of committing torture lingered. Getting inside the mind of a sick and twisted *each uisge* was no joyride. I needed a minute to catch my breath, and put my head back on straight.

Double Marvin disappeared, returning a moment later with a daisy that he lay on the ground beside me. Smart and sweet, he'll be a real lady killer once his facial injuries heal. He was going to be fighting the girl trolls away.

*****

After a short break, I stumbled to my feet and we headed north toward a section of marsh where Jenny Greenteeth, one of the local water hags, was rumored to live. She wasn't known for her hospitality, but I hoped that I could persuade her to share any information she may have regarding the *each uisge*. If we had time, then I'd also call upon Peg Powler of the Trees. But Peg's grove was further upriver, so Jenny was first on my list.

Water hags may not like humans, unless they're being served for dinner, but a pack of bloodthirsty fae encroaching on their territory was bound to piss them off. Hopefully, that would make us allies, for a time. If that didn't work, then I was putting my faith in Marvin's intimidating size to make the hags pause before trying to eat us. It might just give us time to run away. *Maybe.*

No one ever said my plan was foolproof.

The walk from the bridge to the marsh was unpleasant. Heat and fear sapped my patience and I swore an oath to send a letter to the parks and recreation department about trail maintenance after stumbling, not once but twice, over loose rocks and exposed tree roots along the gravel path.

After about a half mile of following designated walking trails, we left the path and wandered deeper into tall grasses and thickets of rosa rugosa. The narrow trails we had left now seemed like highways paved with gold, by comparison. Blades of saw grass and thorns of sea roses grabbed at my legs, leaving bleeding scratches that attracted the unwanted attention of nearby mosquitoes. Brambles and insects didn't seem to bother Marvin, but I was ruing the decision to wear a skirt.

Things didn't improve much when we reached the marsh. A haze hung over land dotted with pools of water and deadly patches of wet sand that could swallow a person whole. I pinched my nose at the stench of the place, the air thick with salt brine, rotting sea life, and vegetation. Marvin chuckled and walked on, careful to stick to the solid ground that continued to sprout prickly bushes and the sharp blades of fen-sedge.

I watched as a sea bird swooped down to pluck a clam from an area of wet sand, breaking the monotonous background hum of insects as it cracked the shell against a nearby rock. I turned away, feeling queasy, as the bird removed the small piece of pink flesh from its shell pulling it into its mouth. There is no place safe to hide when a predator designed to hunt you down and eat you is set on your destruction.

I hurried forward, taking the lead, thankful to leave the bird and its meal behind. Dunes rose in the distance, bright beneath the sun. It was a relief to finally be reaching an area of shifting scenery. Even the air held a promise of cool, clean ocean waters.

We were nearing a tidal area, where storms had left deposits of seaweed and driftwood, and the river had cut deep troughs through the sand on its way to meet the sea. Veering to the left, I decided to take the easier route around. Lush greenery grew here, close to the water's edge. After the tall reeds and bushes, the section of low-lying ground cover was a blessing. Busy swatting stinging gnats, who had joined the mosquitoes swarming my arms and legs, I stumbled into Marvin.

How did he get in front of me so fast?

"Wait," Marvin said, raising a halting hand.

He poked a long piece of driftwood at the ground in front of me and I was amazed to see a stagnant pond revealed below a layer of green vegetation. What had appeared to be a field of clover and moss turned out to be a web of lily pads, duckweed, and frog's-bit. As I watched, slime covered plants moved back together, their floating roots and leaves intertwining, hiding the murky waters below.

If it wasn't for Marvin's keen sight, I would now be immersed in those dark waters, trapped beneath a thick layer of plants that blocked out the sun, and all chance for survival.

Drowning in that filthy water would be a horrible way to die. I took another step back, distancing myself from the watery grave. I owed Marvin a lot of sweet maple syrup and honey. Heck, I should buy the kid an entire candy store.

Eerie laughter bubbled up from the water to my right and I edged closer to Marvin. A slime covered head rose to meet the phlegm-filled cackling. As the hag continued to rise, rust colored water and green strings of algae dripped from her long, straggly hair. It hung in sickly clumps, exposing patches of corpse-gray skin that clung too tightly to her skull. Her laughter trickled to an end as she laid eyes on us and a fiendish grin spread across her lined face. Thin blue lips pulled back to bare sharp, green fangs.

We had found our water hag, Jenny Greenteeth.

It was no wonder how she had come by the name. Her mouth was filled with crooked, overlapping, green teeth resembling a jumble of moss and lichen covered bones, not unlike the mass grave that likely lay at the bottom of her pool. This dentistry nightmare was framed by a pair of impressive fangs.

Well, at least she was smiling. The view was horrifying, but it was something. I lifted my chin and put a steely courage that I did not feel into my voice.

"We have come offering information and requesting the same in return," I said.

"She says she has information," Jenny muttered.

"Eat the girl."

"No, listen to her...then chew on her bones."

" Hush, you'll frighten the child."

Great, Jenny appeared to be crazy. I suppose it made sense. I would have gone insane too, if I had to live in a pool filled with the remains of my dinner. I imagine it must be a bit like wallowing in a dumpster filled with old burger wrappers, but really wet and containing a lot more bones.

"No eat," Marvin said, frowning. "Talk."

"Yes, we just want to discuss the recent activity of the *each uisge*," I said. "We suspect that they are planning to invade our city. Have they set foot in your territory?"

"*Each uisge* in our marsh?" Jenny asked. "They wouldn't dare."

"Are you blind? Saw them clear as day."

"Skinny horses didn't look appetizing, but the girl looks tasty."

"Such a...sweet girl."

A swollen, grub-like tongue darted out to lick at black silt and clay that oozed from the side of her mouth.

It seemed that I was losing the battle between the voices in Jenny's head. Too many of them wanted to eat me, and those filthy green fangs made me reluctant to give them a taste of my fist. No, I needed information, not a staph infection.

If the voices were being truthful, then Jenny had seen the *each uisge*. I just needed to jog her memory.

"Did a large, black horse come through your marsh?" I asked. "You may not have realized that it was an *each uisge*, from a distance..."

"Of course I know what an *each uisge* looks like," Jenny said. "I was riding *each uisge* before you were born."

"Braggart."

"She makes it sounds so easy, but we're lucky to have our skin."

"Do pay attention. She's asking you a question."

She rode an *each uisge*? Well, wasn't that just dandy? The very idea was totally freaky, and more than a little terrifying. If I had to put money on whether or not anyone, fae included, could ride an *each uisge* and survive, I would have bet no. I knew the water hags were older than dirt, but it was easy to forget the power that they were able to wield. I would do well to remember that, and try not to make her angry.

"That's...impressive," I said. Perhaps playing to her vanity would work. It was worth a try. "I have never heard of anyone taming such a creature. You must be a very talented rider."

"Oh, yes," Jenny said, hand fluttering to her face. "I was one of the best water riders in Mab's court. *Each uisge*, hippocampi, kelpies, mermen...I rode them all."

Ewww...that sounded so wrong, especially coming from a green toothed hag.

"Not this story again."

"Those were the days."

"It's sad that The Queen no longer holds court. Mab always did know how to throw a party."

She knew Queen Mab? Jenny was definitely older than dirt.

The faerie king and queens disappeared centuries ago. The disappearance of the heads of both courts, Seelie and Unseelie, has caused wild speculation amongst the magic community. No one knows where they went or why, except for their royal highnesses. Some claim that they have all gone into hiding, deep in the bowels of the world, to avoid frequent assassination attempts at court. Others whisper that the faerie monarchs have left our world entirely, following in the footsteps of the Queen of Elphame who led the elves from this land long ago. One thing is for sure, they have not been seen by fae or man in over three hundred years.

They may be absent from their thrones, but Oberon, Titania, and Mab still rule over the Otherworld. Their word is law, and somehow royal missives continue to reach the hands of loyal retainers and knights of the realm. Over time, absence of the royals has become part of the peculiar Byzantine workings of the fae courts.

The Otherworld, a magic place between human occupied earth and the fiery pits of Hell, is dominated by faerie creatures of every possible shape, size, and temperament. The fae are split into two groups, Seelie and Unseelie, each with its own kingdom and ruled by the royalty of its court.

Oberon and Titania rule over the Seelie court in the verdant heart of the summer kingdom while Mab rules over the Unseelie court deep within the dark reaches of winter. The fae courts are as different as night and day, but they are both a place of immense power within the Otherworld. That power, the excesses natural to faeries, and the decadence of court life make each court a place of extreme danger and wanton extravagance.

Neither domain is safe for humans.

The summer kingdom may be lovely at first sight, but the majestic trees, lush vegetation, and blooming flowers are often just as likely to drain you of your blood as the fae lurking within their leafy branches. Titania herself has a reputation for dallying with her human servants only to reward them by wrapping them in poisonous vines which slowly squeeze the life from their bodies, then revive them with her magic.

And the Seelie court faeries are the good guys.

The fae of Mab's domain are often walking horrors, dark and twisted, but at least you know to run away. Whether you are able to, is another story. Playing with humans is a favorite sport of the fae and they are very, very good at it. They've had millennia to perfect the art of luring unwilling souls, and the games of torment that follow such imprisonment. The Unseelie court is particularly adept at breaking the minds of their human pets.

The fact that Jenny had spent time at the Unseelie court, and in Mab's presence, made me especially wary.

"The *each uisge* should know their place then and not invade the territory of such an esteemed member of Mab's circle," I said. "I am sorry to have troubled you with my questions."

I bowed at the waist and began slowly backing away. Marvin tilted his head, giving me a sidelong look, and raised his brow quizzically. I gave him a quick nod to follow my lead.

"Wait," Jenny said, holding up a skeletal hand.

Well, color me pixed. We almost made it out of here in one piece. I stopped in my tracks and prayed she hadn't decided to have us for dinner. It would be no mystery what, or rather who, would be on the menu.

I swallowed past the lump forming in my throat and tried to look subservient. It wasn't easy. My natural appearance is more of a defensive scowl or glare to keep people at a distance, but I made the effort to look sweet and unthreatening. Judging by the quirk of Marvin's lips, I probably just managed to look constipated.

"Yes, ma'am," I said.

I didn't enjoy groveling, but if it meant getting out of here safely with the kid, I'd do some grade-A bootlicking. Sycophant, thy name is Ivy.

"I have seen the wretched beasts lurking about," Jenny said, pinching her nose and squeezing her eyes shut tight. "If I could just remember when..."

"Well, that isn't likely. You can't remember where you've put your shoes, and we live in a mud puddle. It's not like there's a lot of places you could have left them."

"It was during the full moon, silly."

"She's right. We could see the beasts clear as day, though it had to be going on midnight when they passed through."

"The *each uisge* were here during the full moon?" I asked. That coincided with Ceffyl Dŵr's disappearance. "Did they have a man with them?"

"I don't know what you are all talking about," Jenny said, throwing her hands up in the air.

"Yes, a handsome kelpie man."

"Wouldn't mind riding that one..."

"He was a fine specimen of kelpie masculinity, all rippling muscles...and the smell of fear coming from him was like exquisite cologne."

All of Jenny's personalities seemed aquiver over Ceffyl Dŵr. They may not have given the *each uisge* much notice, but the kelpie king had definitely attracted attention.

"Did they happen to mention where they were taking the handsome kelpie man?" I asked.

"I don't remember..." Jenny said.

"His wrists were bound with rope and tethered to *each uisge* guards who were laughing, bragging that soon he would be wrapped in chains of iron."

"They mentioned a place with lots of lights and music, said that even if they gave him the freedom to speak, that where they were going no one would hear his screams."

"Two were discussing a human amusement where children ride in circles on false horses."

Huh, apparently the kelpie king had made quite the impression. They, or rather Jenny, had remembered a lot. I already knew from my psychic vision that the *each uisge* had chained Ceffyl Dŵr in iron, a cruel way to torture any pure-blood fae. The gold token that I received the vision from came from an arcade. The mention of lights, music, and carousel ride, seemed to indicate that they were heading for an amusement park, like the one at the pier.

We had a definite lead on where to find the kelpie king. Now we just needed to escape Jenny Greenteeth before she remembered her hunger for human flesh.

The mention of children had put a wicked gleam in her eye. If the old folktales were to be believed, water hags preferred their food young and tender. I had often thought the stories of Jenny Greenteeth and Peg Powler grabbing children by the ankles and pulling them into the water, where they eat their flesh and gnaw on their bones, a cautionary tale to keep wayward kids from venturing too close to the water's edge. But perhaps there was some truth to the tales that went beyond basic water safety.

"Uh, thanks, we'll just be going now," I said. "Do you have any messages for the attractive kelpie man?"

"An attractive man?" Jenny said, preening.

"It's not likely the *each uisge* will let him live, but if they do, I want what's left of him."

"I'd like to give him more than a message."

"Do tell the man to visit."

Marvin shuffled his feet, obviously uncomfortable. Poor kid. I just didn't know of any other way to distract Jenny. If I could have thought of anything else, I wouldn't be encouraging her crush on Ceffyl Dŵr. It was creepy, in so many ways.

"Sure, thanks for the info," I said, backing away. "I'll be sure to deliver your message."

Marvin and I made our escape while Jenny talked to herself about whether or not she preferred kelpie men in their equine form. I hustled to get beyond ear shot. There are some things I just do not want to know.

CHAPTER 12

I was anxious to discover what Hob was able to learn from his eavesdropping, but most dockworkers would only just now be heading to the pubs. It would be a few hours, and a pint or three, before their tongues loosened. No, Hob wouldn't return to The Emporium until late tonight.

Marvin and I would just continue our trek across the city, heading toward my office where Jinx was working on our client schedule. She had phoned earlier to ask if I could squeeze in a quick lost and found case tomorrow. According to our account books, the money from the kelpies, after Forneus' cut, would cover our rent for the next month, but we still needed to see other clients if we wanted to eat.

My stomach growled when Jinx mentioned our grocery budget, punctuating our need for food and reminding me that I'd skipped lunch again. I didn't admit to forgetting to eat, but did agree to meet with Mrs. Hastings about her lost engagement ring, tomorrow afternoon. Who knows, we might be fighting off an *each uisge* invasion by then. Now that's a happy thought. I shook off the gloomy mood and kept walking.

There was still an hour of daylight left, but the sun hung low in the sky. Tall brick and stone shop buildings, containing wares of every description, cast long shadows across the streets of the Old Port. This was a good thing.

We were in a shopping district heavily traveled by tourists, mostly day-trippers off the ferryboat, and Marvin had a tendency to stand out in a crowd. Trolls are huge and, even with an active glamour to make him look human, Marvin was intimidating. Some of his bulk was hidden beneath a large olive green trench coat, but it stretched uncomfortably tight across his shoulders and was way too hot for the stifling evening heat. He looked like an overgrown teenager, but his glamour couldn't entirely hide the oversized brow, broad shoulders, and enormous hands and feet.

I was also drawing unwanted attention. Somewhere between Jenny Greenteeth's pool of water and the edge of the marsh, I had lost my sunglasses. My rush to be rid of the water hag and her incessant talk of kelpie man-parts versus equine-parts, had me running through the briars without any heed for the sun in my face. Now that we were back to civilization, I was ruing my lack of camouflage. My eyes were a peculiar amber color that tended to draw stares. Or maybe it was the bloody scratches that lined my legs.

We made an odd pair, me shielding my unusual eyes while self-consciously tugging the short skirt to cover my legs and Marvin huge and menacing in his army surplus gear. Our best bet was to stick to the shadows where we were less likely to be noticed. The last thing we needed was someone reporting us to the police as suspicious persons. I kept my private investigator license up-to-date, but Marvin was an underage homeless orphan, and a bridge troll to boot. I was betting that he didn't carry any legal form of identification. Faeries, wingless or not, didn't usually need a driver's license and I was pretty sure that the Otherworld didn't issue social security cards.

"Come on, big guy," I said. "We're almost there."

I felt bad for Marvin who was obviously suffering beneath the trench coat. His brow was beaded with perspiration and his round cheeks and nose were bright red as he puffed his way up the hill that led away from the water. Most people would be complaining by now, but not Marvin. I suppose living on the streets meant he was used to discomfort. Thinking about the kid curled up under a bridge alone, made my chest ache. I was definitely treating him to something sweet.

As we turned up Wharf Street, I had a brilliant idea.

"You have any food allergies?" I asked.

Marvin lifted his head and rolled his eyes. I'd take that as a no. I had never heard of a Troll having allergies, but fae were tricky. Things that are totally safe for humans can be deadly to faeries. A benign flower, such as prickly gorse, can kill some of the small faerie breeds, so why not a type of food? Marvin didn't seem concerned, so maybe trolls have stomachs with linings as tough as their hides. Considering their size, that would make sense.

"Okay, wait here," I said.

I left Marvin, fanning himself and gasping for breath, in the shadows alongside an empty building. The front windows had been taped over with butcher paper that was yellowed and curling at the edges. It was unlikely that he'd get into trouble in the few minutes it would take me to duck into the ice cream parlor across the street, but I hustled anyway.

Once inside, I found the end of the queue wound back and forth through the small shop. I let out a sigh, folded my arms, and got in line. I shouldn't have been surprised, not with the current heat wave, but the close proximity to other people made my skin itch.

At least the long line gave me plenty of time to decide what to order. With temperatures persisting in the nineties, I didn't trust an ice cream to last the walk back to the office, not without melting into a gooey mess. Jinx deserved a cold treat though. Looking over the board, I found just the thing. I left the shop, juggling a chocolate sugar cone for me, a cherry shake for Jinx, and a huge banana split for Marvin.

The smile on the kid's face was priceless. His teeth were broken and his lips were marred with bloody scabs, but at that moment his smile was the most beautiful thing I'd ever seen. I rapidly blinked away tears. Heck, spending time with Marvin was making me soft.

We ate our ice creams in silence, trying to eat faster than they could melt. It was quite the race against the heat and didn't leave much opportunity for talking. Marvin was nearly skipping as he bounced along, all sign of fatigue gone. In our sugar-induced glee, we made good time.

Marvin was licking his fingers as we approached the office, looking curiously at the Private Eye logo on our front window. He pointed to the picture and at me with brow raised, before stuffing his fingers back in his mouth.

"Yes, this is the place, Private Eye psychic detective agency," I said. "I run this place with my friend, Jinx. I think you'll like her. But, um, let me go inside first and take down some of our ward charms. I'll be right back."

Crap. The place was so cluttered with anti-faerie charms I didn't know where to start. With a sigh, I headed for Jinx's desk where she was getting up from her chair.

"Wow, you're back," she said smiling. I handed her the plastic cup filled with cherry shake. "Oh my gosh, thanks! I've been so busy, I forgot to eat lunch."

Huh, that made two of us.

"We stopped at that new ice cream parlor up the street," I said. "Their sugar cones are to die for."

"We?" Jinx asked.

"Um, I brought a friend," I said, biting my lip. "He's outside and he's...well, he's not human. Marvin is a troll."

"Dude, like, for real?" Jinx asked. I nodded. "Well, don't make him wait outside. It's a million degrees out on the street."

"About that, we need to take down some of the anti-fae stuff first," I said, waving my hand.

Her gaze took in the room, and the implications of what I'd said, and her shoulders slumped.

"Really?" she asked.

"Really," I said. "He's worth it. The kid saved my life today."

I felt a chill as I remembered my foot hovering over the brink of the water hag's lair. If it wasn't for Marvin, my bones would be lining the bottom of that cesspool. Goose pimples pricked my skin and I fought to keep my ice cream in my stomach where it belonged.

"Girl, what are you waiting for?" she said, tying a checkered apron around her waist. "We have some serious work to do."

*****

Fifteen minutes later, we were achy and sweating, but all of the iron and anti-fae charms were safely tucked away in the back storage closet. I even found my spare set of sunglasses. *Go me.*

Jinx pushed a few stray strands of hair from her face and went to open the door. She waved Marvin inside with a smile.

"You must be Ivy's friend, I'm Jess," she said, hooking a thumb at her chest. Seeing a look of confusion on his face she added, "But some people call me Jinx."

"It's okay, Marvin," I said. "She won't bite. And we packed up everything iron, so it's safe to come in."

His face was flushed from the heat, but he managed to blush a shade darker as he walked past Jinx. Poor kid, she had that effect on guys. He pulled off the trench coat with a sigh, hanging it on the coat rack, and stepped in front of the fan that sat on top of the metal file cabinets beside the fedora wearing phrenology head. Closing his eyes, he let the fan wick the sweat from his face. The room filled with a slightly animal-smelling musk, but it wasn't too gross and the kid had obviously been suffering.

I pretended to ignore Marvin's attempts at personal cooling and turned to Jinx.

"You are not going to believe what happened today," I said, sinking into the client chair in front of her desk.

I proceeded to tell her about the token we found, my vision at the bridge, our hike through the marsh, and the audience with Jenny Greenteeth. Jinx sucked in air and whistled when I told her about Jenny's multiple personalities and how we made our escape.

"Wow, I always thought she was something my Gran made up to keep me from playing near the water," she said.

"I wish," I said, shaking my head. "She had an unhealthy obsession with water men, of every shape and size. I'm going to have nightmares for a week, after that visit."

Jinx covered her mouth with one manicured hand and giggled.

"Sorry," she said, wiping tears from her eyes. "I'm sure it was horrible, and dangerous, but the way you distracted her is kind of hilarious, especially considering the source. I can't imagine you talking about the *hot kelpie man*. You never talk about hot guys."

"I do too," I said, folding my arms across my chest.

"No, you don't, ever," Jinx said.

"What about that guy at the dojo," I said, remembering an evening not long ago.

"You admired his technique, while I admired his butt," Jinx said. "It's not the same thing."

I glanced at Marvin who had turned a shade redder.

"Um, can we change the subject?" I asked, flicking my eyes at our guest.

Jinx just shrugged. She was never going to give up on her attempts to make me more normal, which included matchmaking, but now was not the time.

"Okay, so what next?" Jinx asked.

"I hate to ask, but were you able to finalize a contract with Forneus?" I asked.

"Yes, not that the demon bastard was much help," Jinx said. She turned to Marvin and added, "Pardon my French."

"What am I contracted to do exactly?" I asked.

I needed to know precisely what the job was. Not that I wouldn't stay on the case if I felt my actions could save the city, but I needed to know the terms of our agreement. It would be just like a demon to let me do all the work, then weasel out of paying.

"You must use your second sight to help locate the bridle belonging to Ceffyl Dŵr, King of the Kelpies," Jinx said. She used finger quotes, a pompous voice, and funny, bird-like gestures that made me think the words came direct from Father Michael.

"Okay, so I'm responsible for using my second sight and locating the bridle," I said. "I've already had visions using the piece of bridle and the token found at the scene of the crime, so now I just have to find the rest of the bridle."

"Yes, and Father Michael used his Deffakus thingy to make sure the demon was straight with us," Jinx said. "That worm, Forneus, tried to slither out of every deal we made that involved him actually paying us for the job, but we finally found terms we could all agree on."

She looked smug and I was suddenly glad not to be in Forneus' shoes. He had finally met his match. There was a reason that Jinx handled all of our contracts. It's not the fact that I suck at typing, which is not entirely my fault. Have you ever tried using a keyboard while wearing gloves?

Jinx was a natural at running the face-to-face client side of the business. Her smile was sugar sweet, but don't let that fool you. Even without the mystical aid of The Deffakus, she had a finely honed nose for bullshit and a backbone made of steel. She set people at ease then made sure the terms of the job were crystal clear, and signed in triplicate. If someone tried to skip out on paying, she'd hound them like a Cù Sìth.

With her skills and Father Michael's knowledge of the demonic, we should have a solid contract. I still crossed my fingers, toes too. We really needed to make rent next month and I wasn't hopeful to get the cash elsewhere during this heat wave.

"Good, I should probably run upstairs and take care of these scratches," I said, waving a hand at my bloody legs. "After that, Marvin and I will head back to The Emporium.

Hob should be back in a few hours. We can hit the books until then. Hopefully, Hob's spying or Kaye's calls to contacts in the hunter world will pay off."

"I'm ordering us some take-out," Jinx said. "You run on up and disinfect those scratches while I call for Chinese. It's probably going to be another long night."

As usual, she was right.

CHAPTER 13

I winced as Marvin let out another foul smelling belch. Trolls may not have deadly food allergies, but apparently, they do have trouble digesting MSG. Kaye lit another stick of incense before coming back to sit at the table.

We were all seated around the table in Kaye's kitchen, updating nautical charts and city maps with information we had discovered throughout the day. According to our new intel, the situation was much worse than we had first imagined. The timetable for saving Harborsmouth had been moved up, and none of us were happy about it. We needed a plan and we needed it yesterday.

Kaye pulled off her head kerchief, twisting it in her hands, black and silver hair sticking out in every direction. She looked like a raven with its feathers ruffled.

"By my wand, I don't know who else to contact," she said, sounding tired. "I've put out the call, by magic and mundane means, to every mage on the eastern seaboard and all hunters left in the city, but that is not enough."

She slammed her fist on the table and a few sea glass markers bounced off the map. Kaye was worried. We all were. The bridle controlling the kelpie king needed to be located and the *each uisge* stopped, but we were running out of time. Meanwhile, the *each uisge* army was preparing for a battle that we could not hope to win on our own.

We needed the help of the kelpies, who would not fight without their king, their allies, and anyone else that we could convince to risk their lives. Kaye was waiting to hear back from her hunter contacts, but it was a depressingly short list. Most of the men and women whom she fought with in the past were either dead or retired. She was hoping to drag a few out of retirement, but even with the help of a dozen hunters, we remained vastly outnumbered.

Our maps indicated a feeding frenzy along beaches to the North and South. Emergency personnel were responding

to multiple sites where human livers were reported to have
washed up onto the shore. Local government officials had, as
of this morning, declared beaches up and down the coast closed
until the "shark threat could be fully ascertained and
neutralized."

We were also monitoring reports of possible human
remains showing up in fishing nets in the waters just off the
bay, so it was likely that commercial fishing operations would
be effected as well. Hob had eavesdropped on more than one
fisherman drowning his memory of hauling a human liver onto
his boat. Some of the more superstitious fishermen were
overheard saying that the waters off Harborsmouth were
cursed, while others blamed the heat wave saying that it had
brought man-eating sharks to the bay. Whatever the reason,
human organs caught up in fishing nets definitely didn't seem
sanitary and, let's face it, gave a whole new meaning to "catch
of the day." The local fishing industry would be lucky to
survive, even if we did win this war.

If you added missing person reports to the picture, it
was likely that the *each uisge* were responsible for over fifty
deaths in the past twenty-four hours. The deluge of
unexplained violent deaths, especially when tempers were
escalating due to the ongoing heat wave, was a ticking time
bomb. The fishermen were already muttering about curses and
local news networks were running the story non-stop while
flashing screen stills from the movie Jaws. It wouldn't be long
before mass hysteria broke out within the city and surrounding
seaside towns.

An angry panicked mob would cause unnecessary
violence and destruction of property. In the ensuing chaos,
more people would die. That was unacceptable. The *each uisge*
had to be stopped now, before people had an opportunity to
realize what was happening. Ignorance is bliss, right?

We also had a responsibility to keep the fae, and the use
of magic, out of the public eye. Not only would evidence of
faeries and witchcraft cause increased hysteria, it would also
create an easy scapegoat for frightened humans. Men, women,
and children were being attacked and devoured by vicious
creatures that the average human could not understand. If
they became aware of any unnatural beings residing within
their city, they would probably shoot first and ask questions
later.

There were hundreds of harmless fae people in and around the city, and a few magic users who call Harborsmouth their home. They would all be in grave danger if the human populace caught wind of their true nature.

It would be The Burning Times all over again.

We needed a plan for stopping the killing and halting the *each uisge* invasion into our city. The one advantage we had was the knowledge of where the enemy army would likely strike first. *Each uisge* are strongest in the water; they would launch their attack from the harbor, where the piers and jetties reach into the bay. If we could find a way to block their movement at the harbor, we stood a chance of breaking their momentum and possibly saving the city.

Taking that kind of stand would take numbers, both in the water and on the docks. My hands started sweating and I absently rubbed gloved hands futilely on my pant legs and cleared my throat. It was time to take some risks.

"Do we know any water fae willing to fight?" I asked.

Kaye pinched the bridge of her nose as all eyes turned to her. She was our most likely link to any benevolent fae, but those were few and far between and tended to have magical abilities like making flowers grow more quickly—not really the most helpful skills in battle.

In my opinion, we needed strong soldiers who knew how to fight. Call me crazy, but I wanted someone or something with some serious power at my back. Unfortunately, most powerful fae don't play well with others. In fact, most of them had crossed blades, or claws, with Kaye in the past. I had my doubts about whether the monsters Kaye used to hunt would be willing to help if she asked.

I also didn't think she'd be willing to request a favor of the more powerful faerie. There were always risks when dealing with faeries. The older and more powerful the fae, the more dangerous they are...and the more adept at tricking you into a deadly bargain. Trading "just one dance" for a fae army at your back may sound like a good deal, until you discover that faeries enjoy tormenting humans by making them dance until they die. Being compelled to dance on bloody stumps was not something I wanted in my future, but someone needed to do something to save the city. If a deal needed to be made, I was ready.

"A few mermaids may fight alongside us, if it amuses them," Kaye said. "But most water fae will not stand against the *each uisge* without the kelpie army. We must locate and recover the bridle."

"Da kelpie king is being held 'neath yonder pier," Hob said. "Dis we know."

Fishermen weren't the only ones Hob had spied on tonight. Dockhands, shop workers, and taxi drivers all had strange stories to tell and the nexus of bizarre activity appeared to be the amusement park on the pier.

"Yes, my vision and the information Jenny Greenteeth gave us seems to confirm this," I said.

"I reckon dis bridle be dere as well," Hob said with a wink.

"Really?" I asked. "You think the *each uisge* would keep it close to where they're holding Ceffyl Dŵr? Why? Does the bridle need to be near the kelpie king in order to control him?"

According to Kaye's books, anyone who took possession of a kelpie's bridle gained control over them. More than one folktale describes a human farmer who steals a kelpie's bridle in an effort to force the creature to plow their fields. A kelpie, whose bridle has been stolen, can use their incredible strength and speed to prepare an entire field for planting in one day. Of course, according to the stories, if the enslaved kelpie ever managed to trick the farmer into giving back their bridle, they would meet out their revenge. I couldn't remember any mention of the bridle needing to be within close proximity of the kelpie to control him or her, but it was possible I had missed something.

"No, lass, but it be a cruelty," Hob said.

"Yes, mean," Marvin said, nodding.

Oh, right. Dangling the item representing the kelpie king's enslavement just out of reach would be especially cruel.

"Okay, let's say the *each uisge* are playing with Ceffyl Dŵr like he's a shiny new toy," I said. "They have him under one of the piers near the amusement park, wrapped in iron chains. As an added torment, they're probably keeping his bridle nearby, possibly within sight, but out of reach. Does that sound about right?"

"Aye, lass," Hob said.

Marvin nodded, but looked away. Talking about this stuff couldn't be easy on the kid. Heck, I was having a hard time picturing the kelpie king being tortured like that. Iron was anathema to the fae, causing extreme pain and damage to their bodies. The chains had probably completely burned through his skin by now. The memory of the *each uisge* from my vision, drooling over Ceffyl Dŵr as he suffered beneath the iron chains, struck me suddenly and my stomach churned. I swallowed hard and regretted eating that second egg roll. I couldn't imagine what poor Marvin must be feeling.

"Kaye?" I asked.

"Yes, you may be right," Kaye said. "The *each uisge* are known for their depravity and barbarism. They are true sadists. Not only do they achieve social status within their hierarchy for their actions, but they also derive pleasure from tormenting others. Cruelty, in all its forms, is something that the *each uisge* revel in and aspire to. It is in their nature."

"So the bridle is probably there too," I said. "Any idea how many guards they'll have on Ceffyl Dŵr and the bridle?"

"Too many," Kaye said with a sigh. "Even on land and armed with my most powerful offensive charms, you would likely only survive against two or three of the beasts. In the water, against even one *each uisge*, you would be dead in seconds."

Gulp. That did not sound good.

"Judging from the amount of feeding activity, and the sightings that Hob reported, there are bound to be over a score of *each uisge* surrounding that pier and five or six times that many in the bay," Kaye said, continuing.

I searched my memory for the obscure measurement. Right, score represented twenty units of something. More than twenty of the torture-happy killing machines around the pier and over one hundred swimming around the bay? I was going to be sick. I focused on the tops of my boots and breathed deeply, in through my nose and out through my mouth.

"Here, lass," Hob said, pressing a hot porcelain cup into my hands.

"Tea?" I asked. Why was Hob handing me a cup of tea?

"Chamomile, girl," Hob said, placing one knobby finger against the side of his nose. "Will help calm ye nerves."

He said the last in a whisper for my ears only. With a conspiratorial wink, he scarpered off to fuss over Marvin's muddy feet. I sipped the warm, fragrant liquid and tried to calm the organ dancing the mambo in my chest.

"Okay, we know where our enemy is located, where they're keeping their hostage, and we have a theory for where the bridle is being kept," I said. "Now we just need to find an army."

I was oversimplifying, but if I let myself dwell on all of the obstacles to our survival, I'd become paralyzed with fright. Better to focus on the task at hand—retrieving the bridle. If we took the kelpie king's abduction out of play, then the local kelpies and their allies, the merfolk and selkies, would stand against the *each uisge*.

"Vampires?" Marvin asked, shyly.

Okay, not water fae, but it didn't hurt to think outside the box.

"Why vamps?" I asked.

"They have a lot...at stake," Marvin said, devolving into fits of laughter.

Marvin mimed fangs with his fingers and Hob pretended to stake him with the handle of his duster.

"He has a point," Kaye said. This only set off more giggles and snorts from the troll and brownie. Kaye sighed, but continued on. "The vampires of this city have a vested interest in protecting their properties, and their food supply. They may come to our aid, if the right person asked."

She looked at me pointedly (snicker) and I groaned. I really did not want to make another trip up Joysen Hill, especially not to call on one of the dusty old bloodsuckers. The undead were creepy. I'd much rather deal with fae monsters.

"Fine, I'll add a visit to The Hill to my list," I said.

"Just keep in mind that they will not be able to help with your extraction of the bridle, or rescue of the kelpie king," Kaye said.

"Why not?" I asked.

"Think, dear," Kaye said. "What things in this world are the bane of all vampires?"

"Vamp kryptonite?" I asked. "Garlic, sunlight, holy symbols, stake through the heart..." I noted each deadly item with the fingers of my left hand. "Oh, right, running water!"

"Yes, the vampires may be willing to help in the final battle, but only on dry land," Kaye said. "They will be unable to assist us at the bay, since the ocean would incapacitate them. Vampires cannot cross moving water."

"We need de murúch," Hob said.

"Murúch?" I said, rolling the Gaelic word around the back of my throat.

"You may know them as merrow," Kaye said. "They are indeed powerful water fae, but they will not answer our call. The merrow are high bloods who scorn humans. They live in the deepest ocean waters, where they remain isolated from their cousins the merfolk."

"So, are they like mermaids on steroids?" I asked.

"It is true that they are larger and more powerful, but there are similarities, though the merrow would be loath to admit any," Kaye said. "Merrow and merfolk are physically alike in that they appear mostly human from the waste up and have the body of a fish from the waist down. In fact, the merrow have a similarity to selkies as well. The Roan, or selkie people, wear their seal skins around their waist when out of the water, but they must put on their skins in order to swim in the ocean. Merrow also have an item, a red scarf, which allows them to survive in the ocean. If a selkie's skin or a merrow's scarf is taken, then they must remain on land and are beholden to the one who possesses it. That is where the likeness ends though. All merrow believe selkies and merfolk are foolish creatures who waste their time playing silly games with humans."

"Silly like when they drown humans, or silly when they sleep with them?" I asked.

"Both," Kaye said. "Merrow avoid humans, blaming man for polluting their oceans, but they do not believe in senseless murder. The merrow are a serious people who, though skilled at killing, do not take lives senselessly. They kill for food and to protect their waters, not for sport. When they must take a life, they honor the dead and ask for forgiveness."

"Wow, that definitely doesn't sound like any merfolk I've ever heard of," I said.

"No, they are quite different," Kaye said. "Are you aware of the modern decline in fae birthrate?"

I used to have nightmares about changelings and had read some of Kaye's books on how to prevent the exchange. Information about the interbreeding of fae and humans to avoid extinction had been a hot topic in those books. I nodded and Kaye continued.

"While merfolk maintain their numbers with the occasional dalliance with a human, the merrow have turned to other methods. Merrow men and women have been known to mate with dolphins, fish, and even giant squid. Interbreeding with creatures of the sea has made them all the more detached from human and fae society."

"But I bet they're fierce in battle," I said.

"Yes, they are skilled hunters, especially in the water, and savage when cornered, but there is no reason for them to fight with us," Kaye said.

"Perhaps there is," I said.

*****

It took awhile to explain my idea, but Kaye finally admitted that it might work. At this point, anything was worth a shot.

When Kaye was describing the similarities between merrow and selkies, I realized that they also had something in common with kelpies. Each clan of water fae had a weakness, an item that rendered them a slave to anyone able to steal it.

In most circumstances, this probably wasn't a big problem. I'm sure that, like the kelpies, most humans and faeries were unlikely to try to steal something from a powerful merrow. But the *each uisge* had already demonstrated their ability to steal a kelpie king's bridle. It wasn't unrealistic to suspect that this pack of *each uisge* may try again, this time attempting to steal scarves from the merrow. Such a wild, honorable, and strong-willed people would not be able to bear being enslaved to the twisted, bloodthirsty *each uisge*.

It was my hope that the merrow would see this pack of *each uisge* as a threat. If I could get a message to the nearest tribe of merrow, there was a chance that they could be convinced we faced a common foe. In my opinion, it was our best opportunity for gaining the help of a powerful group of water fae.

"Do we know how to contact the merrow?" I asked.

Hob and Marvin shook their heads in the negative. Kaye harrumphed as she shuffled over to a stack of dusty books. She pulled one old tome from the stack and returned to settle it on her lap. After much squinting and wiping at old dirt and grime with one of her skirt layers, Kaye found what she was looking for.

She thumped the book down on the table in front of me and tapped the page with a smudged finger.

"Here," Kaye said. "No sane person has tried to communicate with the merrow in years, but there is mention of a way—for anyone foolish enough to try."

The leather cover was crumbling at the edges and the pages of the book were yellowed and filthy with old candle soot. It may be a reference guide, not a magical compendium, but I was careful not to touch any portion of it. I most definitely didn't want to be thrust into a vision. Something with this much age and wear had to contain secrets best left unseen. In fact, the ink with which someone had made notations in the margin looked suspiciously like dried blood.

My mouth went dry and I reached for another sip of tea before turning to face the dreaded book. Kaye had pointed to a black and white lithograph depicting a creature hunched over, wearing a large, peculiar cloak. The figure was on a beach, the waves of the ocean in the background, staring intently at a large shell resting on the sand at its feet. Well, I guessed it had feet. The creature, listed beneath the diagram as a "shellycoat," was not anything I recognized.

"What's a shellycoat?" I asked, glancing up at Kaye.

"Shellycoats are an amphibious fae who live near the ocean," Kaye said. "They can be found along nearly any stretch of sand collecting shells and other sea detritus, most of which they add to the heavy coat that they wear. Their name comes from these unusual coats and if you know what to listen for, you can usually hear the clinking of shells as they approach. To the average human, they appear to be nothing more than a harmless beachcomber with a cart or bag filled with empty bottles."

"It says here that a shellycoat is able to locate the *blaosc*," I said. "Is that the seashell in the picture?"

"Yes, the merrow communicate by sending out special magic shells," Kaye said. "Shellycoats are beach scavengers adept at finding any type of shell, even the merrow message shells."

"Is it like a message in a bottle?" I asked.

I had a case last year helping a young woman with romantic intentions locate the original owner of a letter she'd found in a bottle washed up on the beach. Though not a romanticist myself, the case had a surprisingly happy ending and I found the notion of a message in a bottle charming. It would, of course, be impractical to our needs. The man who sent the bottle adrift had waited five years for someone to answer—we didn't have five years, we'd be lucky to survive the next five days.

"More like a magic cell phone," Kaye said. "Once you lift the correct *blaosc* or shell to your ear, the magic will connect you with the nearest merrow. You do not have to wait for the sea to carry your message, as with a letter in a bottle."

I was liking this magic shell thing. Now I just needed to meet with a shellycoat who could find one for me.

"Are shellycoats nocturnal or diurnal?" I asked.

It was getting late, or early, depending on perspective. I was bone tired, but if shellycoats were nocturnal, I'd have to comb the beach for one tonight. This couldn't wait another twenty-four-hours.

"They venture out during the light of day," Kaye said.

Thank Mab. I could sneak in a few hours of sleep before dawn, and my trip to the water's edge.

CHAPTER 14

I wasn't really a beach person. I know; it doesn't make a lot of sense. I live in a harbor city, surrounded by the sights and smells of the ocean, with miles of white sand beaches to the north and gorgeous rocky cliffs to the south. I really should love the beach, but I don't.

I was a native of Harborsmouth and, for me, the beach has always been a place where tourists fight for ridiculously expensive parking, then tromp miserably through sand that burns the skin off the soles of their feet. Once they reach the water, they stake out their spot with an umbrella and other accoutrements they've had to carry from their car. Odds are good that this same umbrella will catch the wind and risk skewering at least one passerby during the course of the day. Jinx couldn't go near the beach without being injured by one and I didn't want to add death-by-umbrella to my list of reasons why this day sucked. Going to the beach was bad enough.

I hit the boardwalk early, and was already trudging through dry sand as the sun rose in the sky. I hoped to avoid the crowds of tourists that, even with the swim ban, would be swarming to the beach and its promise of cool ocean breezes by mid-morning. Once they shower and stuff themselves with a free continental breakfast, most families make a mad dash for "the perfect spot." By noon there wouldn't be one scrap of sandy ground left uncovered. Tourists would be crawling over one another like roaches on a dung heap.

I shuddered and pushed on, careful to keep an eye out for growing crowds or deadly flying missiles. Thankfully, I encountered neither.

As the sun rose higher in the sky, a figure I had mistaken for a large seaweed and mollusk shell covered rock emerged from the gloom. He or she, it was impossible to tell gender from this distance, was definitely a shellycoat.

Kaye had been correct. If I glanced at the creature from the corner of my eye, I saw an old beachcomber waving his metal detector over the damp ground while trundling a small pushcart filled with bottles. The empty glass bottles seemed to rattle together creating a bell-like tinkling as he walked, but I knew the true source of the sound was the cloak of shells that he wore.

Looking at the shellycoat directly, his (I was now going with he, since, ahem, that wasn't a metal detector he was swinging around) glamour melted away to reveal a bipedal creature with large eyes, dark, slimy skin dotted with green and yellow spots, and elongated limbs. Kaye had remarked that a shellycoat looked a bit like a humanoid salamander wearing a bumpy turtle shell, and I had to agree.

A pale bulbous belly peeked out of a gap in his cloak, making me wonder what shellycoats ate. I should have asked Kaye, but I had been too tired to think straight. I hoped that whatever this creature ate, it didn't look like me. It was nerve wracking enough being this close to roaring ocean waves which may conceal deadly *each uisge*.

I shook my head and strode toward the shellycoat. I kept my chin up and arms splayed, palms out, at my sides to show that I was confident, but not a threat. Wind slapped at my back, whipping my ponytail against the bare skin on my shoulders.

The cooler air felt wonderful, and I sent up a silent prayer of thanks that I wasn't facing the shellycoat in a stifling sweatshirt or, even worse, one of Jinx's retro rockabilly sundresses or poodle skirts. I had arrived back at the loft late last night to find that Jinx had left me a basket of clean laundry, the magazine clipping of her dream shoes set on top. At this rate, I'd end up having to buy her two pairs, but it would be worth the clean tank tops and jeans.

"Ahem," I said, clearing my throat as I approached. "Excuse me."

The shellycoat looked up from its scavenging, cocking his head to the side.

"Yesss?" he asked. A long, thin tongue darted out as if tasting the air. "What isss it? Can't you sssee I am busssy?"

"Sorry to bother you, but it's urgent," I said. "I need to find the *blaosc*, the merrow message shell." I held up a bag and gave it a shake so he could hear the clinking sound of shells within. "I'm willing to pay you for your trouble."

It was a gamble, but I figured that shellycoats valued seashells more than human currency. Luckily for me, there were plenty of twenty-four hour gift shops in Harborsmouth that sold touristy trinkets. I found a net bag filled with assorted shells at Sand Dollar Joe's, where everything was a buck or less. The shells were cheap. Hopefully, they weren't fake. Fae tended to take bargaining very seriously and I didn't think offering plastic seashells would be considered a fair trade.

A pink membrane slowly blinked over one eye, then the next, as the shellycoat stared intently at the bag I held. His hands flexed open and shut as though he were grabbing at something. Apparently, I had brought the right kind of bait.

"Can find the *blaosc*, yesss," he said, bobbing at the waist in a nod like movement. "A ssshell firssst?"

I pulled a small, pale orange shell from the bag and set it on the ground between us. I didn't want to touch the faerie or his coat. He didn't seem to mind, or even notice me, as he leaned forward and snatched the shell up in one deft movement.

He held out his cloak with one skinny arm, looking for a place to add his new treasure. I jumped back a step when a stream of water sprayed out from one of the shells, surprised to realize that, on closer examination, much of his garment was actually alive. The shellycoat's cloak was a woven mesh of seaweed, algae, kelp, and discarded fishing nets covered in an assortment of hard shells and other sea detritus. I recognized periwinkles, sand dollars, starfish, crabs, blue mussels, and razor clams. The overlapping layers of seashells probably provided a protective barrier similar to medieval chainmail armor for the shellycoat's delicate body.

With the new shell firmly in place between a chunk of driftwood and a cluster of barnacles, he started humming and set off down the beach. He seemed to know instinctively when to step out of the way of incoming waves, perhaps it was fae magic, but I ended up trudging along with soggy sneakers.

After twenty minutes of searching, the shellycoat stopped humming and started digging through a pile of debris. Brushing away a layer of dried seaweed unveiled a rose colored conch shell. The shellycoat bowed low and gestured to the shell with one black and yellow hand.

"Is that it?" I asked.

"Yesss," he said.

I don't like touching strange objects, but I didn't have much choice. Kaye said that my skin would have to make contact with the shell in order to activate its magic. Hopefully, the shell, and its former inhabitant, hadn't born witness to anything too heinous.

I knelt in the sand and lifted the shell to my ear. It was warm, rather than cool to the touch, and seemed to vibrate with its own energy. There was definitely powerful magic at work here.

"Hello?" I asked.

"Who disturbs our slumber?" a woman asked. Her voice seemed bubbling and unreal, as if piped up from the depths of the sea and carried on the waves.

"Ivy Granger, ma'am," I said. "I'm sorry to bother you, but it's an emergency."

"The merrow are not 9-1-1," she said, haughtily.

Great, this was off to a fabulous start.

"I think your people may be in danger!" I blurted. "Please don't go."

"We are listening," she said.

I wasn't sure if that was the royal we or if I was on speakerphone. Do magic seashells have that feature? An image of wild sea faeries swimming around a shell and listening to my voice, made me want to giggle. I bit my lip and tried to think.

"Do you know who the *each uisge* are?" I asked.

"Yes, vile creatures," she said. "Why?"

"A local pack of *each uisge* have attacked the kelpie king who rules the waters near Harborsmouth," I said. "They stole his bridle."

"This kelpie king, does he have a name?" a man's voice asked.

Huh, maybe I really was on speakerphone.

"Yes, I was told his name is Ceffyl Dŵr," I said.

A high pitched burbling filled the shell and I had to pull it away from my ear. The merrow were definitely upset.

"Are you certain?" a young woman's voice asked.

"Yes," I said. "His people have hired me to find his bridle. I think I've located it, and the kelpie king, but the *each uisge* are powerful...and I am not water fae."

"...Ceffyl a slave," a woman said.

"We cannot let this go on!" a man shouted.

"The merrow will not fight," a woman said. "Our people believe in peace and the sanctity of life. Senseless killing would make us as bad as the *each uisge*."

"...but it's Ceffyl," a young man said.

"We could be next," an older man said. "These *each uisge* must be stopped!"

I waited for the voices to calm down before speaking again.

"I know that you are an honorable people and that you will not enter into a war lightly," I said. "But I see no way to rescue the kelpie king, or defend the fae and humans living in Harborsmouth, without your help."

"Ceffyl Dŵr is an honorable king," a woman said. "We will listen to you."

I told the merrow what I knew of the *each uisge*, what they had done so far and what I feared would happen next.

"We don't have much time," I said.

"Yes, we will come," a woman said. "This pack of *each uisge* must be stopped. The merrow and our kelpie friend are not playthings to be enslaved and tortured. We will help you retrieve Ceffyl Dŵr and his bridle, and we will fight. If we are too late for a rescue, then we will make the *each uisge* regret ever entering this world."

The shell went ominously silent. I stood and brushed sand from my pant legs, frowning at the dark circles where saltwater had soaked into my jeans from the damp ground. I had planned to take the shell with me, but a jolt of electricity struck my hand as I tried to take a step away. The shell fell from my hand and landed in the pile of debris. As I watched, the seaweed and sand swallowed the shell back into the very fabric of the beach.

"Wasss it the right ssshell?" the shellycoat asked, shuffling forward.

"You couldn't hear us talking?" I asked.

"It sssounded like you were sssinging underwater," he said.

Interesting, the shell must have some kind of privacy barrier. I had worried about the shellycoat eavesdropping. With his large eyes and slender arms, he wasn't overly threatening, but looks could be deceiving, especially with the fae. I had seen him move with terrific speed and it had to take incredible strength to carry that shell covered cloak. It was best to be careful.

"Yes," I said, reaching for the bag of shells. I didn't want to tell him too much, like about the kelpies, merrow, and the upcoming battle, but he deserved a warning to stay clear of the water. "Um, you may want to be careful around the ocean for awhile. There have been *each uisge* hunting the waters around here."

"Ah yesss, they mussst be the onesss resssponsssible for the liversss," he said. "Very tasssty."

Great, now I knew something shellycoats like to eat—human livers. The knowledge didn't make me feel any better. I dropped the subject of the *each uisge* and tossed the remaining shells at his feet.

"Here is your payment," I said. "Fresh breezes and safe travels."

"Sssafe travelsss," he said, distractedly.

His attention was on the shells I had thrown. I hurried away, hoping that collecting the shells would keep him busy long enough for me to make my escape. I didn't want to become another one of his tasty treats.

I kept my fingers crossed all the way to the boardwalk.

CHAPTER 15

On the way to visit my new client, Mrs. Hastings, I stopped at Fountain Square. After grabbing a coffee at Higher Grounds, I found an empty bench at the edge of the concrete park. Fountain Square was a great place to people watch in the heart of the city. Even in today's heat men and women in business suits hustled to and from work, parents walked babies in strollers, and some people even played Frisbee with their dogs as traffic roared by to the east and west. Students from the nearby college of music were playing instruments with the cases open and a girl clapping and twirling to the song let her leashed ferret climb into one of the cases where it fell asleep.

It was a typical summer day in the square. The skyrocketing temperatures hadn't discouraged locals from their routine, though I saw more than one person dip their hands in the cool fountain waters as they passed. My stomach twisted and I looked away.

The worn patch on the bench, pedestrian crossing signal buttons, and greasy hand prints on lamp posts and shop windows. I couldn't imagine touching any of these things with bare skin. Just ordering a tall latte was risky enough, though this morning it was worth it.

The late night at Kaye's and fitful few hours of nightmare-riddled sleep, followed by a hike to the beach and back, had left me feeling sluggish. The spike of adrenaline I'd felt as I left the beach, was long gone. I needed caffeine if I was going to meet a new client...and face the city vampires this evening.

With a sigh, I unlaced my shoes with gloved hands. I upended each sneaker, dumping sand out onto the concrete at my feet. I was glad to have my shoes relatively sand-free, but my feet felt swollen as I tried to squeeze them back inside. My legs still itched from the bug bites and scratches I accumulated on our walk through the marsh the day before.

If I survived my meeting with the city vamps tonight, I
was taking a break to put my feet up later. Maybe I'd even
take a bubble bath. Jinx would think I'd been abducted by
aliens. Bubble baths were her thing, but right now I was ready
for Calgon to take me away.

I slugged back the last few gulps of coffee and tossed my
cup in the metal trash bin. I considered ordering another, but
dismissed the idea. Public restrooms gave me the horrors.
Instead, I dragged myself up onto swollen feet and started
walking north.

*****

Jinx had given me the directions to my new client, Mrs.
Hastings. According to my phone, I was in the right place. I
kept a wary eye on her lawn ornaments as I made my way up
the short path to her door. The grinning garden gnomes in
their bright red hats reminded me of my recent encounter with
the red cap, and his nasty bloodstained dagger. I swallowed
hard, remembering the carrion smell of the red cap.

I squared my shoulders when I reached the door. Using
my sleeve to cover my finger, as well as my gloves, I rang the
doorbell. It was answered by a plump, white-haired lady who
barely reached my shoulder.

"Hello, Mrs. Hastings?" I asked. "My name is Ivy
Granger from Private Eye. Did you make an appointment with
us?"

"Yes," she said. Her round cheeks blushed red as she
nodded. "Please, come in."

She stepped back, opening the door wide and I lifted my
hand to my mouth to stifle a gasp. The place was crawling
with pookas. Every bit of chintz, silver, and china was being
haggled over by the small faeries.

Careful not to let on that I'd spotted them, I followed
Mrs. Hastings through the living room, past more than a dozen
pookas, and into a small kitchen. The woman spoke with a
slight accent, and I wondered if she inadvertently brought the
faeries here from abroad.

It was a well-known fact that the fae used to favor the
British Isles where the veil between our world and the
Otherworld, where faeries originate, was at its thinnest.
Imagine a family's surprise to leave an accursed home behind,

only to bring their problems with them as they settled in a new land. The story was a common one.

"Tea, dear?" she asked.

"Yes, please," I said.

I didn't have any intention of drinking anything from a cup in this house, but I knew the ritual of making tea would help calm the older woman.

"My assistant mentioned that you were missing something and hoped that we could help you locate it," I said. "Could you tell me about the item?"

"Well, I must be going daft, but I keep misplacing things," she said, shaking her head. "Normally I don't mind, but I promised my granddaughter that she could have my engagement ring when the time came. Now she's gone and met a nice young man and..."

"And you can't find the ring," I said.

"Yes, that's about right," she said.

She brought a tray laden with teapot, cups on saucers, sugar, cream, and a plate of cookies. I felt a pang of guilt that I wouldn't be drinking any, after she'd gone to the trouble, but I made sure to busy myself with the cup so she wouldn't notice.

I was surprised, with so many pookas in the house, that the old woman had any nice belongings left. It wouldn't be long before the rosebud trimmed teacups would be missing as well.

Pookas are mischievous little faeries. Due to their antics, they are often mistaken for poltergeists. They make silly noises, get into drunken brawls with house pets, and steal anything that isn't nailed down with iron. Pookas are insatiable kleptomaniacs.

They are also skilled shapeshifters. Pookas can take animal form, often choosing the guise of a squirrel, rabbit, goat, dog, or bird.

"This may seem like a strange question, our methods at Private Eye are a bit unorthodox, but have there been any stray animals around lately?" I asked.

She nodded.

"Oh, don't worry, love," she said, smiling an impish grin. "You can speak plainly. I know there are things that most people cannot see, but that doesn't mean that they don't exist. When I was a girl, we were all aware of such things. People forget."

I breathed a sigh of relief and felt my shoulders ease. It was so much easier when a client had an open mind.

"It's a lovely day for a stroll," I said, winking. "Could we take a walk while our tea cools?"

Actually, it was so hot you could roast an egg on the pavement outside. I'd rather go for a stroll in Hell, but I pretended to want nothing more than to go for a ramble around the black-topped streets of her neighborhood. Mrs. Hastings caught my wink and played along.

"Yes, dear," she said. "That's a lovely idea."

Once outside, her impish grin returned. In fact, she looked ten years younger.

"It's a relief, you know," she said. "At my age, I expect some forgetfulness, but I was beginning to worry. When my ring went missing, I thought my granddaughter might try to put me in one of those homes."

"No, I don't think you'll need to leave your home," I said. "Well, not permanently, anyway. But could you go visit your granddaughter for a week or so? Or stay with a friend somewhere outside of Harborsmouth?"

"I could do that, yes," she said. "Shall I leave as early as today?"

"Is that possible for you?" I asked. "I could help you pack. I don't think the pookas know why I came to visit. I can pretend to be a friend come to collect you."

"Ah, so it's pookas then," she said, nodding.

Oops. I hadn't meant to fill her in on all the details, but I was worried about the old woman. With a house full of mischievous pookas, and the looming *each uisge* threat, I'd feel better knowing she was out of town.

"Have you heard of them?" I asked.

"I heard stories as a girl," she said. "Frightful little creatures, aren't they?"

"Yes," I said. "I don't think you are in any real danger, but they're a nuisance, and difficult to get rid of."

"Good, then it's decided," she said. "I'll surprise my sister in Rockland. I could use a holiday away from the city. It's been miserable here in this heat."

We finished our walk around the block, Mrs. Hastings chatting away about her sister. Once back inside the house, we kept up our charade. The pookas didn't seem to react, except to fuss when she put a shiny brooch in her overnight bag. I helped Mrs. Hastings pack up her things and walked her to the corner of Congress Street where she could catch a cab to the train station. She was almost giddy with excitement at her plans for a holiday.

I helped her into the cab when it arrived and she pressed an envelope into my gloved hand.

"Here you are, dear," she said. "That's my spare house key, so you can come and go while I'm away, and your fee. There's a little something extra for relocating the...pests. If I owe you more, we can settle up when I return Friday next week."

"Thank you," I said. "Here's my card, in case you want to check in regarding our progress with your pest problem."

"I'll call you next week," she said.

I closed the taxi door and watched her go. I liked Mrs. Hastings and hoped I could locate her ring. Pookas stash stolen loot in their nests. I was willing to bet that her ring was tucked beneath a pile of shredded newspaper in her attic. I would come back equipped to explore the attic, clean out the pookas, and search for the ring.

Smiling, I turned to walk south toward the Old Port. With the money in my pocket, I could stop at the grocery store on my way home. My appointment with the city vampires wasn't for a few more hours. I had time for shopping.

With an empty fridge, and nearly bare medicine cabinet after Jinx had a nasty fall last month, we were not prepared for an assault on the city. I headed to the grocery store to buy food and emergency supplies for the office and apartment. Jinx would definitely think I was an alien clone when I arrived home with groceries, bottled water, hammer, iron nails, flashlight, batteries, and a new first aid kit.

Up until now, I had been narrowly focused on how to stop the attack on our city. After spending time helping Mrs. Hastings pack and lock up her house, I realized just how foolish that was. Bad things happen in our city every day. I wasn't giving up, but it was time to face the possibility that things could go terribly wrong.

It was time to prepare for the *each uisge* invasion.

CHAPTER 16

The only thing worse than wondering if a walking salamander wants to eat your liver, is waiting for an audience with a vampire. In the case of the vampire, there's nothing to wonder about, you know he wants to eat you. He wants to drain all of your blood like a giant, big gulp slurpee.

I was nobody's dinner, damn it. I crossed my legs, for the tenth time. Leather creaked as I clenched my fists in my lap. What was taking so long?

I was sitting in the world's most uncomfortable chair set in an alcove outside two heavy wood doors. The doors were reinforced with large iron bands and protected, if the buzzing sensation was any indicator, by a powerful magic ward.

I wanted to get up from the hard chair and stretch my legs, but couldn't risk triggering the door wards or angering my host. Vamps tended toward archaic, overly formal social rituals and I didn't want to start things off on the wrong foot. I had been told by the creepy servant ghoul to sit in the chair and wait, so I stayed fidgeting in my chair.

I was inside one of Harborsmouth's oldest mansions. Most local historians and antiquarians would probably kill to get a glimpse inside this dusty old mausoleum. Personally, I thought it was overdone. Vampires, no matter which century they are originally from, tend to embrace the dramatic medieval Gothic Revival aesthetic of the Victorian era. The walls were cold, damp stone and the alcove was lined in heavy burgundy damask that was stained and mildewed from moisture seeping through the fabric.

At least I hoped those dark red stains were from weeping condensation. Inside a vampire's lair, blood splatter on the walls wasn't outside the realm of possibility. If walls could talk, these would probably scream in terror. Thankfully, Jinx had convinced me to wear a long-sleeve turtleneck over my tank and jeans. She had worried about a vamp wanting to munch on my neck, but right now I was glad for the extra

material between me and a multitude of horrifying visions. I
checked that the wrist straps on my gloves were secure and
shimmied forward, inching away from the wall to perch on the
edge of the chair.

The alcove, and its pointy chair, was a small annex off
the main hallway—a long, gradually descending, rib-vault
monstrosity that gave the impression of walking through the
belly of the beast before being vomited out onto the vamp's
inner doorstep. The floor of the hallway had been at a
noticeable incline, and I had walked behind the ghoul for over
fifteen minutes. That meant this alcove, and the chamber
beyond, lay deep beneath the earth of Joysen Hill.

I sucked in a ragged breath and tried not to think about
the immense weight of the city streets, people, buildings, and
stone above me. Bright, glowing spots were forming at the
edge of my vision and I struggled to slow my racing pulse. If I
passed out now, there wouldn't be a turtleneck thick enough to
keep a vamp's fangs from my neck.

Something dropped onto my shoulder and I squeaked,
brushing it away. A small black spider righted itself and
scuttled into a dark corner. Great, now I was jumping at
shadows and harmless insects.

I settled again, but this time didn't have to wait long. A
door slammed in the distance and the reverberating echo was
joined by a shuffling sound and the clank of keys, or chains.
The noises grew closer and a figure emerged from the gloom.

A second ghoul came limping toward the doors, dragging
a gangrenous foot and carrying a large ring of keys.

Ghouls are disgusting creatures. They are a type of
revenant created when a vampire turns a person who is dead,
rather than alive. Unlike a living person turned vampire, the
animated corpse doesn't retain the memories of its former life.
These walking dead have no ability for higher thought (It's all
"feed me" when your brain has decomposed to wormy pudding),
but they obey basic commands, without complaint. No asking
for a raise or needing a sick day. Ghouls do whatever their
creator demands. This makes them favored servants for any
vampire old and powerful enough to create one.

My host obviously had at least two ghouls under his
control. The newbie vamps must all be green with envy. As for
me, I knew to use extra caution. I was now the guest of a
vampire old enough to create more than one ghoul, and he

didn't mind flaunting that fact in my face. That made him both arrogant and dangerous. Judging by the state this ghoul was in, he also had no sense of smell.

The butler ghoul, who met me at the front door and guided me to the alcove, had been well preserved, but the one approaching stank of sickness and rotting flesh. The downside of using ghoul servants was that they required regular feeding to keep them in tip-top shape. Since they eat human flesh, some vamps will feed a pet ghoul their table scraps, but many don't bother. An unfed ghoul will continue to obey orders until it completely rots away. This one obviously hadn't fed recently. I held my nose, fighting the gorge rising in my throat.

Stinky unlocked the heavy doors and pushed them inward on creaky hinges. No surprise there. I was just surprised there wasn't organ music or the endless flutter of bat wings—vamps were all about the drama.

Stinky waved me forward, dead eyes not quite meeting my own. Was he embarrassed by his state of decay? Were ghouls capable of emotions? Probably best not to think about it.

I rose from the chair, wiped creases from my salt-stiff jeans, and stepped onto the red carpet runner. It was time to make friends with the city vampires.

After the darkness of the alcove, the light coming from the adjoining room was blinding. I blinked rapidly, trying to bring my eyes back into focus. As my pupils adjusted to the bright illumination, a large banquet hall was revealed just beyond the doors.

The source of the light was a series of tall lancet windows on the left and right-hand walls of the room. Sunshine seemed to stream in from panes of clear and multi-colored glass. That, of course, was impossible since this room was deep beneath the ground. Sunlight was also highly impractical for a room designed to house the undead. Legend and folklore may not have all of the details right, but vampires definitely did have a sun allergy.

Although the lighting was illusory, the stained glass was beautiful—if you didn't let your mind linger on the unspeakable acts depicted in those panes. Though I suspected the glass pictures to be pure fantasy, bodies just did not bend that way, the disturbing images promised to return in my dreams, or nightmares. I was going to need some serious brain bleach when this case was finally over.

I dragged my eyes from the vamp idea of art and checked out the rest of the hall. The entire room was impressive. The walls rose at least three stories to meet an ornate fan vault ceiling. It looked as if huge, fossilized ginkgo leaves held the ceiling aloft. With regret, I turned my curiosity from the incredible room and focused on its inhabitants.

I had seen the figures as soon as I entered the room, but it took a moment to realize that they were my hosts. Vampires don't look like the pop culture idols found in books and on television. Sure, they like to dress like dandies in lace-cuffed and lace-collared shirts, fancy cravats, and heaps of velvet, but vampires are not handsome rogues who will sweep you off your feet. Vamps do not have beautiful alabaster skin, nor do they glitter. They don't have dark, soulful eyes and they are never sexy.

Oh, Mab's bloody bones, they are so not sexy.

The vampires seated at the table in the center of the room were a perfect example. Yellowed skin the texture of dried parchment lay over skeletal bodies, like scarecrows filled with sticks and straw. Skin pulled tight across cheekbones gave them a sinister, fanged rictus grin below a gaping sinus cavity and empty eye sockets.

Handsome? Sexy? Hell no.

Of course, most people couldn't see what vampires truly look like. Similar to the fae, vamps have a magic glamour that shields humans from their grotesque visage. My second sight cuts through the glamour. Aren't I the lucky one?

There *is* a way for regular humans to see past their glamour without a psychic gift. You just need a mirror. The rumor about vampires not having a reflection was probably created by the vamps themselves to create an excuse to avoid mirrors. If you look at a vamp's reflection, you'll see past the ethereal beauty to the dried husk that lies beneath.

That dried husk of a body is the reason why fire is so dangerous for vamps. They're essentially kindling with fangs. They may have supernatural strength, speed, and immortality, but a single spark could turn each one into a ghastly torch. I checked my pocket and was comforted by the cool plastic of a disposable lighter. I wasn't planning on a fight, I had come for a favor after all, but it didn't hurt to bring an insurance policy.

Fire would incapacitate any vamp, but a wooden stake through the heart would put it down for good. Ashes to ashes, dust to dust—in seconds. I didn't think my host would take kindly to a tool belt filled with a mallet and stakes, or a flamethrower for that matter, but the pencils nestled in my back pocket were made of wood and needle sharp. In a pinch, they would work just fine.

Good thing I had sharpened the entire package. My host had invited friends.

Three vamps sat at the long banquet table. The Boss sat at the head of the table farthest from me. To his left sat a short vamp who was either a child when he died or from a time period when men didn't reach over five feet tall. Either that or the dead furry thing draped over his shoulders was really, really heavy. Across from Shorty sat a vamp with an elaborate wig.

They were so still, I nearly screamed when the one to my left, the boss man's right, lifted his hand to dust his face with powder from a compact. Oberon's eyes! I would do well to remember that a vamp can go from zero to a gazillion in under sixty seconds. But why would something that made even king tut look bloated need face powder? The bewigged figure was nearly made of powder, why would he want to apply more? Forget it, I didn't want to know. It was probably filled with something freaky like rat poison or grave dust.

Dusty continued to powder his face while Shorty waved a boney hand in disgust. I got the impression that the two did not get along.

"Corpse candle," The Boss said.

Okay, that was definitely creepy. The head vampire's voice clattered up through his ribcage and past his fangs like the dying breath of a rattlesnake. And what did he mean by, "corpse candle?"

"Um, hi," I said.

"Why have you come to us?" The Boss asked.

Dusty put away his compact and fussed with his wig. It was distracting. I took a deep breath and tried to think.

"The city of Harborsmouth is about to go to war," I said.

"Why should we care?" Shorty asked.

"Of course we should care, it will make a terrible mess," Dusty said. "It always does, you know. Best to be prepared, forewarned is forearmed and all that. Perhaps we should take a holiday to the country."

Go away on holiday and let the humans die? That would be typical of the undead, though they may want to keep an eye on their real estate investments, and their food supply. I was counting on that.

"Going to war with whom?" The Boss asked.

"The *each uisge*," I said.

Well, that shut them up. Dusty closed his mouth so fast that a puff of face powder formed a mini cloud around his head.

"How did you come to be involved with this matter?" The Boss asked. "Whom do you represent?"

I had debated my reply to that question while sitting on the world's most uncomfortable chair. I could go with shock value and answer that I represented a demon. I did, in fact, work for Forneus who, in turn, worked for the kelpies. After twenty butt-numbing minutes, I'd decided that it would be best not to mention demons or other powerful allies such as the merrow. I needed an ace up my sleeve and I didn't trust vampires.

Vampires are the worst sort of monsters. They possess all three personality traits of the Dark Triad: Machiavellianism, narcissism, and psychopathy. What was there to trust?

No, I had decided that my best option was to keep things simple and hold my cards close to the chest. But the vamps were long-time inhabitants of Harborsmouth. There were some details, such as my friendship with Madam Kaye and my work at the psychic detective agency, that would not have escaped their notice. I figured a salting of easily known facts would give my story the spice of truth, without making it obvious that I wasn't revealing everything I knew about the case.

"I have the gift of psychometry and use this talent in my private investigations business," I said.

"Yes, yes," Dusty said. "We know all about 'Private Eye' and it's horribly tacky sign."

The Boss gave him a look which made the fop shut up and slouch lower in his high-backed chair. Dusty's wig, of course, still won the ribbon for highest item at the table.

"Pardon the interruption," The Boss said. He pulled his face into a wider grin that revealed another inch of fang. "Please continue."

Thank Mab, my pockets were filled with sharp pencils. Those fangs had to be over three inches long. I scratched at my side, keeping my hand within easy reach of my improvised stakes. My other hand nestled in my pocket, gripping the lighter like it was the Holy Grail.

"I was hired by a local clan of kelpies to help them retrieve an item using my special skills," I said. "I discovered that a pack of *each uisge* had stolen the item in question. During my investigation, I also became aware of the intent of the *each uisge* to invade Harborsmouth."

"And what would you have us do?" The Boss asked.

"I am here, as a potential friend and ally, to warn you that the *each uisge* army will be invading soon," I said. "They have already hunted and killed over fifty humans in our area and will probably begin their attack at the docks within the next twenty-four to forty-eight hours. My hope is that you will want to protect your real estate investments and your, um, blood supply by standing with us to defend the city."

The vamps were so quiet that I figured they were planning how best to serve me, and my blood, for dinner. Maybe, if I was particularly unlucky, they'd feed me to one of their pet ghouls. Wouldn't Stinky be a happy boy.

I waited, thumb on the strike of the lighter, ready to serve up these vamps extra crispy. I'd start with Dusty. That wig was bound to go up like napalm.

"Your heart is racing," The Boss said. "There is no need to worry. We immortals do not come to decisions as rashly as humans. Give us a moment to converse."

Vamps could communicate telepathically? That was news to me. Having Dusty rattle on inside your brain with his inane chatter, for all eternity, would be torture. It was no wonder that Shorty despised him.

I took a slow breath, in through the nose and out through the mouth, trying to calm my racing heart. My pounding pulse probably sounded like I was ringing a dinner bell. I so didn't need that kind of trouble.

I focused my gaze on the top of Dusty's wig and waited for the vamps to so much as twitch. When they came out of their telepathic huddle, Shorty nodded and Dusty shrugged.

"Our servants will keep close watch at the docks," The Boss said. "When the battle begins, we will assist the kelpies in an effort to defend our own interests. However, we make no promises of allegiance. Also, keep in mind that our kind will go no further than the storefronts on the land side of the waterfront."

Right, I knew that vampires couldn't cross moving water. It made sense that they would stay clear of the actual docks and pier. The ocean would make them vulnerable if they got too close. They may be motivated to protect their own selfish interests, but wouldn't go out of their way risk their own safety. Vamps weren't altruistic—far from it.

But I tried to sound gracious. Hanging out with Kaye was finally rubbing off. The old woman could be gruff when she wanted too, but was always polite when making a deal. In fact, it was when she was most frightening.

"That's generous of you," I said. "Now, I need to return to The Emporium and make preparations."

"You may take your leave of us, *this time*," The Boss said. "My servant will see you out."

Shorty started chuckling an evil, raspy laugh and Dusty tittered.

Whatever. It was time to go and I didn't have patience for vamp theatrics.

"Later," I said.

I stood and strode to the heavy doors which swooshed open as I approached. Stinky held the door for me as I left the brilliance of the banquet hall. The doors shut on my heels, thrusting me into the dark and near blindness. Not bothering to wait for my eyes to adjust to the gloom, I followed the bump-drag sound, and stench, of the ghoul servant as he led the way to the exit.

CHAPTER 17

I had never been so glad to step out onto the streets of Joysen Hill. The combination of decadence and poverty of this street usually ignited a fire in my belly, but after the oppressive hours underground, Bernard Street seemed positively quaint. Even the urine smell that lingered beside the stone steps of the mansion was a relief after the scent of decay and rot that clung to my ghoul guide.

Stinky slammed the door closed behind me as I scanned the cracked sidewalks for possible threats. Since it was now past twilight, I hustled back to The Emporium. I may have survived the vampires, but there were other things that hunt the shadow darkened streets of The Hill.

A wailing cry rose from an alley to my right, raising gooseflesh along my arms and sending a chill down my spine. It wasn't a cat out prowling for a good time.

I turned left and walked quickly, keeping my eye on the shadows and a hand in my pocket. A lighter may not work against all monsters, but they didn't know what I was toting.

*****

I made it to The Emporium unmolested, but exhausted. I could feel eyes on me the entire walk from the vamp mansion to Kaye's shop. I circled the block twice, hoping to lose my tail, before slipping inside.

The vampires knew that I was working with Kaye, but I didn't like the idea of leading monsters to her doorstep. Not that she couldn't handle a few baddies. Heck, she could do that in her sleep, but we didn't have time for the cloak and dagger games vamps are so fond of.

When I arrived in Kaye's kitchen, Hob was sitting astride the pot hook above the hearth telling Marvin a story. The young troll was listening with rapt attention as Hob told the tale of an epic fairy battle. The brownie was waving his arms and Marvin whooped with delight.

I smiled at my two friends and went to sit with Kaye. She looked tired, her olive skin taking on a grayish cast and new creases lining her face, as she watched Hob and Marvin at the hearth.

"They have no idea the wickedness of battle," Kaye said. "I would spare them if I could, but war leaves no innocents."

"They're not fighting!" I said.

"It is their city just as much as it is ours," she said. "They have a right to defend their home."

It was naïve of me, but I hadn't considered Hob or Marvin joining the fight against the *each uisge*. I knew that I had to be there. I could sometimes see things that others could not and I had taken on the job, after all. Kaye would be there as well, using her magic to defend the city. It was what she swore to do as a young woman. A few wrinkles hadn't changed that. But Hob, Marvin, maybe even Jinx? That terrified me worse than anything.

"Can we give them something to do here then?" I asked, lowering my voice.

"Of course, I'm not daft," she said. "I have already requested their help in preparing certain spell ingredients. They'll be working in my garden, inside the courtyard walls, safe as houses. But if the *each uisge* break through our defenses at the waterfront and make it into the city, then they will get their chance to fight."

I couldn't let that happen. I'd rather die first.

"Is there anything else that I can do?" I asked. "Anyone else I can ask to fight with us?"

Kaye sat in silence, tapping a finger against her bottom lip, deep in thought.

"There is one place we haven't gone for help," she said. "I had hoped to find other allies, but we've run out of time. To be honest, they're sitting right on top of a ticking bomb. Even if they do not aid us in this battle, The Green Lady and her people deserve to know the danger circling beneath their home."

"Who is this Green Lady and where can I find her?" I asked.

"The glaistig, a powerful faerie known to her people as The Green Lady, rules over the misfits and wanderers of the carnival," she said.

"The amusement park down at the pier?" I asked.

"Yes, the carnival has long been home to trooping faeries," she said. "And the circus sideshows that grew up around carnivals are home to many of the more unusual fae. Though rare, there are some faeries unable to create a glamour to protect their appearance from mortal eyes. Some of these poor creatures have found a home in the sideshow tents."

"Of course, flaunting their true forms would not have been tolerated by the courts," she said. "Revealing the secrets of faerie society is punishable by death, but the glaistig intervened. Rumor has it that she is just as old and powerful as Oberon himself. Whether that is true or not, the faerie king and queens agreed to let the glaistig rule over any fae who call the carnival their home."

Huh, that gave a whole new meaning to running off to join the circus.

"And she's here, in Harborsmouth?" I asked.

"She arrived last year, I have no idea why, but yes," she said. "The Green Lady resides here with her people. If you wish to save your friends, then I suggest you pay her a visit."

"How will I know where to find her?" I asked.

"You haven't been to the carnival in the past year, have you?" she asked.

"No, I hate crowds," I said.

My voice came out sounding angry, but it was true. Crowds were potentially painful and to be avoided whenever possible. There were too many chances for unwanted visions, and embarrassment, in crowded places. I would never pay the cost of an admission ticket for the experience.

"The Green Lady is part of the sideshow," she said. "You can't miss her tent. It's the one covered in a large painting of a woman with green skin, golden hair, and the legs of a goat."

Green skin and the legs of a goat? Great, just great.

"Anything I should know before I pay her a visit?" I asked.

Like if she breathes fire or eats humans for breakfast...

"The glaistig is very powerful," she said. "Never forget that. She is also very fond and protective of her people."

"But she makes money off of their misery, doesn't she?" I said.

"Don't ever say that where the glaistig, or her people, can hear," she said. "Most carnival fae credit The Green Lady with giving them a home when no other doors were open to them. She protects and provides for her people. If they must endure a bit of staring in return, what is the harm in it?"

It rang of exploitation, but Kaye was right. Who was I to judge how a powerful faerie ruled her people?

"Okay, anything else?" I asked.

"She dislikes any human who uses magic," Kaye said. "And absolutely detests hunters. As you can imagine, there have been more than a few misunderstandings between her people and mine over the years."

Well, now I knew why Kaye wasn't volunteering to go with me. I never realized how many enemies she had in this town, though it made sense. She had joined forces with hunters to protect our city. Hunters often kill in the course of doing their job. Their targets may be monsters, but that doesn't mean they don't leave behind families and friends of their own. Friends and families have a tendency to hold a grudge when you kill someone they love.

No, I couldn't ask Kaye to join me. I also didn't dare ask Hob or Marvin to come along. It was dangerous for fae to enter another's domain without permission and technically The Green Lady and her people had been granted the carnival grounds as part of their kingdom. I couldn't risk the possibility of having their presence anger the glaistig and put our mission on bad footing.

I even considered calling Jinx. My roommate had dated a guy a few years ago who worked at the carnival. Unlike me, she'd know her way around. Jinx loved the chaos of lights, sounds, and people at the amusement park. She'd think this trip was a freaking blast.

I went as far as pulling my phone from my pocket, but with a heavy sigh shoved it back in my jeans. My friend may be able to charm her ex into helping us gain entrance to the glaistig and could probably navigate the carnival chaos with her eyes closed, but she was only human. Jinx didn't have any magic powers or superhuman strength. That was fine when wielding a reception phone and appointment book, she was damn good at that, but the amusement park sat like a beast sprawling along the waterfront and pier. Those waters were filled with *each uisge* and the pier was ground zero.

As much as I could use the company, Kaye, Marvin, Hob, and Jinx wouldn't be going with me. I would be visiting the carnival alone.

CHAPTER 18

I grudgingly paid the exorbitant ticket fee and used my hips to push through the squeaky turnstile. Hundreds of kids and their families touched those metal bars each day. There was no way in hell that I'd touch any part of it with bare skin. With my luck, I would probably get whammied with a vision and a nasty case of the flu. Wouldn't that be fun?

Glowering to keep passersby from edging too close, I continued to follow the press of bodies until I reached a hub where different pathways branched off delivering patrons to a multitude of attractions. I had to wait for a family of five to move out of the way before reading the signs posted on a weather-beaten directory board. Red arrows pointed to rides, games of chance, and the video arcade.

Not surprisingly, there wasn't an arrow indicating deadly *each uisge*, but I kept their close proximity in mind. My stomach churned as I looked down at the wood planks beneath my feet, imagining the bloodthirsty fae circling in the dark waters below.

Finally, I found directions to the circus sideshow. According to the sign, The Green Lady was located past a row of concessions. I followed the smell of grease, fried dough, and cotton candy.

The concession booths were busy. Lines of people waited for their heart attack in a basket or tooth decay on a stick. I lost ten minutes trying to dodge hungry tourists and parents who looked ready to drop from exhaustion. I checked my watch again. It was nearly midnight. Shouldn't these families be home, and their kids in bed?

I finally made it past the line of food vendors and followed an arrow pointing to my right. The sideshow tents were down a narrow plank path which had been dusted with wood shavings once upon a time.

The first attraction was a fortune teller. The flaps of her colorful tent were open wide and she sat huddled over a large, glowing crystal ball. Swaddled in layers of glittering scarves, skirts, and head kerchief she resembled Kaye. The woman looked up, meeting my gaze, and I was suddenly sure that she was nothing like my witchy friend. No, this fortune teller wasn't even human.

Kaye had prepared me for the fact that many fae would be residing within the tent city of the carnival, but the woman was still startling. Her disconcerting eyes were multifaceted, like an insect, and each orb seemed to move independent of one another. One glittering eye continued to watch me while the other looked for potential customers walking up the path.

I hurried on, keeping watch for the painted tent featuring The Green Lady. I didn't have to travel far. Looming at the center of a ring of low tents and colorful caravan wagons towered a large green tent just as Kaye described. A folding sign announced evening show times at six, eight, and ten o'clock. Hopefully, the glaistig would still be in her tent.

When I tried to approach The Green Lady's pavilion though, I found myself veering to the left and circling the tent until I ended up where I began. Well, that was frustrating. I didn't have time for games. The glaistig was obviously using a "keep away" spell to deter unwanted visitors. I could understand wanting one's privacy, especially when you were subjected to slack-jaw humans gawking at you three shows per day, but I needed to speak to the faerie now. Not willing to wait for an invitation, I looked around for any carnival fae who may know how to gain access to their queen.

I struck off toward a tent advertising a vaudeville variety show. A slender male faerie with fair hair stood beside the tent playing a stringed instrument while a voluptuous female succubus in burlesque costume danced hypnotically to the music. Passersby swayed to the entrancing show.

I waved to the musician letting him know I'd like a moment of his time and flashed a few bills. The faerie smiled greedily and gestured to his partner. The succubus dancer bent low, giving me a wink and a long look at her cavernous cleavage. I could feel my face burn with embarrassment. Mab's bones; maybe flashing money to get their attention wasn't the best idea. I was now almost certain that the two were running a little prostitution side act—and they thought I was their next mark.

The song came to an end and the humans were ushered inside the tent, gladly paying the extra admittance fee. They probably didn't even know what show was playing inside. The faerie and succubus had made the small crowd of humans so open to suggestion that they'd probably walk off the docks and into the harbor if asked. Glad of the charms hanging around my neck and in my pockets, I smiled and asked if the glaistig was available.

The succubus looked disappointed. She pushed her large, bee-stung lips into an exaggerated pout. Well, she could sulk all she wanted, but I wasn't touching her with a ten-foot pole.

Succubi were the offspring of faeries and demons and had appetites that would make both parents proud. A succubus feeds on sexual energy and emotions. Dining on the feelings of her risqué burlesque show audience would keep this one alive, but succubi and incubi, their male counterparts, were known for being insatiable. To touch them often meant death, and that was without the unwanted visions. Horrific visions would be my own special psychometry bonus prize at the bottom of that Cracker Jack box.

I bit my lip and focused on the faerie bard. I'd pay the two for information. That was all.

"Her Ladyship usually rests after her last show, but she may be ready to accept a visitor by this hour," the musician said, scrutinizing me from head to toe. "Is she expecting you?"

"No, I don't have an appointment, but it's urgent," I said. "I believe that you are all in danger. The Green Lady needs to know."

The succubus whispered something in his ear and he nodded.

"Right," he said. "Our Lady thought someone would come. She told Delilah to keep an eye out for strangers with a keen interest in the center tent."

The succubus, Delilah, made a purring sound in the affirmative.

"Follow me," he said, waving me forward.

The tent decorated with a painting of The Green Lady stood behind me and I stopped in my tracks. Should I follow this faerie into the darkness, away from curious eyes, or run toward the tent shouting for the glaistig. After a moment's hesitation, I decided to follow the musician and continued forward. Delilah brought up the rear, which seemed fitting since hers was fully exposed.

The back alleys of the carnival were a maze of rope, canvas, tools, carts, and machinery. It was obvious that any non-carnie outsider would be lost as soon as they stepped off the marked pathways.

We nodded to off-duty faeries who sat smoking, drinking, and playing games on upended buckets and overturned crates. Creatures of every shape and size could be found in these secret avenues that ran behind the main tents, but I was the only human in sight. I hadn't seen another non-fae since leaving the sawdust covered path by the vaudeville tent.

A small part of me held out hope that I might bump into Jinx's ex. It would be nice to see a familiar face, even if that face was covered in tattoos, piercings, and attached to a well-muscled body. Brice hadn't been my favorite of Jinx's long line of boyfriends, but he wasn't the worst either. He was just a compulsive flirt with an overgrown sense of self-worth. Heck, that described nearly every guy Jinx dated.

Too bad he was nowhere to be seen. Maybe the faeries had a spell that kept humans from bothering them here. With a mental shrug, I continued on. I was a big girl. I could do this on my own. So why was my heart trying to beat its way out of my chest?

Stepping gingerly over a griffin's tail, I followed the faerie bard around the corner. I continued to watch the dog-sized creature, who looked bored with his chess game. He was resting his eagle head on a cat's paw attached to a furry body that resembled a lion—except for the large, feathered wings sprouting from his back. Fascinated with the griffin, I nearly stumbled into the bard who was kneeling just beyond the corner, head bowed, before a petite woman dressed in a long green dress and cloak.

The Green Lady was surprisingly tiny, but that didn't mean she wasn't formidable. Even the smallest pixie can bring a man to his knees in seconds. Remembering my own run-in with a pixie hive, I lowered my eyes and gave a slight nod of my head as a show of respect.

"Rise," The Green Lady said, gesturing with one slender hand. "Who is this you have brought to shed light on my grove?"

"She was asking questions and said she had urgent business with you, My Ladyship," the bard said.

"You have done well," The Green Lady said. "Now go and enjoy a wine cask with Delilah for your troubles."

Obviously dismissed, the bard took the succubus by the hand and left the way we had come. Delilah licked her lips suggestively and gave me a wink as they left. I rolled my eyes and turned back to the glaistig.

"Please don't be offended by their bad manners," The Green Lady said. "They are like naughty children." She smiled proudly as she watched them go. "Now, who are you and why are you here?"

A faerie who gets quickly and directly to the point? Now that was refreshing. As if reading my thoughts, the glaistig answered.

"Yes, I do not have time for games," she said. "I am spread too thinly as it is. I rule over every carnival, fairground, and amusement park on this green planet and my presence is often required at each of my kingdoms simultaneously."

She waved a hand at herself and suddenly her small size made sense. The glaistig had literally split her own body into tiny shards to rule over her people who were sprinkled over the world. She must truly have a mother's love for the carnival fae to be willing to weaken her body that way, putting herself at such risk.

I couldn't see Mab, Oberon, or Titania doing the same. They would never expose themselves to that kind of danger. No, they'd rather hide safely away in the shadows.

"I promise, I'm not here to waste your time," I said. "My name is Ivy Granger. A pack of *each uisge* recently came to Harborsmouth, kidnapped and stole the bridle of the local kelpie king, and killed numerous humans. I was hired by the kelpies to help find and retrieve their lost bridle. During my investigation to find their property, I learned of the kidnapping of Ceffyl Dŵr. I also believe that the *each uisge* are preparing to attack the city."

"And you wish for my help to defend your city?" she asked.

"Yes," I said. "The *each uisge* are holding the kelpie king prisoner beneath this pier, the same pier on which your kingdom stands. I don't know if you care about Harborsmouth, but I do think you care about your own people."

I clamped my mouth shut and waited. Hopefully, I hadn't said too much already. Fae were easy to offend and I had a tendency to blurt out everything that I was thinking. I did, at least, try to be polite.

The Green Lady's cloven hooves scraped the ground as she began to pace. She didn't strike me down, turn me to stone, or order "off with her head" which I took as a positive sign. I started to relax for the first time since stumbling into her grove.

"So it is true then," she whispered.

The glaistig slumped forward, her shoulders bowing as she seemed to draw in upon herself. Her long golden hair hung in a flaxen cascade that hid her face, but I could tell from the way she held herself that this had come as a blow. I gave her a minute to collect herself, not wanting to intrude on her grief.

"Some of my people have recently gone missing," she said, turning back toward me. Her green skin had taken on a sickly sheen, but she raised her chin and met my amber eyes with her emerald ones. "I had hoped that they were just out wandering, it is common enough behavior among the trooping faeries, but in my heart, I knew that they were dead. Each one had disappeared without saying a word to anyone and they left all of their treasured belongings behind."

Hitting the road without bragging about their destination and leaving everything they owned behind? That definitely didn't sound like any fae I knew. It was especially worrisome that they'd left without packing up their prized possessions. Faeries were like magpies, collecting everything that caught their fancy. They might wander off without telling their friends, but faeries would never walk away from their hoards of treasure.

"It had to have been the *each uisge*," I said, pounding my fist into my gloved hand. Mab's bones. Those bastards would kill and eat anything that moved—and not necessarily in that order. "There has to be something we can do to stop them taking over the city."

"What are you willing to give me if my people join you in this fight?" she asked.

Oh, of course, the bargaining. Faeries have made an art of haggling over deals. They even give demons a run for their money. But what did I have to bargain with, my soul?

The glaistig was staring at me hungrily with green, gleaming eyes waiting for my answer. I sucked in a deep breath, preparing to offer what I could to save the city, when my phone jangled loudly from my pocket. Damn, I'd forgotten to turn off the ringer.

I felt my face flush, cheeks burning in frustrated embarrassment, but was saved the full force of the glaistig's anger. One of her servants, an ogre armed to the teeth, came rushing to her side. While she turned to confer with her guard, I used the opportunity to check my phone. The name "Kaye" was flashing on the screen so I hit the button to take the call.

"Kaye?" I asked. "Um, can this wait? Now's not really a good time."

"Mab's bloody bones, lass!" Hob said. The brownie was out of breath and sounded terrified. "Listen, girl. Kaye's been cookin' her seein' spells. Says yer under attack. Get out o' there. Kaye and her hunter friends will meet ye near Wharf Street."

Mab's bloody bones, indeed. I could tell from the harried look of the glaistig, and the orders she was shouting to her guards, that Kaye's spell had seen true. Prophecy spells were usually too convoluted to make sense of, and cost the caster dearly, but my friend must have felt it was worth the risk. It would have been a nasty surprise to discover the *each uisge* planned to launch their attack tonight.

"Okay, got it," I said. "I'm with the glaistig, um, The Green Lady, now."

"Ye got cotton in yer ears, lass?" Hob asked. "Run!"

The line went dead and I ran to the glaistig who was now standing beside a wooden chest filled with weapons. Spears, swords, and arrows appeared to have been carved from trees and tipped with stone. When most of your army are allergic to iron, you got creative. These looked more like art than weapons, but I was sure that in fae hands they were plenty deadly.

"I have to leave, so I'll take that answer now," I said. "My friends are waiting for me. Will you stand with us against the *each uisge* or will you run? I have it on good authority that they're about to attack Harborsmouth."

"We will fight alongside you if you give me a boon," she said.

"Sure, whatever," I said, shrugging one shoulder.

"A wish to be granted at a later date," she said.

She wanted me to owe her a favor that she would collect in the future. It didn't seem like a bad bargain. In fact, it was a total no-brainer. If the glaistig and her army of carnival fae didn't help us fight the *each uisge*, there would be no future. What was there to lose?

"Yes," I said. "I promise."

She looked amused. Well, bully for her.

"Since we are allies in this battle, I will bestow upon you a gift of knowledge," she said.

"For what price?" I asked.

"One more favor?" she asked. "The information is not widely known and would give you a potential advantage over our opponent."

"Sure," I said, gesturing with my hand for her to continue.

"You are aware of how stealing a kelpie's bridle removes his or her free will, so this should not be a difficult concept," she said. "Every *each uisge* wears a piece of seaweed with similar powers. Steal the weed from an *each uisge* and they will no longer be your enemy."

Great. If the pictures in Kaye's books were accurate, then the creatures wore seaweed like a clown wears make-up.

"How will I know it's the right piece of seaweed?" I asked.

"When he stops trying to eat you," she said. "And, Ivy? That is two favors that you now owe me."

I agreed to her terms and she nodded. The bargaining was over. It was now time to fight.

CHAPTER 19

The screams of terrified families were quickly drowned out by an electronic shrieking and wailing. The loud sound blasts, like a car alarm on steroids, were coming from an observation tower that stood overlooking the pier. Someone had triggered the severe weather warning siren. Good thinking.

The emergency warning system could be set off by radio transmitter, or, as I suspected in this case, magic. The alarm system was tied into a network of speakers and flashing beacons attached to navigation buoys and atop buildings, lighthouses, and water towers up and down the coast. That would get humans traveling out of the harbor and moving inland to higher ground. Nobody wanted to be standing at sea level when a hurricane or tsunami hit ground.

Little did they know that the true threat was much more eager to draw blood. Nature could be cruel, but the *each uisge* took death and destruction to a whole new level. A hurricane or tsunami could kill you, and leave the city a wasteland, but at least nature didn't take pleasure in torturing you for a few days before letting you die.

The cacophony of sounds nearly blistered my ears and, for the length of one ragged breath, stopped all higher thought in its tracks. My imagination running wild with images of bloodthirsty *each uisge* probably wasn't helping either. Thankfully, my lizard brain was working just fine.

"Fight or flight, idiot!" my body screamed at me. I raised a shaking hand to wipe my brow as traitorous perspiration slid into wide, unblinking eyes. My heart beat against my ribs like a wild beast trying to escape captivity. Even my saliva abandoned ship, leaving my mouth dry as desert sand.

Okay, right. It was time to run like hell, definitely, but which way? I was lost in a sea of tents with armed faerie creatures running, flying, and slithering in every conceivable direction.

I turned back to where the glaistig had been standing, thinking to ask her what path was the quickest way to the exit, but she was no longer approachable. The diminutive lady had disappeared, replaced by a seven-foot-tall behemoth. Glowing phantom glaistigs flew like angry specters toward the faerie queen. She was gathering pieces of herself, retrieving the tiny shards she had scattered throughout the world to watch over her people. As she drew in more power, the glaistig came to resemble a true fae leader, one to rival Oberon in stature and Mab in ferocity.

While I stood, mouth gaping, she grew even larger in size, now a twin to The Green Lady painted on the main attraction tent. But where the painting invited guests inside with a quirk of the lips and a dancing pose, this Green Lady snarled with rage and used her goat legs and cloven hooves to stomp a wagon, and an approaching *each uisge*, to dust.

A second *each uisge* galloped into sight, which made my stomach churn. I had read about these creatures in Kaye's books and watched them in my visions, but nothing prepared me for seeing one in the flesh. The monster was death incarnate, from the milky orbs of its dead eyes to the dripping fangs, sickle claws, poisoned spines, razor sharp exoskeleton of its legs, and dark mangy fur stretched thin over jutting ribs and hips.

For the second time tonight, I froze. I felt like someone had replaced my blood with strawberry slushie, causing a chill to creep up my spine and turning my veins to ice.

With a stroke of luck, the approaching *each uisge* didn't target me as his first victim. A running satyr wasn't so lucky.

The satyr was moving fast, carrying an armload of weaponry and a satchel containing messages. He, (Satyrs are always male, a fact evident for anyone with eyes. They never wear clothes, preferring to display their manhood for all adoring female fae to see. Normally that fact would have me throwing up a little and reaching for extra-strength brain bleach, but not today. I was too busy being terrified by the *each uisge* invasion.), never saw the attack coming.

Spears and staves went flying as the *each uisge* launched itself onto the satyr's back. The satyr struck the ground hard, but immediately tried to turn itself around to reach its attacker. Little did he know, he was already too late.

When the *each uisge* leaped onto the satyr, it latched on using the shredding and gripping power of its barnacle and chitin covered forelegs. Shimmying up the satyr's back with amazing speed, it managed to straddle the poor creature. As soon as the *each uisges'* rear legs were close enough, it hooked its wicked sickle claws into the satyr's hind quarters.

The satyr flailed, but couldn't dislodge the water horse. It twisted to face its attacker, knife in hand, but the fight was already lost. While the *each uisge* climbed up the satyr's back, it drove the long, needle-like, barbs of its forelegs into the flesh along the satyr's spine. The fast-acting neurotoxin was already causing paralysis in the satyr's extremities. It would only be a matter of seconds before he would lose the ability to move at all, but he would remain conscious. The *each uisge* liked their prey to be aware, as they flayed the flesh from their bones.

This one was in a hurry—no time for flaying. That didn't stop it from making a snack of the satyr's shoulder. The black horse-like head lunged forward, fangs and needle-teeth gleaming in the carnival lights. The *each uisge* continued to chew on muscle and bone as it reared back on hind legs, the helpless satyr dangling from its mouth. The faerie finally dropped its knife, fingers twitching against empty air. Not bothering to finish the satyr off, the *each uisge* flung the man to the ground to fall like a bloody ragdoll.

As he turned to search for more humans and faeries to hunt, the *each uisge* gave the satyr a vicious kick to the face, crushing his jaw. Something inside me shattered, releasing a burning rage. This is what happened to Marvin—the poor, innocent, sweet, smiling kid that I'd come to care for in just a few days. One of these plague infested, overgrown sea horses had kicked in my friend's face, just like this asshat was doing to the dying satyr. Kicking a man when he's down wasn't very sportsmanlike, now was it?

Bastard.

I let the rage build in my chest. Anger burned away the ice in my veins and salt laden air rushed in to fill my chest as I released a breath I hadn't known I was holding. Strength returned to my legs and I ran. It may have seemed cowardly, but I vowed to do everything I could to rid my city of these monsters. I wouldn't do anyone any good, if I was dead.

I had lost my chance to ask for directions, the glaistig was no longer in sight, so I picked the path farthest from the blood-crazed *each uisge*. I searched for any familiar scenery in the strobe flashes of buildings, people, and amusement rides that were there, then gone again, as I ran past narrow pathways between the tents.

Finally, I caught a glimpse of a familiar Harborsmouth landmark. Dodging around rope and canvas, I came out before a row of low, wooden booths containing games of chance. The skyline, which had been obstructed until now by carnival tents, shone brightly in the distance. I could clearly see the steeple of Sacred Heart church high atop Joysen Hill. I now knew in which direction to run.

I ran.

My lungs burned and leg muscles screamed in protest, but I ran. I continued running even when I rounded a corner to find a pile of discarded corpses. The scene was both grotesque and sad. Mothers and fathers still held pieces of their children in their arms—an evening at the amusement park gone horribly wrong. Wiping tears from my eyes with the back of a gloved hand, I ran. The dead would be mourned when this was all over, if any of us survived, but, for now, I focused on the living. There were still lives that could be saved.

I ran.

With every pounding thrust of my legs, I sent up a silent prayer that my friends were still alive and safe. When it came to praying, I was no expert. I knew a few anti-demon prayers, so I started with those. Then I decided not to discriminate. I prayed to God, the Goddess, Zeus, Oberon, Titania, Mab, the Easter Bunny, and Santa freaking Claus. I didn't think I could bear stepping over the bodies of my friends, like I had the bodies of strangers. I remembered a pale, bloodied arm ringed with an intricate rose tattoo. It reminded me of Jinx. I shook my head and prayed harder.

Still running, I searched my pockets for my phone, but came up empty. It was urgent that I pass along the information the glaistig had given me. If Kaye had known about the magic seaweed, she'd have mentioned it earlier. I needed my phone, now. Oberon's eyes, where was the damn thing? I checked each pocket again. Nothing but pocket lint, No.2 pencils, and the lighter I'd brought to my meeting with the city vampires.

I pushed myself into a sprint as I burst out into the open stretch of pier beside the Ferris wheel and carousel ride. This section of the park, so close to the entry gates, was abandoned. The lack of laughing families, and abundance of blood, cast an eerie pall. Even the carousel horses seemed to leer as they bobbed up and down in their perpetual dance.

The emergency siren continued to wail over the discordant carousel music, but I heard another sound, could almost feel it vibrating up through the soles of my boots. It thundered like an avalanche, which even my fear-addled brain recognized as out of place here at sea level. I turned my focus from the spinning carousel to the sky, and nearly fell.

The ground heaved at my feet, deck planking thrusting upward and thin tarmac breaking apart, as something forced its way up from the churning waters beneath the pier. The white carousel horse was replaced by its midnight cousin; if that cousin were a serial killer decorated in ropes of blood and seaweed rather than blue and gold paint.

The *each uisge* climbed up through the broken planks and pavement like a spider. Alighting on the ground in front of me, it blocked my path. I tried to focus on the milky white eyes that sat like eggs in the *each uisges'* face, rather than the dripping fangs and sickle claws. My friends needed the glaistig's information. I had to survive.

Tilting its head to the side, the *each uisge* regarded me with curiosity. I wasn't screaming, peeing my pants, or running away. I was, however at risk of passing out with fear. I pulled in a deep calming breath and tried to focus.

I grabbed hold of my anger and embraced it. Stoking the fire of my rage, I remembered my vision of Marvin being beaten by these creatures. The tension in my shoulders released. I shifted my weight, letting my hands hang loosely at my sides. The *each uisge* were swift and deadly, but I knew their weakness. I also could see through their glamour. This one was trying, ironically, to look like the carousel horse behind him.

I narrowed my eyes and searched his body for seaweed. If I could grab the correct slimy clump, then I might live. In a matter of seconds, I came to a realization. Even with the tip from the glaistig regarding the *each uisges'* Achilles heel, I was screwed.

Trying to find a piece of magic seaweed on an *each uisge* was like searching for a needle in a haystack. A haystack that was looking at me as if it wanted to skin me alive, eat me like a screaming fudge brownie, and pick its teeth with my bones.

I was staring into those hungry eyes, trying to ignore the saliva dripping from black fangs, as an arrow plunged into one milky white orb. The arrow came from my right, striking the *each uisges'* left eye. The *each uisge* stumbled as it turned to face the direction of its new attacker, no longer curious about the tiny fly in its web. I took a step back, wondering if I could make it around the *each uisge* unnoticed.

No, probably not. Even blinded in one eye, the *each uisge* was a powerful killing machine. This one was tearing up the pavement as it stomped its feet and swung its head to dislodge the arrow.

I continued backing up, hoping to distance myself from the enraged beast, until the heel of my boot struck metal. My retreat came to a halt. I was out of room to move. Colorful lights shone from hundreds of electric bulbs and movement stirred hair on the back of my neck. I didn't want to take my eyes from the primary threat, but was almost certain that I had backed myself into the still operating Ferris wheel.

The *each uisges'* nostrils flared as it scented for its prey. It was moving, heading to my right, when a second arrow struck its right shoulder. Shrieking, it turned in the direction the shot had originated. Mab's bones! The arrow had come from the area where I stood. The creature moved to face me, lips drawn back to display the full length of its fangs. I hadn't been the shooter, but try explaining that to a furious *each uisge.*

It charged toward me, the arrow in its shoulder not slowing it down one bit. I retreated a single step, having to climb onto the metal support beam bolted into the pavement, but there was nowhere else to go. With a ragged sigh, I pulled the No.2 pencils from my pocket and, with a quick flick of the wrist, slid them down between my fingers to rest securely in the palms of my hands, point outward. I spread my feet hip width apart, bent my knees, and raised my fists preparing to strike.

There was no hope of surviving close combat with an *each uisge*, but I planned on finishing this one off with my dying breath. It was already injured, which gave me a fighting chance at taking it out of the current battle. Its eye was an oozing, useless mess and the arrow in its shoulder was embedded deep enough that it was probably scraping bone as it ran. If I could jab a pencil in its remaining good eye, it might become one less monster my friends would have to fight today.

It seemed like a decent plan, as far as split-second near death strategies go, but I never got a chance to find out if it would work. The *each uisge* was so close that I could feel the pounding of its hooves vibrate up through the metal framework into the soles of my boots, and smell the carrion on its breath, when two hands grabbed me from behind.

CHAPTER 20

Have I mentioned that I am not fond of heights? Yes, I'm more than a little bit neurotic. I have an aversion to touching or being touched (psychometry's a bitch), dislike waiting in narrow hallways far beneath our city streets with tons of bedrock overhead (hello, claustrophobia), and am prone to panic attacks. Oh, and swinging to and fro while flailing above a hungry *each uisge* makes me sweat buckets.

I was lifted into the air, my feet dangling within inches of the *each uisges'* snapping jaws. With a vertiginous tilt, I continued to rise as the open air Ferris wheel car, that I suddenly found myself in, swung back and forth. The faerie bard I'd met earlier dropped me, without ceremony, onto the gondola seat beside the succubus, Delilah. Not my favorite amusement ride companion, but I was alive.

There was that.

Without a word or glance, the faerie bard climbed out onto the front of the car. He was barefoot and I idly wondered if he were part gecko. What else could explain his ability to walk with ease on such a slippery surface?

Slippery surface. I peeked over the side of the gondola to watch the ground move away at a rapid pace. I squeezed my eyes shut not wanting to look, but forced them open again.

The faerie continued walking along the top of the metal and fiberglass car, settling into a crouch as he reached the oval tip. As he leaned out precariously, the entire gondola swung forward. I let out a little squeak of terror, gripped the safety rail with gloved hands, and held on for dear life.

He raised the bow and drew an arrow back to his pointy ear. In one graceful movement, he released the bowstring allowing the arrow to dive down more than two hundred feet to thrust deep into the *each uisges'* single functioning eye.

If I hadn't witnessed it myself, I would have sworn it was an impossible shot.

Judging from the effect it had on the *each uisge*, the arrow probably traveled all the way into its brain. The last thing I saw, before the arc of the Ferris wheel blocked my view, was the *each uisge* dropping lifeless to the ground.

"Um, thanks," I said, voice shaking. "Ni-ice shooting."

The faerie bard slung the bow over his shoulder and sat cross-legged, where he'd stood, on the front of the swinging car. Delilah purred happily in the seat beside me and I inched away. I was thankful for the rescue, but wasn't about to repay the favor with a life-essence-sucking embrace. If Delilah wanted to cuddle, she could cozy up with her faerie friend.

"The Green Lady charged us with finding you and offering our protection while you remain within the boundaries of her domain," the faerie said.

My very own bodyguards? I wasn't sure if the glaistig had assigned my safety to these two to keep them out of trouble, or to safeguard her wishes. Either way, I was grateful for the help against the *each uisge* and would gladly accept an escort to the carnival gates.

"Okay, great, I can use the help," I said. "As soon as we're off this thing, I'm heading for the park exit. I already lost time facing down that *each uisge*. If you're coming with me, we need to move fast."

I didn't want to waste any time getting off the Ferris wheel. People thought these contraptions were entertaining? I guess it's all fun and games until you fall to your death.

I was already planning the escape route in my head. I'd been able to see the entrance turnstiles, before the *each uisge* came bursting up through the pavement to block my path. There were a few obstacles, including the dead water horse, spinning carousel ride, and piles of debris, but with the faerie and succubus covering my back, I felt confident that I could make the run unscathed.

I bent down to check my boots, making sure that they were tied tightly with the laces tucked out of the way. Tonight an untied shoelace could mean my death. I pulled up my pant leg, determined to quadruple knot my laces before we hit the ground running.

"Wait," the faerie said, reaching out to grab my arm.

I pulled out of his reach. Arm already extended, he fluidly altered the movement to point at the bay below. His eyes were fixed on something in the water. Irritated, I stopped fussing with my boot laces and followed his gaze.

Oh.

From the Ferris wheel, we had a bird's eye view of the ensuing battle below. I looked on in horror, overwhelmed by the vastness of the destruction already beset upon the harbor. Something had found its own means of entertainment—and it had nothing to do with amusement park rides.

Every boat, down to the smallest dinghy, had been torn from its moorings and ripped apart. Docks and boat slips lay empty, an ominous portent for the city that lay beyond. But the destruction of property was nothing, a momentary distraction to wet twisted appetites, compared to the slaughter taking place in deeper waters.

The night carnival cast flickering light on much of the bay, from its position atop the pier, and the lights of waterfront businesses and residences reflected here and there, casting an eldritch glow on the water...illuminating the abominations within. Waves crested, holding aloft battle detritus. Spined, furred, and scaled bodies swam past the floating corpses of the fallen, to face their foes.

Though it was impossible from this distance, and with the constant blare of the alarm, I could imagine weapons ringing as they clashed above the surf. Everywhere I looked, fae creatures fought. Blades, tridents, harpoons, teeth, and claws gleamed beneath the city lights before sinking into flesh and disappearing beneath the waves.

Hundreds of *each uisge* had attacked the water's edge, but were driven back out to the center of the bay by another fierce species of water fae. The merrow had kept their promise.

The dark waters of the harbor continued to swell with their numbers as more merrow joined their tribesmen. Even in the half-light, it was simple to tell the merrow and *each uisge* apart. While *each uisge* were a nightmare form of water horse, the merrow were a beautiful, if deadly, mating of sea life and water faerie. Similar to merfolk, the merrow resembled attractive humans from the waist up. From the hips down, the merrow took after their non-fae parentage. Everywhere I looked, tentacles and fish tails lashed out.

They had come, and just in time. The merrow were savage fighters, but the *each uisge* had their secret weapon: Ceffyl Dŵr.

I recognized Ceffyl from my visions. He was in his water horse form, just as he had been while ruling over his court. During that vision, I had seen his reflection in the dark pools of water at his feet. I had been impressed when I first saw him in this form. Sleek seal-like skin covered his well-muscled body from equine head to seaweed entwined tail. He was larger than the other members of his court and his eyes held wisdom in their dark green depths.

That had been before the *each uisge* had their fun. Ceffyl's beautiful gray coat was now striped with jagged ropes of pink scar tissue. Blisters and open sores, unable to heal, lined his skin where he had been wrapped in iron chains. This regal man had suffered greatly at the hands of the *each uisge*. I felt sorry for him.

The visions that I previously experienced through his eyes, when I touched his bridle, had made me sympathetic to the kelpie king. He had served his people well and had the misfortune of feeling a great deal of pain during his immortal lifetime. That pain had imprinted on his bridle, embedded into the leather grain alongside sweat and tears. And let's not forget, he had been married to a child-killing bitch.

No, Ceffyl Dŵr, like my friend Jinx, was not a lucky soul.

Now he was being forced to fight for his torturers. The kelpie king, pulled along by the puppet strings of his stolen bridle, lead the *each uisge* army. No kelpie would join this fight with Ceffyl Dŵr leading the enemy, and the merrow I had spoken with, via the magic seashell, had sounded fond of the kelpie king. None of the fae wanted to go up against him, which was too bad. Ceffyl Dŵr was a formidable opponent.

The situation looked grim.

How many would be killed before this was all over? And, at the end of the day, who would be left standing?

Concerned, I pulled my eyes from the water battle to assess the damage along the waterfront. That's when I noticed it, the absolute absence of humans. The pier and waterfront had been bustling with people out enjoying the summer night, and trying to beat the heat by staying close to the water. Now, there were no humans in sight.

The emergency weather warning alarm system was effective, but it wasn't one hundred percent effective. Though it seemed like an eternity since the first *each uisge* appeared, not much time had gone by since the sirens began their wailing. Most crowds don't move that quickly and efficiently in a crisis. Also, there were always stragglers. Whether dissenters stubbornly refusing to do what they are instructed, wounded persons immobilized by their injuries, good Samaritans wanting to help, criminals looking for opportunities, or people remaining behind to protect their property from potential looters—there were always people who stayed at the scene.

I was glad that the streets weren't teeming with panicking humans, but their absence went beyond the realm of normal possibility. It almost seemed as if someone had cast a "keep away" spell on the entire waterfront and pier. But that was impossible. The amount of magic skill and harnessed power needed to fuel such a spell was unthinkable. No one was that powerful, right?

I cast a glance for the far side of the waterfront, where I was due to meet with Kaye. Kaye, and her hunter and magic wielding friends, should be there by now. Could they be responsible for keeping the human population in the dark, and out of harm's way? Hunters took their vow to protect the people of this city very seriously, and no member of the magic community would want to risk knowledge of the supernatural finding its way into the general populace.

Had they found a way to cast the "keep away" spell together?

I had to concentrate, but finally caught sight of Kaye and her friends. They were cloaked in mist and shadow, but my second sight, with some effort, allowed my eyes to cut through the thick fog. Obviously, someone had thought to cast more than the "keep away" spell. And now I had a good idea how they had come to accomplish such a thing.

The entire magic population of Harborsmouth stood in a circle, with Kaye at its center. There were hundreds of them, standing with hands linked and heads bowed. I had no idea that there were so many magic practitioners in Harborsmouth. Every minor hedge witch and magician's apprentice had turned out, ready to face the *each uisge* threat against our city.

Now that I could see past the dark shadows of the cloaking spell, the lines of magic shone brightly. Green, blue, and silver bands of power snaked between each member of the circle. Every time Kaye raised her hands, the lines of power would lash out to strike her chest where she drew the energy into herself. Magic licked over her body like blue flame.

I was both incredibly proud, and concerned for the safety, of my friend. I had no idea what support I could lend to the casting, but I felt certain that I had a role to play. There must be something that I could do to help. I desperately needed to get off this ride and make it to where the magic ritual was taking place.

Before the Ferris wheel reached the bottom of its arc, I was out of the gondola car. I hit the ground running. Without looking over my shoulder, I knew that the faerie and succubus were close on my heels.

"Hang on, Kaye," I whispered. "I'm coming."

CHAPTER 21

The faerie quickly overtook me, leading the way as we ran. I considered myself in good shape—went jogging daily, when the job allowed, ran sprints up and down our stairs and around the block, practiced self-defense moves in the open space of our loft apartment, and didn't over eat—but had to struggle to keep up. I was fast for a human, with decent stamina, but no match for a faerie. My pride kept me running full tilt, as we passed the carousel ride and leapt over broken pavement, but I suspected that the faerie wasn't even trying. He was more focused on potential attackers than his running speed.

With a grimace, I pushed myself to run faster. I wouldn't be able to keep up this pace much longer, but at least I'd reach Kaye sooner rather than later. That was the upside of quickening my pace. The downside was that I sounded like an overweight dog on a hot day.

I tried to control my panting breaths, since it seemed to excite Delilah. The last thing I needed was to turn on a succubus. I inhaled hot briny air in through my nose then exhaled slowly out my mouth.

I nearly stumbled when the emergency weather siren stopped blaring. The silence, as the alarm cut out, left my ears ringing. I shook my head and continued to run, with Delilah at my hip.

We were drawing close to the exit, the metal turnstiles within sight, when the succubus abandoned her place at my side to veer toward our left. I slowed, but she looked back at me with a wink and nodded her head toward the park entrance.

Turning back to face her prey, Delilah seemed to grow in size. Not in the way that the glaistig had become physically larger, by calling separate parts to join together, but as if she suddenly had presence. Her aura seemed to envelop the entire pier, as she set her sights on an *each uisge* who was attempting to ambush us.

The black horse leapt toward us from its hiding place, but Delilah was already blocking its path. The *each uisge* had been completely silent, moving like a living shadow as he raced in for the attack. How had she known that the monster was waiting for us behind that ticket booth?

Lust.

The succubus, equipped to sense lust in all of its forms, could sense the bloodlust of the water horse. He was frenzied from battle, foaming at the mouth, scraping the ground eagerly with razor-sharp hooves, and focused his gaze on his new opponent with nostrils flaring. In fact, the *each uisge* was looking at Delilah with a hunger that bordered on desire.

Each uisge enjoyed the perversion of mixing pain with pleasure. Tearing apart a sexy succubus was probably this guy's wet dream—twisted son of a bitch.

The water horse lunged toward Delilah only to pull away at the last second. He was like a cat playing with a mouse. Too bad for him, she was a tiger in mouse's clothing. Delilah let her flirtatious mask slip away to reveal the face of a killer—a very hungry killer.

When was the last time that she ate?

Her manicured fingernails had been replaced with talons and she dragged one across her wrist, drawing blood. She now had her opponent's undivided attention. The *each uisge* fixated on the blood dripping down her arm.

Delilah strode forward without hesitation and, with one acrobatic leap, jumped on top of the water horse's back. Gripping his head, the succubus stilled the beast. The *each uisge* was no longer fighting—he appeared to be in a trance.

Delilah's pupils widened and dark veins stretched out across her chest and down her arms and hands. Riding the *each uisge* bare back, she gripped him tightly with her legs and dug her fingers into his tangled mane.

"You do not want to see this," the faerie said.

His voice broke the spell. I had been rooted to the spot, watching on with a mixture of horror and curiosity. The succubus started rocking back and forth on the back of the entranced *each uisge*, and I looked away. I turned to face the faerie, rather than continue to watch the embarrassing Delilah train wreck. Judging from the moaning coming from behind me, I had turned away just in time.

The faerie had come to stand silently at my side, hand resting on his bow. There was tightness in his stance, and a crease in the middle of his brow, that hadn't been there before. I wondered how he felt about Delilah's method of feeding. If he had feelings for the succubus, it would be difficult to watch her seduce, and kill, another man to sate her hunger.

"No, I don't think I do," I said, shaking my head.

"We are nearly at the exit," he said, turning to face the turnstiles. "I will lead you the rest of the way, but there we must part."

I gestured the faerie to lead the way and fell into step behind him. It didn't take us long to reach the gates. At the turnstile, I bit my lip wondering how best to say goodbye. We may not have been friends, but this man had saved my life. I felt that I owed him some kind of thanks, but my mouth was dry and mind blank. I wished, at that moment, that I were better with words, and with people.

"Um, thank you," I said. "Safe travels."

"Safe travels and good hunting," he said.

He watched over my exit through the turnstile and out the gate, then pivoted on one foot and was gone. The faerie had kept his promise to the glaistig, nothing more. He had watched over my safety until I reached the boundary of The Green Lady's kingdom. He was a faerie skilled at killing, and had only been doing his duty for his queen. That was something best not to forget.

Standing on the empty sidewalk, I suddenly felt very alone.

CHAPTER 22

The waterfront was a ghost town, sans tumbleweeds.

Ever wonder what it would be like if the zombie apocalypse hit your city? I had a nagging suspicion that it would look something like this.

Streets that were normally filled with people out enjoying a summer night were empty. No couples holding hands as they strolled along the boardwalk, no rowdy drunks stumbling along their nightly pub crawl, no smokers standing in clusters outside doorways, and, most strange of all, no police. The Old Port normally has a strong police presence at night, with mounted cops, bike cops, and the regular cruiser and SUV patrols.

During a threat to the city, such as a hurricane or tidal wave, emergency personnel would normally assist in evacuations, medical triage, and the prevention of looting. But there were no police, or EMTs. There was no one in sight—not a living soul.

Lights remained on, shining out from shop and restaurant windows, as if no one could spare the time to turn them off. That was unusual. During a weather emergency, most business owners would normally make an effort to shut down electricity to prevent fires. I think, deep down, people could sense that something more than a storm threatened out there on the bay.

If preparing to face the *each uisge*, would you want to be left in the dark?

People had been here, less than an hour before, and they obviously left in a hurry. A sandal sat on its side, in the middle of the sidewalk. Someone had run out of their shoe, and hadn't bothered to stop and retrieve it. Who continues to run half barefoot along city streets, leaving their shoe behind? A person terrified of what was coming—that was who.

There were similar signs of panicked escape all up and down the waterfront. Doors hung open on their hinges, radios and televisions continued to play, and upended chairs lay where they had fallen. Café tables held half eaten meals and hundred dollar bottles of wine. Cash tips fluttered from under salt and pepper shakers, never to be retrieved by wait staff. Even thieves had passed the source of easy money, in their rush to evacuate.

With the dark, churning water of the harbor to my left and businesses topped with apartments to my right, I ran. I was like a ghost sprinting along the waterfront—a specter flitting from shadow to shadow. A lone survivor left behind.

At least, I had thought myself alone. A dark figure leapt down from atop a three-story brick building, to stand in my path. With a yelp, I stopped running and took an involuntary step back.

The man was tall and slender and moved with a grace and agility that I attributed to fae reflexes. He reminded me of the faerie bard I'd just left behind. Sweeping his long coat behind him like a cape, he strode toward me.

What did he want? Was he a messenger carrying a directive from the glaistig? I really didn't have time for this. I needed to reach my friends before the *each uisge* overtook the merrow, an eventuality that seemed more than likely by the screams and snickers coming from the water. I clenched my fists and tried to tamp down my impatience.

As the man drew closer he smiled, showing a flash of fang. Ah, not a faerie then. Illuminated by a flickering street light, I could now see through his glamour to the details of his corpse-like visage. No self-respecting faerie would be seen with skin that dry and dusty. I slowly moved my hands closer to the pockets that held my lighter and makeshift stakes.

The man towering over me was a vampire.

"You made a deal with The Green Lady," the vampire said.

It was a statement, not a question, but I answered just the same.

"Yes," I said. "It doesn't change the promises made by your boss."

The vampire hissed. This guy answered to someone, so it made sense that his boss, or his boss's boss, was one of the bags of bones I'd met with. Funny, he didn't seem happy at the mention of his superiors. Most megalomaniacs don't appreciate being reminded that someone is higher up than them on the food chain. This vamp wasn't any different.

"You should not have made a bargain with the faerie queen without consulting the vampire council," he said.

I shrugged. I wanted their help to protect the people of this city, but if the vampires decided to revoke their promise to defend Harborsmouth, there really wasn't much I could do about it.

"Is that it?" I asked, tapping my foot. "Your bosses are bent out of shape because I made a deal with the glaistig, and now they're refusing to fight?"

The vampire cleared his throat, a strange left-over nervous habit from the days when he still had flesh. It sounded like a cat coughing up a fur ball that was wrapped in a paper bag.

"Well, no, not exactly," he said, pulling at his collar. "The vampires of this city will fight, if this battle reaches land, but I was sent to voice the displeasure of the council. In the future..."

"Look, I don't have time for this," I said. "If you don't get out of my way, now, there won't be a future."

Without waiting for the vampire to move, I circled around him at a jog. I tensed as I ran past, but he didn't try to stop me. After running two blocks, I looked back over my shoulder to see him still rooted in place.

Vampires are not the most adaptable monster. I suspected it had something to do with mixing immortality with human stubbornness. Whatever the reason, they tended to become easily flummoxed when things didn't go their way. This one would probably stand there, in that creepy, super-still vampire way, until birds came to nest in his straw-like hair.

The council of dusty leeches was upset with me? I felt a slow grin spread across my face. Well, they could just take a number and get in line.

As I ran, the ringing in my ears lessened and my hearing returned. I wish it hadn't. Nightmare sounds came from all over the bay. Splashing, shrieks, and cries were growing louder which meant the battle was drawing closer to shore.

I hurried on, nearly at the edge of the cloaked hunter encampment. At this range, I could see the waves of flickering power running up and down the magic barrier. I hoped there was a way to pass through the curtain of blue and purple flames. I didn't come all this way to be fried extra-crispy by friendly fire.

CHAPTER 23

As I approached the enchanted barrier, a woman on sentinel duty came into sight. She was younger than me, perhaps in her late teens or early twenties. I wouldn't be surprised if she wasn't old enough to buy beer, but that didn't make her any less of a badass. Her freckled face and flame red hair cut into a pixie-cut would have been cute on anyone else, but she was a hunter. Hunters are always deadly serious— they don't do cute.

She stood with feet hip-width apart and left hand at her side, within easy reach of her weapons. She wore a sword at her hip, knives in forearm sheaths, and a gun holster strapped around her thigh. Her right hand held a crossbow that was trained at my head.

Most monster movies promote the idea of shooting through the heart to kill supernatural creatures, but a head shot is more reliable. Even if it doesn't finish the monster off, a head wound will usually make them pause long enough to come in for the kill. Of course, there is always the chance it will just piss them off. There's a reason why Hunters have the average lifespan of a fruit fly.

Wariness and knowledge of their enemy is often what keeps a Hunter in one piece. Hunters have libraries of supernatural info that they study, like the encyclopedia I borrowed from Kaye, to make monster identification easier, but vision isn't foolproof. I was gifted with second sight, but that was a rare ability in humans. And Hunters are always human. They may ally themselves with supernatural races at times, but their membership is made up exclusively of Homo sapiens.

This Hunter was sizing me up, but not letting down her guard. Kaye would have told them I was coming. This young woman had probably been given a description of me, possibly even a photograph, but Hunters know to distrust their eyes. Glamours and shapeshifting were too prevalent in the supernatural community for her to believe what she saw.

"I'm really not a big fan of piercings," I said, raising my voice to be heard across the distance. "Would you mind lowering that thing? I'm here to see Kaye."

No laugh. No smile. She didn't even blink.

"State your name," she said.

"Ivy Granger," I said, letting out a sigh. "If you don't mind, I'm in a hurry. There's a war going on, in case you hadn't noticed, and I need to see Kaye, now."

Yes, I was getting, as Jinx would say, a case of the grumpy pants. I was tired, my legs were cramping, and I didn't want to stop here long enough to think. I felt in my gut that that way lay insanity. The image of corpses, families torn apart, strewn across a carnival pathway, was already creeping in. I needed to keep moving. There would be time to fall to pieces later.

The Hunter pulled something from her vest pocket with her free hand. Keeping her crossbow aimed at my face, she started scrolling down through something on her phone. Each flick of her thumb was like nails on a chalkboard. I tried to distract myself by looking for patterns in the wall of magic flickering behind her. I could just make out a lopsided butterfly when she grunted, stopped playing with her cell phone, and slipped it back into her vest pocket.

"Your name is on the list," she said.

I knew that Kaye wouldn't forget to mention me to the guards. Looked like I had permission to pass the barrier and enter the encampment.

"So, how do I get through that thing?" I asked, gesturing at the wall of magic.

"You can see it?" she asked. Her eyebrows raised and for a second she seemed impressed. The expression took a few years off my earlier assessment of her age placing her squarely in high school. Mab's bones, she was just a kid.

"Yes, and I don't feel like having my brain short-circuited," I said.

"Right," she said, returning to her stoic, unimpressed self. "Hold out your hand."

I did as ordered and she came forward...and dumped a sports bottle of water over my hand. Nothing happened.

"Holy water?" I asked, wiping my hand down the front of my shirt and pants.

"And a few other things," she said vaguely. "You can go ahead. The magic will let you through."

She stepped out of my way, lowering the crossbow to point at the ground. She didn't, I noticed, remove her finger from the trigger. I felt an itching between my shoulder blades as I walked past the guard, to the magic barrier. I could imagine her raising the crossbow again to aim it at my back. If she remained that cautious, she may actually survive until her twenty-first birthday—if we all survived the night.

I squared my shoulders, took a deep breath, and walked through a wall of potentially deadly magic. Though the barrier looked like a curtain of flame, the magic felt cool. It was like walking underwater—if the water was filled with hundreds of stinging jellyfish. My skin tingled where tiny needles of energy brushed over me. I held my breath and rushed forward. It seemed as if the magic had been *tasting* me. That was a disturbing thought.

I felt a sensation of pressure, and a popping in my ears, as I was pushed through and out the other side of the barrier. Rubbing my arms, I checked to make sure I was still in one piece. Except for a whopping case of goose bumps, I was just the same as when I'd entered.

I looked around the encampment for my friends. Part of me hoped to see them here, under the protection of the Hunters and magic community, but I also wished them home behind wards and solid walls.

Before leaving for my appointment with the city vamps, I'd helped Jinx ready the loft. After carrying in armloads of groceries and bottled water, I had put the hammer and nails to good use. I'd secured plywood over our office window, then returned to the loft to add the remaining iron nails to our line of salt and herbs at every windowsill.

Without my phone, I had no way of checking on my friends. I just hoped that Jinx, Hob, and Marvin were all somewhere safe. I caught sight of Kaye and hoped for her safety as well.

Kaye remained at the center of the casting circle. She was standing on some kind of raised platform, making her visible above the bowed heads of every magic user in Harborsmouth.

Well, nearly ever magic user.

A woman jogged toward me. Her thick glasses slid low on her nose as she checked the clipboard in her hand.

"You must be Ivy Granger," she said. "You're prettier than your photograph." I tried not to groan, wondering which embarrassing picture Kaye had circulated. "Kaye informed us that you were coming. Um, how is it out there?"

"Bad, but it could be worse," I said. I tried to forget the image of small bodies held in their parents' arms, and the screams coming from the bay. "The *each uisge* have attacked the carnival, but the glaistig and her people are fighting against them. After the first attack, the emergency weather sirens started blaring and humans left the area around the water for higher ground. The merrow have also joined the fight, pushing the battle back out into the bay and away from the waterfront."

But it was only a matter of time before their lines broke and the *each uisge* poured into the city.

"Glad to hear the city itself isn't under siege, yet," she said. "Most of us have been too busy here to find out if our efforts are having results. That was us, by the way, triggering the alarm system and casting a huge keep away spell."

"I thought so," I said, nodding. "Good thinking..."

Two young men, boys really, ran forward pushing past us. A woman from the casting circle had fallen to the ground unconscious. Blue light flickered from her fingertips, fizzling to nothing as she was pulled free of the circle.

"That's been happening more and more," she said. She gestured at the woman being lifted and carried away. "Everyone is supposed to work in shifts, but that last casting, to encourage all humans to leave the waterfront, required more magical energy. Every practitioner had to pitch in. They should be taking breaks again soon though. It won't help anyone if our circle falls."

"Do you know if Kaye is due for a break?" I asked. "I really need to speak with her."

"She needs to rest now more than anyone," she said. "Stay here and I'll see if I can have a message passed to her through the circle. Just don't touch anything while I'm gone."

With one last glance at her clipboard, she lifted her chin, pushed her glasses further up her nose and turned to face the casting circle. Squaring her shoulders, and holding her clipboard like a shield, the woman looked like she was preparing for battle. Perhaps she was. Convincing Kaye to take a break would not be easy.

*****

I was surprised when the woman returned with Kaye less than ten minutes later. My friend looked exhausted. Even from ten yards away the dark circles under her eyes were evident. Her skin held a sickly gray pallor and a film of sweat reflected off her brow and cheek bones that suddenly appeared too pronounced. She resembled someone who had survived a month starving in a refugee camp.

I bit my lip and tried to force a smile. I was relieved to see Kaye, but her frail appearance was worrying. It was difficult to reconcile the ailing woman before me with the friend whose kitchen I sat in, just hours before.

The woman had an arm around Kaye's waist, helping her to shuffle along. That was surprising. Kaye must really be in dire shape, if she was willing to let someone assist her. Normally, a helping hand would risk a rap on the knuckles from one of Kaye's staffs or kitchen spoons.

The woman and I settled Kaye on an overturned crate. Even then, I didn't receive a cuffed ear or a smack on the wrist. But I stepped back quickly, just in case. The woman with the clipboard walked away at a gesture from Kaye. She was within shouting distance, in case we needed anything, but we had our privacy.

"Ivy," Kaye said. She coughed into a kerchief that matched the blue of the one tied around her head. It came away with dark, wet blotches that turned purple against the vibrant blue. "Did you have any luck with the glaistig?"

"Yes," I said. "I made a deal with her." That received a shrewd, narrow-eyed look and I quickly continued on. "She has agreed to have her people join us in the fight against the *each uisge.*"

"Thank the stars," Kaye whispered.

"The *each uisge* have already attacked the carnival and wreaked havoc on property at the edge of the waterfront, but your spell worked," I said. "Every human has left the waterfront. And the merrow have joined the fight. They've driven the *each uisge* back out into the middle of the bay."

Every living human—the bodies remained where they lay.

"By my wand, I did not think this would come so soon," she said. "But you have done well, girl."

"There's more," I said. "The glaistig shared a secret about the *each uisge*. Every *each uisge* carries a piece of magic seaweed that, when stolen, can render them helpless. The seaweed works similar to the kelpie's bridle. The way I see it, there are two problems. First, we need to find a way to identify the piece of magic seaweed on a creature that wears their own weight in the stuff. Second, getting close enough to steal the seaweed is extremely dangerous."

Kaye sat up straighter and a smile slid onto pale lips.

"I may have a solution to our first problem," she said. Her eyes glittered with a familiar inner light, that only moments before had appeared permanently extinguished.

"Good, because I have an idea about how to deal with the second," I said.

*****

Kaye had returned to the center of her casting circle. An outsider may not recognize any difference from now and thirty minutes ago, but for me, it felt like everything had changed. It's funny how hope can alter your view of things.

With the help of the knowledge imparted by the glaistig, we had identified the major problems to taking down the *each uisge*. The first obstacle was being able to differentiate between one piece of seaweed amidst hundreds. Kaye had found the solution to this with her magic.

Using the channeled power of the huge magic circle, Kaye cast a spell that made the *each uisges'* magic seaweed glow. Runners were already dispatching messages to the city vampires, the carnival fae, and Hunters already out in the field.

Score one for the home team.

Kaye had laughed at my suggestion to use pookas to aid us in stealing the magic seaweed. But it was a throaty laugh filled with hope. If we were guys, and I wasn't touch-phobic, we probably would have chest bumped. Instead, we settled for an exchange of happy smiles.

After borrowing clipboard girl's phone, I placed calls to Jinx and Hob. Both were holding down their respective forts and relieved to hear that Kaye and I were safe. I asked them to stay put and told them about the glowing seaweed. If the *each uisge* made it that far into the city, knowing how to disarm them would be their only chance at survival.

I returned the phone to its owner and checked my pocket for Mrs. Hasting's spare house key. The warm metal was there, my ticket into the klepto faeries' lair. With one last look at Kaye, wrapped in blue and purple magic, I pushed out through the barrier and into the night.

The air was filled with screams.

War cries mingled with the pained shrieks of the dying as the sounds of battle echoed across the bay. I covered my ears, but continued to look out across the harbor as I began my run along the waterfront.

Ink black water churned beneath the night sky as *each uisge* and merrow continued to fight. Here and there, *each uisge* glowed where Kaye's magic targeted every special piece of seaweed. But the battle was far from over, and too many had already lost their lives. Lapping waves were already carrying the bodies of the dead to the shore. It was a relief to turn up Wharf Street and leave the sights and sounds of battle behind.

CHAPTER 24

After I had run three blocks from the waterfront, I started seeing signs of human life again. A curtain twitch here, a face in the window there, but the streets remained empty. With no pedestrian or vehicular traffic to avoid, I made good time.

When I arrived at Mrs. Hasting's house, the windows were dark. She would be at her sister's now, possibly hearing reports of a hurricane on the news and feeling thankful that she had left the city. I stole a look inside, just to be sure. Nobody was home, except the pookas.

I slid the key in the lock, turned the knob, and quietly slipped inside. My eyes adjusted easily to the dim light. Jinx was always lecturing me to eat my veggies, and saying how carrots will help my night vision. I was becoming a health food convert. My night vision had never been poor, but it was improving rapidly lately. It had to be the carrots.

This time though, I wished that my vision hadn't improved, since, speaking of carrots, hundreds of small bodies were humping like bunnies. Pookas filled the room, engaging in every eye-gouging form of debauchery. There were copulating pookas swinging from the curtains, dancing on the coffee table, and hanging from light fixtures. There was also an orgy taking place on the doily covered sofa. The pookas were obviously enjoying themselves. Apparently, stealing wasn't their only favored form of pastime.

Pookas are small faeries that stand at about two feet tall, from bare foot to pointy hat, but the ones in Mrs. Hasting's living room weren't just standing there waiting to be measured. And many had foregone the traditional pointy hat for one that resembled a rubber nipple. Who knew that glow-in-the-dark condoms could make such colorful party hats?

At least their affinity for glowing things was confirmed. Now I just had to convince them to abandon their orgy for a night of seaweed stealing.

I sighed and rubbed my face. I cleared my throat loudly, but the tiny faeries hadn't noticed my arrival. Reaching into my pocket, I pulled out my secret weapon. I was going to need it.

Before leaving the encampment, Kaye had asked one of the Hunters to retrieve one of the glowing pieces of seaweed. The red haired sentinel had been more than happy to oblige. She had returned quickly with one.

After showing the seaweed to the Hunters at the camp, so that they would know what to target in the upcoming fight, Kaye placed it inside a clear Ziploc bag and handed it over to me. I had protested—even wearing gloves and with the seaweed sealed in its container, I didn't want to handle something that had belonged to an *each uisge*. With a wink, that made her resemble the feisty Kaye that I was used to, she remarked that I'd need something to entice the pookas with. I couldn't really argue with that.

Now I was glad to have the pooka bait. I pulled the sealed bag from my pocket, gingerly holding the corner of the bag with gloved fingers. My skin crawled, as if trying to run away from the magic seaweed. I felt dirty, just being in the presence of the thing.

The green eldritch glow of Kaye's magic shone brightly in the dark room, casting eerie silhouettes of gyrating pookas on the floral wallpaper. They didn't continue their amorous dance for long. Slowly, at least to one who has to suffer with the image, each pooka stopped what he or she was doing and turned to stand with rapt faces beneath the glow of seaweed in my hand. Most stood with wide eyes and small hands involuntarily grasping at the air.

I finally had their attention.

"Do you like the glowing thing?" I asked. "There are lots more down in the bay. If you help us steal the glowing seaweed, we will give you an entire pooka house that glows."

That was too much for their tiny minds. They all started talking at once, their excited high-pitched voices sounding like a field of cicadas on a hot summer day.

The pooka house was an afterthought. There was an old tree house behind my parents' home just outside of the city. No one used it anymore, not since I was a child there playing hide and seek with fireflies. I was sure that Kaye would cast her spell one more time to make the interior of the tree house glow.

If not, I'd buy glow-in-the-dark paint. The pookas would be happy with their reward, and Mrs. Hastings would have her home and her sanity back.

I put the bag of seaweed back in my pocket. Covering my ears, I waited. The voices died down to a low thrum and a little man, wearing a loin cloth that suspiciously resembled one of Mrs. Hasting's crocheted doilies and a glowing red condom for a hat, stepped forward. He narrowed his eyes and looked me over from head to toe.

"Why should we bargain with one of The Bigs?" he asked.

His voice had a funny nasal quality, but he spoke perfect English. That was a relief. I assumed that by The Bigs, he meant humans.

"Well, stealing the seaweed would be fun, right?" I asked.

Every pooka, except the leader who had spoken, was nodding their head.

"Maybe," he said, crossing arms over his bare chest.

"And the reward is really awesome," I said. "Every pooka will be envious of your pack's glowing home."

All of the pookas nodded their heads faster while grinning from ear to ear.

"But you are right," I said. "There is a catch."

The pookas sighed sadly. The little man spat and shook his fist at me.

"I knew one of The Bigs wouldn't play fair," he said. "What is this catch?"

"You will have to steal the glowing seaweed from vicious *each uisge*," I said.

One by one, every pooka smiled a shark-like grin. Tiny hands fist pumped the air, slapped backs, or rubbed together in glee. Even their curmudgeonly leader was pleased.

"Well, we could use a new house," he said, looking around the old woman's home. "This one here is boring. I suppose we could help."

"Then it's a deal?" I asked.

"Deal," he said. "We do love a challenge."

That was what I had been counting on. Pookas are like little part ninja, part cat burglar, adrenaline junkies. They thrive on the thrill of an impossible heist. By waiting to mention the danger involved, I had left the best for last.

CHAPTER 25

The waterfront was chaos.

Each uisge had begun assailing the boardwalk and pier when I arrived. They had finally broken through the ranks of merrow in the bay and were climbing rapidly out of the water like spiders intent on a particularly juicy fly. The *each uisge* were so frenzied from battle, and the promise of more bloodletting, that they didn't seem to notice that their magic pieces of seaweed had begun to glow.

Perhaps they didn't care, yet. In the water, once they had taken control of the kelpie king, the *each uisge* were the top predator. It would probably take something really impressive to make the *each uisge* balk. So far, only a handful of *each uisge* had learned the dangers of the magic glow. Too bad those individuals were unable to tell their friends. The *each uisge* were in for a nasty surprise.

Kaye, and her circle of magic users, continued to throw magic at the waterfront. Tendrils of power lashed out at the *each uisge*, continuing to mark the location of every piece of magic seaweed. Each monster's Achilles heel was lit up with a ball of green light, an easy target against the night sky and the ink black water of the bay.

Pookas were zipping back and forth carrying glowing pieces of seaweed. Some were shapeshifted into birds or river rats while others flit about naked except for a glow-in-the-dark condom on their head, but every single one managed to steal a piece of seaweed and bring it to the Hunters. As soon as a Pooka reached the shore, they'd drop the seaweed at the feet of the nearest hunter and race back for more.

Hunters grabbed up the seaweed to hang glowing from pockets, belts, and bandoliers. So long as the seaweed remained in their possession, the *each uisge* owner could not continue to fight. The immobilized *each uisge* were considered prisoners of war, to be dealt with later. Hunters strode past

them to fight the *each uisge* who continued to flood the
waterfront.

Kaye, and the casting circle, had magically forced
human civilians away from the bay, to within three blocks of
the waterfront. The Hunters were charged with keeping the
each uisge contained within that area. A human encounter
with an *each uisge* was something that none of us wanted. But
even the mighty Hunters couldn't stop every one of the beasts.

Vampires raced like living shadows to hunt down any
each uisge that crossed the line into the city. As yet, no *each
uisge* had made it past the vamps to reach higher ground.

We were winning.

The battle could have gone easier if it wasn't for Ceffyl
Dŵr. Many of the merrow had been defeated, lost beneath the
waves, because they would not fight their friend. With no
glowing seaweed to steal, the pookas soon lost interest and left
him alone. The kelpie king continued to fight against us, still
under the *each uisges'* control. The sight of his tortured face as
he tore another merrow in two, would haunt me forever.

The kelpies, represented by their demon attorney, were
my clients. They had asked that I find Ceffyl Dŵr's bridle. It
was this case and the information from the kelpies that had
alerted us all to the danger of an *each uisge* invasion. I owed
my client the return of their missing item. Casting a glance at
the anguished kelpie king, I knew that I didn't want to see him
struck down by Hunters. Right now, he was holding off the
remaining merrow, keeping them from nipping at the *each
uisges'* heels, but it wouldn't be long before he left the water
and joined the attack on the waterfront. The Hunters may
have sympathy for the king's situation, but that wouldn't stop
them from killing him. It wouldn't even slow them down.

I had to do something.

On my next run to the casting circle, I asked Kaye if she
could cast a spell on Ceffyl Dŵr's bridle similar to the glowing
spell used on the *each uisge* seaweed. Unfortunately, unlike
the magic seaweed, kelpie bridles are unique to the individual
kelpie. Kaye had no means of tuning her spell to the kelpie
king.

"Wait," I said. I slid a small wrapped bundle out of my
pocket. "Would this help?"

It was the piece of bridle that I had used my
psychometry gift on just a few days before. I had held it in

safekeeping, not knowing where else to stash it, but hadn't given it much thought other than, "do not touch ever again." I carefully pulled back the fabric to display the piece of leather decorated with archaic runes and a silver vine pattern.

"By my wand, girl," Kaye said. "So much has happened, I completely forgot about this little gem."

Kaye leaned forward and lifted the scrap of bridle to twinkle in the reflected magic of the casting circle.

"Can you cast a targeting spell on the bridle with this?" I asked. I held my breath, afraid her answer might still be negative.

"Yes, certainly," she said. "I'll add a pinch of betony flowers to make the bridle glow purple. That way you can tell the difference between the *each uisge* seaweed and the bridle. Just give us a moment for the ritual..." She was already scratching marks into the ground at the center of the circle, lost in her own thoughts.

When she returned, her face was pulled taut and she held a hand across her stomach as if she was ill, but she wore a pleased smile.

"It is done," she said. "I hope the bridle is nearby. We have done our best, dear. Now it is up to you."

I thanked my friend and ran off toward the water's edge. My heart swelled with the hope of rescuing the kelpie king from his enslavement.

I shifted from foot to foot looking out over the water for the only pooka with frown lines. The next time the pooka leader came near, I caught his attention and gestured him forward.

"Oh no," he said. He came to rest on top of a city trashcan, hands fisted on his hips. "We're holding up our end of the bargain. You can't withdraw the glowing house now." He made to leave and I held up a hand.

"Wait, no!" I said. "Please, I'm not trying to cheat you. I have a second bargain to make."

"Keep talking," he said. He tried to look bored, but I didn't miss the eager gleam in his eye. This was so much more fun than hanging out at an old woman's house.

"If you can find a kelpie bridle, steal it, and bring it to me, I'll give you a large jar of honey," I said. I just hoped pookas liked their sweets as much as Marvin did. I felt a pang of worry at the thought of the troll orphan and hoped that Hob was keeping him safe. "An *each uisge* probably has the bridle."

"Pickpocket an *each uisge?*" he asked.

"Yes and the bridle will be glowing purple," I said.

"And you will give us a jar of honey?" he asked. "Will it be organic honey?"

This pooka drove a hard bargain.

"Okay, organic honey," I said. "Do we have a bargain?"

"Lady, for honey I would even kiss one of The Bigs," he said. With a wink, he was gone.

*****

I went back to running messages, but kept an eye out for the pooka leader, and anything purple. I was looking over my shoulder, wondering if the *each uisge* had thought to keep the bridle secreted far away, when I struck my knee on something the size of a softball.

"Watch where you are going, Big Ivy," a voice chirped.

Gaping down at my feet, I saw the pooka leader rubbing a growing red bump on his forehead. A leather bridle, embroidered in silver and glowing purple, lay in his other hand.

Behind him stood my client, Ceffyl Dŵr.

The kelpie king had changed forms throughout the battle, at the *each uisges'* whim, but was now in the form of a water horse, with fin-shaped ears and a dappled gray coat. His beautiful coat was crisscrossed with a latticework of scars and oozing wounds. I pulled my gaze away from his injuries and into dark green eyes.

Release me, release me, release me...

His plea echoed over and over in my mind. I took a step back, surprised at the anguished voice in my head.

"Here you are," the pooka said. He handed me the bridle, which I held tightly in one gloved hand. I was afraid to be touching any part of the bridle again, after the visions the small piece of leather had induced, but part of me was more afraid of losing the precious item so soon after it was found. "You can leave the jar of honey in my new house."

With a tip of his glow-in-the-dark condom hat, he was gone—leaving me to face a tormented kelpie king.

"Don't worry," I said.

I kept my voice low, hands out at my sides, hoping not to startle him. He didn't move a muscle, but his eyes followed the glowing bridle in my hand. Foolish me. Of course, he couldn't move. I held his bridle, which meant that he was now enslaved, to me. Oberon's eyes. My gut twisted and I fought not to throw up.

"I am going to put your bridle back on," I said. "I am giving it back to you."

Release me, release me, release me...

I moved forward, coming to stand within a few inches of the great kelpie king. I raised the bridle, but realized belatedly that I was too short to slip it over his head. Could I just hand it to him? While in horse form, he didn't have hands to put the bridle into and I was uncomfortable with shoving it into his mouth. They may not have the twisted appetites of the *each uisge*, but kelpies have been known to eat humans. No, I wouldn't be putting my hands into that mouth, no matter how much I wanted to rid myself of the bridle.

I would have to get him to kneel down, so I could reach above his head. Mab's bones. I was going to order a faerie king to kneel before me. I gulped down hot air and felt a tear slide down my cheek.

"I am so sorry," I said. I had to bite my lip before I could continue. "I need you to kneel down, so I can return your bridle."

In one smooth motion, the water horse bent its legs and knelt before me, but his sides quivered and nostrils flared. Without delay, I reached up with shaking hands and placed the bridle over his head. I don't know if I did it right, for all I know it could have been on backward or upside down, but the muscles in the king's neck seemed to ease.

With a sigh, the horse laid its head on the ground. It looked like he was settling down to go to sleep—until he started changing. Muscles rippled and contorted beneath the skin, and limbs moved to accommodate a human form, as he shapeshifted. Within seconds, Ceffyl Dŵr was crouching on the ground in the shape of a man—a very naked man.

I spun away, blushing so hard I thought my face would melt from the heat. I heard something fall to the ground and a rustling of fabric.

"You can turn around now," he said. His voice was deep and smooth, like a river that had worked itself deep into the earth. I shook my head. This was no time to be admiring his voice. The man was injured, having suffered abuse at the hands of the *each uisge* and hours of fighting the merrow against his will.

I turned slowly to see a tired man wrapped from the waist down in a white tablecloth. He had industriously appropriated it from a nearby café table. The makeshift kilt covered the manly bits, but did nothing to cover his wounds. His bridle, I noticed, was wrapped tightly around his well-muscled bicep.

What was wrong with me? I must be more exhausted than I thought to be daydreaming about a faerie king who obviously needed help. I lifted my chin, determined to stay focused.

"You're hurt," I said. "Here, sit down and I'll see what I can find to clean your wounds."

"My people heal quickly," he said. "I must return to battle."

"You can return when your wounds are tended to," I said. I could be just as stubborn. "You won't do anyone any good if you pass out or die of iron poisoning. There are probably iron flakes in those cuts that are festering. Take a seat and I'll be right back with clean water—and don't even think about running away."

Okay, that was bossy, but his wounds looked terrible. And I had to admit, I wasn't ready to be rid of him yet. I wanted more than thirty seconds with the kelpie king before he went off and got himself killed.

I ran into the abandoned café and grabbed bottled water and a stack of freshly laundered cotton napkins. Beneath the sink in the kitchen, I found a box of disposable gloves. Returning outside, I was shocked by the battle that continued to rage all around. For some reason, when talking with Ceffyl it had all seemed so far away.

He remained sitting where I had left him, tablecloth wrapped around his waist. I quickly set the water and napkins on the table. Next, I slid the pair of plastic gloves over my leather ones with a snap and set to work. For someone who was touch phobic, I was a pro at tending to injuries. Jinx was always getting hurt, so I had lots of practice.

"Why are you wearing two pairs of gloves?" he asked. He slumped in his chair, chin-length hair falling forward to cover his face. "You are willing to help me, and yet..."

Oh crap. He probably thought I didn't want to touch a monster. I had seen him in the form of a towering water horse, and had witnessed the terrible acts of violence he'd committed while under *each uisge* control. The truth was that I wasn't afraid of big bad kelpie cooties, and the horror I felt when remembering him tearing merrow limb from limb was reserved for the kelpie king himself, and his victims. I couldn't risk touching him because I didn't want to relive his torture at the hands of the *each uisge*, or see his evil wife toss his child into the flames, again.

"Have you heard of psychometry?" I asked.

Most people haven't, but it was worth a shot. Faeries know more about magic and psychic ability than the average human. I was halfway through cleaning his wounds, which were flecked with iron that had flaked off his chains and burned into his skin. I didn't have time for a long explanation. When I finished cleaning his wounds, he'd be gone.

"The ability to receive visions from touching an object?" he asked. "It is a rare gift."

"I wouldn't call it a gift, but it is rare," I said. "I don't think I'd mind the visions as much if I could control them—turn them on and off like a tap. But the way they come crashing in to invade my mind feels like a violation."

I felt my cheeks burn. I hadn't meant to say so much, but I was tired and I felt better having shared a piece of my own burden. It had been a very long night.

A shadow crossed over his already dark eyes, like a cloud eclipsing the night sky.

"No, you are right," he said. "Some visions would not be a gift at all."

I wondered if I should tell him that I'd already had some nasty visions from his past, but decided to wait. If we ever talked to again, I could tell him then.

CHAPTER 26

Ceffyl returned to the battle and I tossed the napkins and empty water bottles in the trash. For the few minutes that we had talked, I had felt safe. Call me crazy. Like I said before, kelpies have been known to eat people, but when I looked at the kelpie king I didn't see a murderous beast. I saw a man who was worried about his people and struggling with the weight of his own troubles. He was like staring into a mirror fogged by the steam of a shower. Until I wiped the mirror clean, we looked so much alike.

The fighting continued throughout the night. I ran to wherever I was needed, often running messages for Kaye who couldn't leave the casting circle. Everywhere that I went, screams rang in my ears. We may win this fight, but it would leave scars.

At least Ceffyl Dŵr no longer fought alongside the enemy. He too would have mental wounds from this night, guilt was a nasty burden, but at least he now stood a chance at redemption. Though his injuries must have pained him, the kelpie king led the Hunters in their defense of the waterfront. I was sure that he wouldn't let himself rest until every *each uisge* was dead.

At dawn, the magic of the casting circle faltered. The green glow surrounding the magic seaweed fluttered then went dark. The transition from night to day dispelled all of Kaye's magic and no one, including Kaye, had enough power left to begin a new casting. That meant no more easily targeted seaweed, and no magic barrier keeping the city safe in their beds.

As the sun rose over the ocean, a fiery red ball on the horizon, shell-shocked humans began to appear. They would shuffle forward, pale faces frozen in fear, or run flailing their arms in terror and shrieking madly for help. A few dropped to the ground to rock back and forth as they pounded the ground with impotent fists.

I can't imagine what they must have thought. How could their brains process so much horror? Sunrise and blood stained the waterfront red. A dozen *each uisge* continued to fight tired Hunters, who were now weighed down with ropes of seaweed. It was a horrible, confusing sight.

These humans had come innocently to the waterfront to check on storm damage. Instead, they learned that monsters really do exist outside our nightmares. That was knowledge best kept secret—for their sakes and for ours.

The kelpie king and the Hunters raced to finish off the remaining *each uisge*. There were only a few of the enemy left, but those creatures just would not give up—and for every Hunter carrying captured seaweed that fell, a dozen or more *each uisge* were released to rejoin the battle.

A whinny carried on the breeze and I glanced out toward the bay. Fading rose hues shone on gleaming gray coats and long, lustrous hair. Ceffyl must have put a call out to his people. More than one hundred kelpies cut though the waves, finally willing to fight and eager to take down any surviving *each uisge*.

They had had days to worry for their king, so much so that they had hired a demon and a psychic detective to help locate him through his missing bridle. Now they had an outlet for all of that pent up emotion.

Hundreds of hooves struck land in a thunderous cacophony that drowned out all other sound. The Hunters retreated to allow the kelpies their revenge. Kelpies surrounded the *each uisge* and when they returned to the water minutes later, the only thing left of the enemy were smears of blood.

One last kelpie remained standing on the edge of the pier, his silhouette dark against the rising sun.

"Safe travels, Ceffyl Dŵr," I whispered.

"Safe travels, Ivy Granger," his voice whispered in my skull.

The battle was finally over, and we had won, but it was too early for celebrations.

Members of the casting circle tried to calm civilians, moving first to those who were doing themselves harm. Some were pounding their heads against the ground while others tried to gouge out their eyes. The appearance of the kelpies definitely hadn't helped to quell their terror.

Then the vampires arrived.

Leathery hands ghosted over warm skin and fangs sank into human flesh as vamps came out of the shadows to feed. I stepped forward, pencils and lighter somehow already finding their way into my hands, but a Hunter stepped in front of me, blocking my way. It was the sentinel with the bright red hair styled into a cute pixie cut. She was probably the one person on the docks whose hair wasn't in snarled, blood spattered disarray.

I knew it was petty, but that really pissed me off.

"Get out of my way," I said. I was breathing hard and at the brink of unconsciousness, but I would take out as many vamps as I could before I gave up. I blinked away the shadows creeping into my vision and pushed past.

"Wait," she said. "It's not what you think."

"Those leeches are feeding on humans," I said, gesturing at a vampire leaning over a woman like an engorged tick. I swayed, nearly falling over as I lifted my hand. I was practically asleep on my feet. "What is there to think about?"

"I know, it's...unfathomable," she said. She blanched and a wrinkle formed between her eyes. Even that was cute. *Bitch.* "It goes against every oath I have taken and everything that I believe in, but this one time we have to walk away."

"Why the hell would I do that?" I asked.

"Because they are erasing their memories," she said.

Oh. My own memory was sluggish at the moment, but that sparked something I knew about the undead. Venom, released from their fangs while feeding, altered memories. It was probably an evolutionary adaptation to keep the fiery mobs away.

With no one left to save, I went off to find Kaye. We didn't need to speak. There weren't words that could change the things we'd seen. She just directed me to a spatter-free stretch of ground where I sat, thinking to rest my eyes for a moment.

I slept like the dead.

CHAPTER 27

According to Jinx, I slept for three days. During that time, she had meticulously taken down the information from over fifty prospective clients.

While her roommate screamed and thrashed in her bed, Jinx had answered every call. She didn't take a break, never leaving my side, and her penmanship was as perfect and precise as ever. I needed all fifty of those clients, since I was going to have to buy her that pair of dream shoes.

The *each uisge* invasion may have left me with a plethora of bruises and a vast array of permanent nightmares, but it was damn good for business. There was a void in the supernatural community for someone with my skills. Now that the faeries and undead knew I was trustworthy, and up for the job, I was suddenly in high demand.

I was also, most definitely, on vacation.

Jinx agreed to pencil me in for some down time until the end of the week. During that time, I wouldn't see clients. She even told Forneus that he would have to wait.

I had an appointment with the demon for first thing Monday morning. Our contract specified a mandatory meeting to settle accounts. I usually enjoyed talking with clients at the end of a case, giving a final accounting before locking the file away. But Forneus was a fiery pain in my butt. I wished that he would just put the check in the mail, but demon contracts are binding. I had to face him for one last meeting.

I'd rather be pixed.

I did make one exception to my week in hiding. The phone had rung again, but I knew that my roommate would pick it up. I was on vacation from the world. I heard Jinx talking excitedly and assumed it was one of her friends until she came in and handed the phone to me with impish glee. That set off all of my alarm bells.

"Hello, Private Eye, Ivy Granger speaking," I said. Jinx had been taking business calls all day, so I played it safe and answered in office mode. Maybe she had been excited about a proposed case. I knew she was thrilled at our newfound popularity.

"Miss Granger," Ceffyl said. "I am not sure if you would remember me, under the extreme circumstances of our meeting, but my name is Ceffyl Dŵr."

I knew who it was as soon as I heard his voice. A voice that I didn't think I'd be hearing again. Forneus was handling the final matters of the case for the kelpies. Why had Ceffyl called? And why did he sound so unsure of himself? Did he continue to worry that I would treat him like a monster?

"Hi, Ceff," I said. Was it okay to be so familiar with a kelpie king? There were probably faerie rules about that sort of thing, but at the moment I didn't really care. I just wanted to put the guy at ease. He had been through hell. We all had, but Ceffyl more than most. "Everything alright?"

"Yes, there is no pending emergency," he said. "I just wondered...would you meet with me this evening?"

Before my brain could catch up with my mouth, I answered him.

"Yes," I said.

I hung up and grinned from ear to ear. For the first time since the *each uisge* attack on Harborsmouth, I was smiling.

I had plans tonight with a sexy kelpie king. Jinx looked like the cat sidhe that ate the canary.

CHAPTER 28

The night air felt chill as it danced along my legs and face. I shivered and buried my gloved hands deep within my coat pockets. The heat wave was finally over.

The weather had turned cooler as soon as the *each uisge* had been defeated. Kaye had explained it at length, using arcane terms that went over my head, but her final statement on the subject had made sense.

"It is all about balance, dear," she said, with a grin and a shake of the head. "Good and evil, earth and water, fae and human—all things must maintain equilibrium. When something throws the world out of balance, everything is affected, even the weather."

Life had been completely out of balance lately, but now, all around me, there were signs that Harborsmouth was returning to normal. Like the weather, the city was finding its equilibrium again.

I stood on the street corner wondering if my decision to come tonight had something to do with maintaining balance. I had agreed to see the kelpie king, but wasn't really sure why I had said yes to the meeting. It wasn't because of pity, that much I knew, but I did feel something when I thought about Ceff. And, I had been doing a lot of thinking about him.

We had shared an experience that night on the waterfront and now were meeting here again. Maybe coming full circle would bring things into balance. That would make Kaye happy, I thought with a smile.

My life had been chaos these past few days, but everything finally seemed like it was falling into place.

An extremely handsome man walked up from the pier, melting out of the shadows. He was smiling, but I wondered if his shoulders were hunched from more than the cold. Faerie kings probably didn't face uncertainty very often, but it must have been difficult for Ceff to come back to this place. I wondered, for the hundredth time, why he had called.

I didn't have to wait long to find out.

"You look beautiful," Ceff said. His gaze lingered on my legs and I blushed. I knew I shouldn't have let Jinx talk me into the skirt. He smiled and his eyes sparkled like a reflection of the moon on ocean waves. "Have dinner with me."

"Are you asking me out...on a date?" I asked incredulously. Okay, that was one possibility I hadn't prepared myself for. A sympathetic ear or a comrade in arms sure, but not a dinner date.

"Yes," he said.

"Let me get this straight," I said. "You want to go on a date with a human?"

It was too far-fetched to be true. He was Prince Charming and I was the Fairy Godmother's bumbling apprentice. I didn't get picked to be on anyone's team in school and I had never been anyone's date.

"No," he said. "I want to go on a date with you."

What the heck was that supposed to mean? No, I definitely do not want to know.

"You're not really answering the question," I said, thrusting my chin out. "Why would a kelpie king want to date a lowly human? You have your pick of gorgeous immortals. It doesn't make any sense."

Ceffyl may be the hottest guy I'd ever seen, but I didn't trust him. Call me paranoid, but making bargains with the fae, even agreeing to go on a simple dinner date, wasn't something I accepted lightly. There was one thing I had learned during my limited time around faeries. If what they were offering seemed too good to be true, then it probably was.

I'd made a lot of mistakes dealing with the fae, but I was learning. Huh, maybe you really could teach an old Black Dog new tricks.

"You think this is a trick," he said, sighing.

"Well, yes," I said, shrugging my shoulders. "Occam's Razor; the simplest explanation is most likely the correct one."

"There is nothing simple about this, Ivy," he said. He looked serious, and tired. "Can we go someplace to talk? I need coffee and you need answers."

"Um, sure," I said. I thrust my hands deep into my coat pockets and turned to face the shadowed street. It was easier to think when I wasn't distracted by his handsome face and gorgeous physique. "There's a twenty-four hour Starbucks up the hill."

I heard a snort behind me and turned to see Ceff striding up the hill.

"What?" I asked. "Got a problem with corporate coffee?"

"No," he said. He came closer, matching my long strides as we moved deeper into the city, leaving the wharf behind. "I was just thinking that no one in my court would believe I had taken a date to Starbucks. I'm not usually such a cheapskate."

"This isn't a date," I said, eyes narrowing. "It's coffee. In the human world, at least, there's a difference."

"The Human World," he murmured.

I wasn't sure that I'd heard him right. Pitched low, his voice was like the burble of a stream trickling over sand and pebbles.

We walked together up the hill in silence. I felt confused and embarrassed. I had expected our meeting to bring balance and closure, and instead, I felt like I was struggling to stay upright on the deck of a ship in a hurricane.

I was relieved when we entered the familiar coffee shop. The smell of roasted espresso beans and hiss of steamed milk calmed my racing pulse. Ceff insisted on purchasing the drinks, so I gave him my regular order and grabbed us a corner booth.

I studied him while he waited in line, reading the menu board and smiling at the barista behind the counter. The kelpie king was an enigma. I was good at solving puzzles, it was one of the reasons why my work suited me, but Ceff was a jumble of random pieces. I was missing the key to solving the Ceff cipher. The only way I'd solve the puzzle would be to ask him questions.

He beat me to it.

"Can I ask you a personal question?" he asked.

"That depends," I said, blowing on my skim milk latte.

"What do you know of your parentage?" he asked.

That wasn't what I thought he'd ask. Again he'd managed to unbalance me. He was eyeing me intently over his coffee, the dark currents within those eyes threatening to pull me under.

I looked away and took a swig of my latte, letting the scalding liquid burn my throat. Sometimes pain stabilizes me. It's foolish and dangerous and completely unhealthy, but at that moment I needed to feel strong and in control. I gulped down another boiling mouthful of latte and set my cup carefully on the table, placing my hands against the cool surface on either side.

"I don't get along well with my parents," I said. "All of this freaks them out." I waved a gloved hand, the gesture encompassing my second sight and the faerie sitting across from me.

"When you refer to your parents, you mean your mother and step-father," he said. "But what do you know about your real father."

I felt like I'd been slapped. No one ever mentioned my biological father. The subject was taboo, completely off limits.

"I never knew my father," I said. "He left."

I let all the unsaid hurt and disappointment hang in the silence between us.

"So, it is as I thought," he said.

"What?" I asked.

I wanted to rage at someone and Ceff was conveniently sitting within reach. He was also the one poking a stick at the pixie nest of emotions. My dad leaving was a sore subject. I didn't need someone stirring up the past to sate their own curiosity. King or not, if Ceff didn't watch out, he was going to get stung. I'd face the consequences of striking a kelpie king later.

"Your mother never told you," he said. "I guess I cannot blame her for that."

"She never told me what exactly?" I asked. "If you know something, spit it out."

The cool hatred in my voice was misdirected. I knew it and hopefully, so did he.

Ceff was no fool. He flinched at my icy tone, but anger didn't flood his face. Ordering a kelpie king around, especially in a waspish tone, was probably an offense with a death sentence attached to it, but like I said...he was the one waving a big stick. I was just drinking coffee and minding my own beeswax.

Maybe if I kept telling myself that, I might even start to believe it.

"Have you ever wondered why you are different?" he asked.

"Sure," I said, shrugging. "It used to bug me. I got over it."

"Your friend, Madame Kaye, never did a tarot reading into your past?" he asked.

Your past is shrouded in the mists of secrecy. Kaye's words came back to me. She had been disturbed by her inability to read my cards. I, strangely enough, had been relieved. I'm pretty sure that isn't a normal response.

Damn him. Ceff was right. There was something fishy about my past. Something I couldn't remember or chose to forget.

"Kaye couldn't see into my past," I said. Mab's bones. "She tried once, but said my past was *shrouded in mists,* whatever that means."

"Do you remember anything at all about your father?" he asked.

I tried to think back, but it was like hitting a wall—a big, blank, nausea-inducing wall. I hadn't thought about my dad in years. In fact, I couldn't remember the last time I brought him to mind at all.

The realization made me feel mad, and guilty. What kind of daughter forgets her own father? I clenched my fists as my shoulders shook and a lone tear escaped to roll down my cheek.

A cool hand reached out to cover my own. I tried not to flinch. The king of the kelpies comforting me? Stranger things have happened, I think. I moved my hands into my lap. Even gloved, I didn't like people touching me and I definitely didn't want to risk a vision. I'd experienced his pain once and wasn't ready for a second showing.

"It's okay," he said, gently.

"No, it is definitely not okay," I said. Good. Anger was something I knew much more intimately than shame, like a long lost friend. Anger I could use. "I forgot about my own father. Until you asked about him, I forgot he ever existed!"

Okay, my voice was getting shrill and my anger was shifting into hysteria. I was supposed to be on vacation. How did I end up being interrogated?

I closed my eyes tight, hands moving to cover my face, and tried to block out the confusing whirlwind of emotions. Ceff was only being nice, I shouldn't have pulled away. It had nothing to do with him being water fae. His cool touch would have been soothing if I didn't have to worry about sudden visions, and the looming wall blocking my memories wasn't smothering me into claustrophobia. Hopefully, he wouldn't be pissed by my reaction. I didn't need to cause an international incident with the faerie courts. Ceff had been calm so far, but everyone has limits.

I heard the sliding of denim against vinyl as Ceff withdrew from the booth seat across from me. *Good going, Ivy. He's leaving. Happy now?*

I lowered shaking hands to my lap and glanced over to see Ceff's bare feet still standing beside our table. Frayed, sun-bleached jeans dragged the floor. Huh. I hadn't noticed until now that he was walking around the city barefoot. I wonder how he managed to enter Starbucks without any shoes on. Faerie glamour? I'd ask, but it's not like he was ever speaking to me again—not after the way I had treated him.

I had forgotten my own father's existence and insulted an immortal kelpie king. Could this night get any worse?

Bare feet shifted apart and a snort erupted somewhere above me. That snort sounded suspiciously like a snicker. Did he think this was funny?

"You're getting angry again," he said. "Good, you are even more beautiful when you are mad."

"Aren't you leaving?" I asked. I bolted out of my chair to stand facing Ceff. He met my glare with a smile. Bastard.

"After you," he said, nodding his head to the glass exit doors.

"Why?" I asked, immediately suspicious.

Walking out into the night with a water fae was all kinds of stupid. Heck, kelpies eat people. They may not play with their food as creatively as the *each uisge*, but dead is dead.

"The night awaits," he said. He was all charisma until he realized I wasn't budging. With a sigh, he reached for my arm and pulled me toward the door. At least he was careful not to touch any bare skin. "Come on. I saw you breathing heavy and eyeing the exits. You're getting claustrophobic. You need to be under the stars."

Not, I noticed, *you need fresh air*. That was interesting.

"How would you know what I need?" I asked.

"It is in your nature," he said. "This," he said gesturing at the chrome, vinyl, and glass room, "is not."

I hated to admit it, but Ceff was right. I needed to get out of here. The fluorescent lights were humming a room spinning tune.

"Okay," I said, shrugging from his grip and charging toward the door on my own. "Fine."

The door clanged as I burst out into the light pooled beneath an old-style street lamp. Cool, cleansing night air brushed against my fevered face. Moonlight caressed my skin and I drank deeply, nearly drunk on moonbeams and star shine. I had to be sick. How else could I explain the bizarre sensations?

"Mab's children require time beneath the night sky," he said. "Especially when they are under extreme emotional and physical stress."

"Mab?" I asked. "As in The Queen of Air and Darkness?"

"Yes," he said. "The one and only."

"Am I...?" I asked.

"Fae?" Ceff asked. "Yes. You are a half-blood. Your mother is human, but your father was of Mab's court."

"The Unseelie Court," I said.

"Yes, but don't hold what you've heard of the Unseelie against us," Ceff said. "All fae possess the ability for good or evil, just as humans do. Our liege may encourage our dark side, but our court does not define us."

"That's a strange statement, coming from a king," I said.

"We all have our faults," Ceff said, smiling and spreading his hands wide.

CHAPTER 29

My thoughts raced for days, buzzing around my head like annoying pixies. Ceff left me with a lot to think about. We'd met a few more times, usually walking side by side under the stars. It didn't seem that strange anymore, being in the company of a kelpie king.

According to Ceff, I had my own faerie king not so very far back in my family tree. Not far back at all.

My absentee father was William, or Will 'o the Wisp, King of the Wisps. That was a lot to process, but Ceff was helping me fill in the blanks and accept who I was. I'd always been different, that much hadn't changed, but now there were details that explained why. In a way, that made the whole bitter pill of truth easier to swallow.

It would have been easier for both of us if Ceff had never brought up my father. When I asked him why he'd risked upsetting me on our first date, which it turned out to be, he replied that he didn't want to begin our relationship on a lie. If he had pretended that I was human, when he knew that I was wisp, it couldn't last.

So we each set about discovering our own truth with the hope that when we were ready, the other would still be there waiting. Ceff was honest about his feelings during his days of captivity and I shared my confusion over being fae.

I still had more questions than answers, but it was early days yet. There were some secrets that even Ceff didn't know. Would I develop certain wisp abilities? Was I a half-faerie princess? Did my mother know what my father truly was? Where was my father now?

When Ceff didn't know, I tried asking Kaye, but she was unusually tight-lipped on the subject. I was dying of curiosity, but I didn't push the topic, yet. She was regaining her strength, but the battle to save Harborsmouth had depleted her magic reserves and left her physically weak. She had her brownie and troll nursemaids, so I was sure she'd be feeling better soon—if only to escape their attentions.

Hob and Marvin fussed over her like worried mothers over a sick baby. They had both come through the attack on the city without harm. That was a huge relief to me, but I suspected that they secretly felt like they should have done more. That may be what motivated them to try so hard to nurse Kaye back to health and pitch in with odd jobs around The Emporium.

It also gave Marvin a temporary place to stay. Hob had graciously offered the kitchen to Marvin since, "it wouldna do ta send ye home when da madam be sa poorly." The *each uisge* had forced Marvin from his bridge home. I didn't think he was ready to go back yet, he had his own demons to face, but the kid wouldn't go homeless. Hob and I would make sure of that.

There were so many things to worry about. I bit my lip until it bled, and pulled at my hair until Jinx threatened to cut it all off. After a few days I decided I couldn't go on like that. It didn't pay to worry about every little thing. I would have to take each problem as it came.

Speaking of payment, I still owed the glaistig. The Green Lady had held up her end of the bargain. She could ask for not just one, but two wishes, at any time. So far, I hadn't heard from her, but I knew that someday she would collect.

I was the daughter of the king of the wisps. The very thought made my stomach clench. I was sure that with that position came responsibility, even if no one had bothered to tell me who I really was. And now I owed the glaistig two wishes. It was no wonder the glaistig wanted two favors from me. I should have known that was a bad idea. It is always a bad idea when the bargaining goes that easily.

Another lesson learned. There was a lot of that going around.

Our Monday appointment with Forneus had met with disastrous results. There had been an incident, a clash of wills between that Jinx and Forneus, that left me shaking my head at them both. I was surprised there was anything left of the office after that meeting. The place still reeked of brimstone— that smell was never coming out.

It was all because of a job offer that Forneus had made to Jinx...and the things he had written into her work contract as "payment." We may not have a 401k, but our business did alright—and we didn't get paid with demon sex.

Forneus was lucky he still had his pitchfork to offer potential employees. When he tried to make a deal with Jinx for her "clerical skills," she ran him through with a letter opener. Now he wanted her all the more. Unfortunately, silver doesn't do much damage against demons. Judging by the way he was acting, it might even be seen as foreplay.

Thankfully, we had already been paid. That was one detail Jinx made sure we covered as soon as the demon arrived. We would have enough to make rent. Hopefully, we'd have some money left over to cover the cost of cleaning the demon funk from the room. Most of our new clients may be supernatural, but no one except a demon enjoyed the smell of brimstone.

When Forneus finally disappeared in a puff of putrid smelling smoke, his laughter lingered setting my teeth on edge as it echoed around my skull. Finally, his voice faded, but I knew he wasn't gone for good.

Our deal had been profitable for both of us. Representing the kelpies, against the *each uisge*, was seen as a bold move in the legal underworld. Gaining status amongst his demon peers gave Forneus even more reason to pester me for jobs.

I better find a damn good cleaning service.

EPILOGUE

Dating Ceff was never dull. He was full of surprises, like the party we were about to enter. The loft was still off limits for social gatherings, I hadn't changed that much, but I had agreed to renting a space at a hotel owned by one of Kaye's hunter friends. According to Kaye, her friend and his team cleaned out a nest of vamps here over a decade ago and ended up running the hotel when they retired from hunting. I supposed that's one benefit of vamps being into real estate.

A hotel owned by retired hunters seemed like a weird place for a mixed race soiree, but Kaye and Ceff both assured me that our hosts would let anyone in who was on the guest list. That list was surprisingly long.

Jinx was one of the first to arrive. She looked fabulous in a red halter dress that matched her new shoes. It took me a month of saving to buy those shoes for her, but I didn't regret a single penny. Good help was hard to find. Amazing friends were even rarer. In Jinx, I had found both. It was best to keep her happy.

Forneus made a grand entrance right behind Jinx. At least they didn't arrive together. Forneus had shown an interest in my friend which I had tried to discourage. A demon dating my roommate? Over my dead body. Though honestly, he probably wasn't much worse than most of her boyfriends—aside from his brimstone aftershave. No one would ever be good enough for her in my mind. She was a ruby in a room filled with rocks.

Actually, the room was filled with fae, not rocks, though a few resembled geodes and a piece of coral that I had assumed to be decorative was now chatting up a mermaid. Knowing mermaids, the coral was probably the more intelligent of the two.

I looked around the room and shook my head. Things sure can change in just one week. How did I end up with so many new friends...and so many fae in my life? Perhaps like, really does attract like.

It's weird thinking of myself as fae. I am a half-breed, half human and half wisp. I'm not sure how I feel about that. To be honest, I think I'm still in shock.

I had been different for so long. It is a comfort to know that I'm not alone. I still had questions about my past, but for now, I was content to let my friends show me around this new world opening up to me.

A big part of that new world was Ceff, King of the Kelpies and my date tonight. How the heck did that happen? Even from across the packed room, I could feel his presence. He was powerful, confident, gorgeous, and looked mighty fine in a suit. He moved with liquid grace and his muscles rippled beneath his suit pants, yes I had looked, and pulled the fabric of his jacket tight across his chest and shoulders. Mab's bones, he was hot.

Ceff caught my eye and winked. I may have a huge new world to navigate, but I had the most amazing tour guide ever. Blushing, I returned Ceff's wink and went to join him by the dessert table. At least, I think it was dessert. It looked suspiciously like sea foam frothed on top of fishy smelling cupcakes.

I passed Jinx and Kaye who were standing, heads together, beside the punch bowl. Jinx raised an eyebrow and I grinned from ear to ear. I was about to give the girl a heart attack. Turning back to shine my smile at Ceff, I went to hold his hand.

Yes, I was wearing gloves, silk evening gloves instead of my usual leather gloves, but this was progress. This whole intimacy thing was completely new to me. I was still scared, but mostly, I was happy. That was all I could possibly ask for.

It was going to take time to get over my fears and phobias. Looking up into the dark green eyes of my immortal date, I realized that that was okay. For once in my life, the thing I needed most wasn't in short supply. Time was something we had in abundance.

Coming in 2013
The second Ivy Granger novel from

E.J. STEVENS

Ghost Light

Read on for a sneak preview.

What do ghost light, friar's lantern, corpse candle, aleya, hobby lantern, chir batti, faerie fire, min min light, luz mala, spook light, ignus fatuus, orbs, boitatá, and hinkypunk have in common? They are all names for wisps. Corpse candle? Now that was bound to give a girl a complex.

I had recently discovered that I was half fae. My faerie half was wisp, as in Will-o'-the-Wisp—my father, king of the wisps. It was a lot to digest.

Dealing with my newfound princess of the wisps status was stressful, but business was booming and I didn't have time for random panic attacks. I used to see a therapist to help deal with my anxiety. Lately, I visited Galliel at Sacred Heart church.

Galliel wasn't the priest at Sacred Heart, though I usually stopped and said hello to Father Michael while there. Father Michael had helped me with my recent demon trouble, but spending time with him didn't relieve my anxiety like Galliel did. It wasn't Father Michael's fault. He was a good priest, as far as I could tell, but he was only human. Galliel was a unicorn.

I was indulging in my guilty pleasure, Galliel's adoring head resting in my lap, while Ceff spoke with the priest. This was bliss. I had always wondered what true happiness was like, but never thought I'd have the opportunity to experience it for myself. Somehow, during a catastrophic week that nearly brought my city to its knees, I had found my own. Galliel was a big part of that, so was Ceff.

If I were looking for love on Craig's List, my singles ad would begin something like, "Must Love Unicorns." Of course, I didn't have to look for love online. My heart now belonged to Ceff.

Ceffyl Dŵr, or Ceff, was a kelpie. In fact, he was king of the local kelpies. Since discovering my wisp princess birthright, that seemed somewhat fortuitous. It was also extremely dangerous. The kelpie king had plenty of enemies. He also had a murderous sociopathic wife.

I didn't care. For the first time in my life, I felt like I truly belonged. I had a gorgeous date, amazing best friend, business partner, and roommate, a wonderful mentor, fabulous new friends, more clients than I had time, and a pet freaking unicorn.

I should have known that something bad was coming. I have said it before and I'll say it again; Fate is a fickle bitch.

Ivy Granger World

Don't miss these great books set in the world of Ivy Granger.

Ivy Ganger, Psychic Detective Series

Shadow Sight

Welcome to Harborsmouth, where monsters walk the streets unseen by humans...except those with second sight, like Ivy Granger.

Blood and Mistletoe: An Ivy Granger Novella

Holidays are worse than a full moon for making people crazy. In Harborsmouth, where many of the residents are undead vampires or monstrous fae, the combination may prove deadly.

Ghost Light

Holidays are worse than a full moon for making people crazy. In Harborsmouth, where many of the residents are undead vampires or monstrous fae, the combination may prove deadly.

Club Nexus: An Ivy Granger Novella

A demon, an Unseelie faerie, and a vampire walk into a bar...

Burning Bright

Burning down the house...

Birthright

Being a faerie princess isn't all it's cracked up to be.

Hound's Bite

Ivy Granger thought she left the worst of Mab's creations behind when she escaped Faerie. She thought wrong.

Hunters' Guild Series

Hunting in Bruges

The only thing worse than being a Hunter in the fae-ridden city of Harborsmouth, is hunting vampires in Bruges.

E.J. Stevens is the author of the HUNTERS' GUILD urban fantasy series, the SPIRIT GUIDE young adult series, and the award-winning IVY GRANGER urban fantasy series. She is known for filling pages with quirky characters, bloodsucking vampires, psychotic faeries, and snarky, kick-butt heroines.

BTS Red Carpet Award winner for Best Novel, SYAE Award finalist for Best Paranormal, Best Horror, and Best Novella, winner of the PRG Reviewer's Choice Award for Best Paranormal Fantasy Novel, Best Young Adult Paranormal Series, Best Urban Fantasy Novel, and finalist for Best Young Adult Paranormal Novel and Best Urban Fantasy Series.

When E.J. isn't at her writing desk, she enjoys dancing along seaside cliffs, singing in graveyards, and sleeping in faerie circles. E.J. currently resides in a magical forest on the coast of Maine where she finds daily inspiration for her writing.

CONNECT WITH E.J. STEVENS

Twitter: @EJStevensAuthor
Website: www.EJStevensAuthor.com
Blog: www.FromtheShadows.info

Made in the USA
Middletown, DE
16 February 2019